ROGUE MAGIC

(LEGACY SERIES BOOK 4)

MCKENZIE HUNTER

McKenzie Hunter

Rogue Magic

© 2018, McKenzie Hunter

mckenziehunter.author@gmail.com

ISBN: 978-1-946457-88-2

ACKNOWLEDGMENTS

———

I am forever thankful for my friends and family who continue to support me unconditionally and make sure I manage to leave my writer's cave.

I'd also like to thank Oriana for the beautiful cover and Luann Reed, who work so hard to help me tell the best story I can.

Last, but never least, I want to thank my readers for following Levy's (Olivia Michaels) journey and allowing me to entertain you with my writing. I can't thank you enough.

CHAPTER 1

Several moments had passed, and I still couldn't take my eyes off the broken door. Hints of Conner's familiar magic permeated the air and brushed against my skin. Savannah was gone. I couldn't believe she was gone. The events of the past twenty minutes kept replaying in my head, and I dissected every moment, trying to figure out the very minute things had gone wrong. I shouldn't have left her. I should've checked the ward. I should've called Lucas to watch her. The list of "should haves" was growing with every passing moment. I was starting to spiral out of control, and the weight of my guilt was difficult to bear. My attention only moved from the door when I felt Gareth next to me. He was so close his body heat warmed my skin. It should have comforted me, but it didn't.

"Are you sure it was Conner?" I asked again. I knew he was getting sick of the same question—the answer wasn't going to change. Remnants of Conner's magic still lingered in the air. It was hard to grasp that he could be behind this. He couldn't be. I'd witnessed Gareth mauling him. Who lived after something like that?

No matter how many breaths I took, not one of them helped

with my overwhelming emotions, which became harder to control as we walked through the space once occupied by the door to my apartment. Splinters of wood were scattered across the floor, but the rooms I shared with Savannah looked just as they had when I'd left. There weren't any signs of a struggle. He'd just taken Savannah, and she wouldn't have been able to fight back. I blinked several times, fighting back tears.

Gareth was several feet away, talking on the phone, I assumed to the Supernatural Guild. Was this a Supernatural Guild problem? Savannah was an *ignesco*. I didn't consider that a supernatural, because she couldn't do anything but enhance magic. As a magical ability it was useless and simplistic, but when coupled with powerful magic it could be quite dangerous. I wondered if Conner had discovered Savannah's ability when she'd joined it with my magic to heal the supernaturals infected by the virus. If it weren't for Savannah, they would have died. A chill ran down my spine. What if Conner had been involved with the attack at the Solstice festival, and he wanted to ensure Savannah couldn't help the affected during the next attack? Conner probably also wanted to torment me: I'd killed his acolytes—and stopped his plans to do the Cleanse, something he desperately wanted. This was my punishment for it.

"I've notified the Supernatural Guild as well as the Shifter Council to start looking for her. We will find her." Gareth sounded so confident, I wanted to believe him. But bleak thoughts of what Conner was capable of and how angry he was with me reasserted themselves in my head. Hurting Savannah would be the perfect revenge for Conner.

Lucas had a rigid look of barely controlled anger when he walked in. I suspected that if he were human he'd actually be flushed. He usually had guards with him, but this time he was alone. When I'd told him about Savannah's abduction, he hadn't bothered to say good-bye before hanging up.

He examined the broken door, then slowly looked around the

room, frowning. "What happened?" he asked in a strained voice; anger tremored in it. Anger that seemed to be directed at me.

I tried to take a cleansing breath, but Conner's residual magic prickled my nose, a quick reminder of the situation. I told Lucas everything that had taken place. Gareth and I'd had a planned trip. As we'd driven down the street away from my home, he'd noticed something suspicious in the rearview mirror and promptly turned around. We arrived back at the apartment in time to see a white van pull away from the open door of my building. After we'd gone after the van, Gareth had been able to get a glimpse of the driver. Conner.

Lucas's brow furrowed. "I thought you killed Conner!" he snapped brusquely at Gareth.

"I thought I had as well." Gareth's voice, tone, and demeanor started to mirror Lucas's. This happened each time they were in a room together. It was underlying aggression, posturing, and testing the boundaries of each's dominance. I didn't have time for this behavior, nor did I want to have to de-escalate a situation.

Lucas's dark gaze slipped in my direction. The silver around his eyes danced to a spastic beat. Icy. Penetrating. He was having a hard time controlling his anger, and it was starting to uncoil and focus on me. "How could you let this happen?" he snarled.

His accusation slammed into me, a summation of my own emotions. I felt anger, hopelessness, guilt, and sorrow. It was hard to decipher which one I should be feeling, and it was damn hard to tamp them down with Lucas's narrowed eyes on me. It was a good thing I didn't have access to a weapon, because I was positive that Lucas would be feeling the sharp end of anything I could have gotten ahold of.

"How could *I* let this happen? Do you think for one minute I wanted this to happen to Savannah? Do you think I'm not feeling guilty and replaying that incident over and over in my mind to figure out where I went wrong? How dare you come in here and ask me how I let this happen!"

It wasn't until I felt Gareth's hand wrapped around my waist and him pulling me back several feet before guiding me out of the room that I realized I had advanced so close to Lucas. My fists were balled at my sides and I wasn't opposed to using them on him.

"Levy, I need you to calm down," Gareth whispered. His voice was soft and soothing but did nothing to temper my misdirected rage. Misdirected, but I didn't care. Lucas's words had lit the flames of my emotions. And I saw that Gareth was working diligently to control his own. I knew it was for my sake: He had to be enraged that someone had lived after he'd mauled them. But it was even more upsetting to imagine how Conner had survived. He had more tricks up his sleeves than I'd ever imagined. This was a reminder that he had much more untapped magic at his disposal. Which made him scarier and definitely changed the balance of things. Each time I dealt with him, I was faced with the fact that my magic was limited.

"Why are you telling me to calm down? He's the one who came in here and accused me of allowing something to happen to Savannah. Why don't you go grab him and pull him out of the room?" I shot back angrily.

He made a face that was a combination of compassion and incredulity. I knew I was being unreasonable. If he'd made any move toward Lucas, the situation probably would have escalated to something violently confrontational.

"We will find her," he assured me. "With the Supernatural Guild and the Shapeshifter Council helping, we'll find her."

I realized he was being optimistic for my sake, but I hated that he was lying to me. My BS detector was giving off a lot of alarms. How could he guarantee that? Shifters had an excellent sense of smell and could track down anyone in the city, but if Conner used magic, how could they find Savannah? The only thing that gave me some hope was that Conner'd had to drive away. He hadn't teleported, ~~which ordinarily he could have easily done. Was his~~ magic now limited?

"He drove," I said. Gareth waited for me to continue, his brow furrowed with curiosity. "He drove instead of teleporting. I wonder if he's not as strong as he was. If he has to conserve his energy."

Gareth slowly nodded, considering it. "Possibly," he offered in a low voice. He was just about to say something else when a commotion in the other room caught his attention. Multiple voices. Authoritative voices. I assumed that someone from the SG or the Shapeshifter Council had arrived. We hurried to the living room to find that both were there. There were three men from the Shapeshifter Council. I assumed they were—there was no denying they were shapeshifters. One had to be a bear or some other large animal. His human shape was awfully broad and bulky. The other two I suspected were feline shifters. They moved with the predatory agility of cats, lithe and graceful, as they prowled around the room. They inhaled and made faces. Agents from the Supernatural Guild were a few feet away, dressed in their traditional casual attire: dark slacks and a polo or button-down shirt. They were shifters as well, and if it wasn't for the badges clipped at their waists I wouldn't have been able to tell which organization they were from.

None of them bothered with the banalities of a greeting. "We need something of hers," one of the feline shifters from the Council informed us. His midnight hair was cut military short, and his light brown eyes were so close to his khaki brown skin tone that the shifter ring around them seemed ornamental— something to break up the monotony of his appearance. Minus the fixed grimace on his face, his round, mild features would have made him look less menacing than most shifters. The other feline was shorter, thicker, and solidly built. His curly blond hair was tucked behind his ear, and he sported confidence and an air of menace like a badge. Of the two, he'd be my last choice to fight.

He looked powerful, as if a single strike from him would knock one out cold. I was more than happy to have him looking for Savannah.

The dark-haired shifter requested something of Savannah's again. His voice was softer this time, and he'd shelved some of his intensity. When we didn't move immediately he looked in my direction, and he seemed to be putting a great deal of effort into resisting a frown. I wasn't sure if he was frowning because he knew I was a Legacy or if, like Lucas, he'd already attributed fault to me. He waited patiently for me to get one of Savannah's belongings. I knew it should be something she'd worn, but it seemed so intrusive to go through her laundry that I pulled the case off of her pillow and brought it to him. He took a half step toward it and backed away.

He jerked his head in Lucas's direction. "His scent is over-whelming hers," he pointed out, and I was treated to a disap-proving look. I rushed back to her room and found it to be a more difficult task to find something of hers that *wouldn't* have Lucas's scent on it. Pajamas were probably out of the question, and if his scent was all over her pillowcase I was pretty sure it was all over her sheets as well. I couldn't use a towel; her floral bodywash would likely overpower her scent as well. Gareth walked in, and sensing my frustration, he put his hand on my shoulder. His eyes went to the lounge chair in the corner, the blanket tossed over it, and the book on the small table next to it. He picked up the fluffy blanket.

"Her scent is heavy on this," he informed me. My brows inched together. How did he know that Lucas's scent wouldn't be on there? He hadn't sniffed it. Reading my look of curiosity, he gave me a half-grin. "I'm sure if Lucas had the option to be with Savannah on a recliner or bed, he'd choose the bed." Then he tossed another look back at the chair. "It seems like it's her special little place, too."

It had only been hours, but it seemed like an eternity since I'd seen Savannah relaxing in her recliner reading a book or hanging out with me while I insulted whatever gluten-free or taste-depleted food she was trying to convince me to eat.

Don't you dare cry! I scolded myself as tears brimmed in my eyes. I didn't have a problem crying; I didn't see it as a sign of weakness. I just didn't want to cry in front of supernatural authority figures, so I steeled myself as we left Savannah's room. When Gareth handed over the blanket, the shifters moved in closer and took a whiff. Moments later they were headed out the door. After receiving instructions from Gareth, the three SG officers quickly followed behind.

"I think you should put a ward up," Gareth instructed me before he left.

"For what? He can break that, too." I didn't like how dejected and defeated my voice sounded, but that was exactly how I felt. Conner was supposed to be dead—one less problem I had to deal with. My days should have been filled with trying to find other Legacy so we could come out in the open and for once live normal lives. Now I was wondering how many more Vertu were out there and if they were all as resilient and difficult to kill as Conner. What did it take to kill him? If a big-ass lion ripping at his chest wasn't enough, I had no idea how to stop him.

"Levy, let's concentrate on finding Savannah. We'll worry about Conner later." Again, he was being overly positive for me. There was no way he couldn't be concerned that Conner was alive.

I simply nodded and gave him a forced smile. Hesitating, he gave me an assessing look and finally left. I was in the kitchen before the door had completely closed behind him, grabbing a kitchen knife. Slashing it across my hand and working my magic to find Conner, I squelched the fear that rose in me at the idea of having to go up against a guy who seemed indestructible. I closed my eyes and called forth the magic, allowing it to ensorcell me and wrap around me like a gentle cloak before twining around my arms and inching toward my fingertips. A map of the city appeared. Bright lines unfurled along the map. I studied it, waiting for that flash of light that would indicate where another Legacy or Vertu was. Nothing. I knew Conner was in town because he wouldn't miss an opportunity to taunt me over this. He'd be watching the results of the chaos he'd inflicted. He was blocking my magic from finding him.

My thoughts spiraled and became a blend of possibilities, speculations, and dire scenarios. Some were absolutely ridiculous, but I couldn't help but consider them. In the past few weeks I'd seen a lot. Fae could glamour their appearances. Could someone have glamoured their body to look like Conner? I needed to see the spot where I'd thought he died.

I followed the path into the woods. Conner had an odd thing about forests and always had his hideaways there. It made sense: He couldn't put up a ward and hide a secret neighborhood in a major city. It would be too easy to detect, but in the woods, he had free rein. Slowly I walked through the area, anticipating the familiar strong buzzing or the stifling smell of his magic. Nothing. He'd destroyed the beautiful retreat that he'd created for his acolytes and me. Hints of magic lingered in the air—just a whisper. But it wasn't as strong as the magic I'd felt at my apartment. Holding my sai, the twins, tighter, I waited to engage, anticipating him showing up. He did that often. Now you saw him; now you didn't. Of the many things I hated about him, that ranked highest. Sheathing one of the twins, I ran my hand over the empty space, hoping to detect the borders of a ward. Once again, I came up empty. I couldn't ignore the light tinge of magic that lingered in the air. Someone was near. Someone with distinctive magic.

A burst of color flashed in front of me. Words that moved slowly and were dark red, the color of blood. When the air scribbling stopped, I was presented with a message: YOU WILL PAY

WITH YOUR LIFE. I didn't have to guess the author, I knew. Conner. *Guess he doesn't want me to be his baby mama anymore.* I'd thwarted his advances before and mocked his silliness for wanting me to be the woman who bore his children. The person he felt would give him the type of children he believed he deserved. My refusal had bothered him. His absurd sense of entitlement had made me the enemy because I'd dared to deny him. Now Savannah was paying for it. Breathing deeply, I attempted to rein in my emotions as they threatened to slip into guilt. I didn't need that. The message remained visible for nearly ten minutes. Clearly, he wanted to make sure I saw it.

"Message received," I said to the empty space. The words disappeared at the same pace they'd appeared, showing a certain level of control and skill with magic. It was just another addition to Conner's many threats. I continued to search the area, hoping to run into him, ready to engage.

Grabbing my phone as soon as it rang, I heard Gareth's voice, which was uncharacteristically bright, lively. "We found her. Come to the Isles. She's being examined by the physician." I wished they'd taken her to a regular hospital. The Isles was for the supernatural and those injured by supernaturals; she was human. She needed a human doctor.

"Is she okay?"

It took him a moment to answer. I speculated whether he had bad news and was searching for the appropriate way to deliver it or if he needed a place where he could speak privately and freely.

"Something's off with her," he admitted. His voice was devoid of emotion, and I felt as if he were talking to a victim's family member as opposed to his girlfriend or whatever I was to him. "Just get here as soon as possible."

"Is she injured?"

"No." Again, he responded with a professional detachment that made me nervous.

Gareth was waiting for me outside of the Isles when I arrived.

"Who found her?" I asked.

"No one, she just walked into the Supernatural Guild's building." This was the first time he'd shown any emotion, and it was abject confusion.

"She just walked in?"

"Yep. She walked in and asked for me."

He took me to the examination room where she was being kept, and I walked in to find my perky roommate looking normal and uninjured. Her long blond hair was twisted into a messy bun on top of her head and she wore the same clothing she'd had on before I'd left the house: a pair of multicolored yoga pants, a loose-fitting shirt with an open neck that allowed it to slip off her shoulder, and a pair of socks. The moment I entered, her eyes snapped up to look at me. She inclined her head to the side and the smile that was feathered over her lips disappeared. Her gray eyes turned icy cold and sharpened. She lunged at me, pushing past the doctor next to her and knocking me to the ground. The first punch shocked me. When she landed the second one, I wasn't sure how to respond. I was trained to hurt, possibly kill. I didn't want to do either to Savannah. Forced into defense mode, I blocked the next set of blows.

"Savannah! It's me, Levy."

Gareth had his arms around her waist and had hoisted her away as she fought to release herself with the sole purpose of getting back at me.

"Gareth, let me go," she growled through clenched teeth.

She knew Gareth. "It's me," I repeated.

"I know who you are, Anya," she hissed angrily.

I stared at her, wide-eyed, trying not to be offended by the level of ire in her eyes and her frown of disgust.

My presence made her angrier, and each time she thought

Gareth's hold had loosened, she made another ~~attempt to come~~ after me. A low, velvet voice spoke from behind me. "Savannah." Lucas purred her name, and she responded in kind. Smiling, her anger lifted momentarily—until she looked in my direction again. Fire and fury, targeted solely at me.

I swallowed the lump in my throat and blinked several times. Once Lucas was next to her, she hugged him. She knew Gareth and Lucas. What she knew of Anya she hated. What had Conner done to her? What memories had he planted?

"I think you should step out, Levy Anya," the doctor urged.

"It's Levy," I said as I backed out of the room. But I didn't move fast enough to miss the glare Savannah gave me when I corrected the doctor.

"She doesn't know who I am," I said to Gareth after he found me in the waiting room. I was staring at the choices in the vending machine. Each time I looked at the healthy options of nuts, dried berries, and fruit, the image of Savannah looking at me with undiluted hate sparked.

"She knows who you are, but what she knows of you is different. That's what I was saying. She's off. She knows who I am, that I'm the head of the Supernatural Guild, and she believes we are friends. When they asked for her residence, she gave Lucas's address. How could her mind be that messed up in just hours?" Gareth inquired, exasperated.

I closed my eyes and inhaled sharply. "It only takes minutes, and I'm sure Conner's an expert at it. That explains why he wasn't using a great deal of magic to transport. He needed it to screw up her head."

"There has to be a way to undo it."

"I'm sure there is, I just don't know how—" My voice broke. I felt helpless. I hated feeling that way.

CHAPTER 2

"What do you mean, Conner isn't dead?" Kalen asked, leaning against the table, before bringing his large coffee cup to his lips. As usual, he looked as if he'd experienced a moment in heaven from that single sip.

"I'm not sure how much clearer I can be. Conner's alive. He took Savannah and did something to screw with her head, and now she hates me. Really hates me. She attacked me."

Pushing up from the table, cup in hand, he paced the area. He stopped mid-length and frowned. It was the same area where he'd been rendered paralyzed by a Mors, a supernatural assassin that Harrah had sent for me. I knew that image haunted him as it did me. We'd both lain on the ground, powerless. It had given Harrah the opportunity to slash my throat. I brought my hand there and ran my fingers along it, gliding over unmarred skin. Except for the memories, there weren't any remnants of the attack. Conner had made sure of that when he'd healed me. I'd been thankful for his assistance although I knew it hadn't been an act of altruism. He'd wanted something from it. Me.

"Now, I have to figure out a way to undo it," I said.

"Undoing a spell isn't really hard," Blu informed us, walking into the office, her neck stretched over the stack of books in her hands. Kalen quickly placed his coffee on the table to take them from her. He grinned at the mocking glare I gave him.

"What? I would have helped you, too," he asserted.

"Sure, after I'd fallen on my face. I'm not completely confident that you wouldn't check to make sure the books were okay first."

He rolled his eyes at my claim. Once the books were on my desk, I stood to examine the stack. They were old magic books. Their leather bindings were worn, and there was a distinctive smell of aged vellum along with a light scent of sage and tannin. I'd forgiven myself for being so reluctant to learn everything I could about my magic. It was a juvenile act of rebellion over a situation that my parents couldn't help. Because of it, I was tasked with learning what I could as an adult. I was lucky that Blu had a wealth of knowledge to give.

"Reversal spells are easier than they sound, if you have access to a great deal of magic"—Blu smiled—"which you do."

"What if the person who cast the spell is stronger than I am?" I asked. She looked flummoxed, as if she couldn't imagine anyone more powerful than me. I'd be lying if I didn't acknowledge that it was flattering.

Kalen's lips fanned out into a scowl of derision. "You're thinking of yourself as a superhero, aren't you?" he teased at my silence at Blu's comment.

"Of course not." I winked and then grinned.

"Liar." I was happy for Kalen and his levity. If he was concerned about Savannah and Conner, he was good at hiding it. I'd come to work just to do research. I couldn't stay in the house with all the things that reminded me of Savannah and not constantly think about her attack on me the previous day. This morning, I'd made the decision to see her again, which Gareth urged me against.

Lucas's position in the city and various connections had made it easy for him to quickly make changes in his home to make it look as though Savannah had lived there. It probably hadn't taken a great deal of effort. Although he spent most of his time at our home, Savannah had spent considerable time there. Even if she'd really lived with him, I doubted he would have been willing to change his modern black and gray–themed home, with stylish stainless steel appliances and expensive white furniture, for her. It fit who he was—one of the oldest vampires in the world and Master of the city. Gareth had been convinced it was the best thing to do, but I'd disagreed. I felt if Savannah saw that Lucas's home wasn't set up as her residence, it would jar her memory. Gareth and Lucas felt it would traumatize her more. It had been two against one, and I was willing to do anything to make the situation better for Savannah, so I'd conceded.

I also suspected that Lucas wasn't opposed to having Savannah in his home permanently. His interest in her seemed to be more than just a conquest, or something fleeting that he had no intention of allowing to last very long. His adulation for her was hard to ignore. It probably had a lot to do with Savannah's adoration of vampires and her overly traditional ways. When he'd sent us flowers, I'd been okay sending him a text message to thank him. She'd felt the need to accept his dinner invitation and send him a thank-you card. A real card—one that you had to leave your house and go to a store to purchase. He'd appreciated the effort and thoughtfulness of it. From the look he'd given me, it had been apparent he knew the only hand I'd had in it had been signing my name, after she'd done all the hard parts. A smile came to my face as I remembered the dinner, and then I felt a sharp ache as images of Savannah attacking me surfaced. The rage and anger that had shone in her eyes unsettled me.

Stop thinking about her, I chastised myself. It wasn't that I didn't want to think about her, but it was a distraction from what needed to be done. I needed to help my best friend.

"There are people stronger than a Legacy: Vertu."

Blu nodded slowly. She knew who they were, but I assumed

she thought we were equal in strength but had different types of magic. And perhaps we were. Maybe I hadn't tapped into all of mine and I was just as strong as Conner. Cynicism rose in me and I quickly squashed the idea. In this situation, I'd rather be a cynic and proven wrong than an optimist and proven foolish.

"But I don't need to be that strong. If I can use Savannah, it will boost my strength enough." I ignored the underlying problem of getting close enough to Savannah to allow her to help. I just needed to find a reversal spell. I'd figure out the rest later.

"Leslie made you food," Gareth informed me as soon as he entered my apartment. "I'm sure you haven't eaten," he said, looking at the stack of books on the coffee table.

"Thank you," I said, taking the dish and setting it on the table next to the pile. It smelled delicious, but I had more pressing things to deal with.

I pushed two books at his chest and placed multicolored strips of paper on top of them. "Look for all reversal spells," I instructed. "Once you find one, just slip a strip of paper in to mark it." I would have highlighted them if they were my books, but they were loans from Blu.

With a half-grin, he gave the books and then me a look. "Good evening, Anya."

I glared at him.

"Levy. Do you ever plan to use your birth name?"

I shook my head. I was Levy, and even if the Legacy were out, I'd been Olivia far longer than Anya. Pain was attached to the name Anya. Not just my parents' deaths, but years of running because of it.

Although I disliked his greeting, at least he'd given me one. I couldn't say the same for me. Leaning forward, I gave him a light kiss on the cheek before sitting down and grabbing the plate of food.

"Thank you," I added as I yanked off the cover, and started picking at the mac and cheese. I hadn't realized how hungry I was until I'd smelled the food.

"Sexy," Gareth mocked as he headed for the kitchen. "Why don't I get you a fork, since that's what most people use when they eat macaroni and cheese. Maybe I'll get a knife to keep you from clawing at the chicken, too." He mumbled loud enough for me to hear, "*I'm* supposed to be half animal."

"I heard that," I shot back, laughing.

"Wasn't trying to hide it," he said, returning with the utensils and napkins, handing them over as he sat next to me.

I wiped my hands on the napkin and used the fork to finish the rest of the mac and cheese.

I smiled. "I appreciate it. Tell your nanny it's delicious."

"House manager."

"Fancy word for *nanny*. She cleans your house, prepares your food, grocery shops, and maintains your home. I call that a nanny. But if you want to call her house manager, so be it," I countered with a smile.

He shook his head and turned to the books. "I'll let her know you didn't bother to use any utensils. After her initial shock that I'm dating a cavewoman, she'll be flattered."

"Betty Rubble is hot," I said. When he picked up one of the books I had already gone through, I informed him, "There are a number of reversal spells. They are very specific. I thought there would be a global one—there isn't. So I need to find one specific to what happened to Savannah."

"Her mind was altered. How hard can that be?" He frowned as he thumbed through the book, looking at the various spells that Blu, Kalen, and I had found earlier that day.

"I've modified memories before, but I don't know what memories were implanted in her." It was something I'd done to the Trackers from the Brotherhood of the Order who had come after me. Their name made it seem more respectable than what it really was: a bunch of radical supernaturals whose sole purpose was to find Legacy and kill them. Gareth had been part of that organization. He'd left because he said he couldn't blindly follow their tenets, but it was still a topic of contention between us. I'd like to say it lessened with each day and was easier to accept, but it wasn't. I still had a hard time dealing with it. "Did Savannah say anything to you?"

He nodded, his face grave. Sympathy coursed through his words as he spoke. "She thinks you're evil. In her mind you've killed people indiscriminately. She has an unreasonable amount of fear and hate toward you, and I can't explain it. It's hard to interrogate her because she gets upset the more you're defended. Caution is needed when dealing with her."

"Did you tell her that she's my roommate?"

He ran his fingers through his hair, mussing it. His frown deepened, and as his eyes darkened, the shifter ring seemed to dance a little brighter. It was rather off-putting, as if his eyes were lit from within. "I tried to, but each time she got more and more upset and accused me of lying. And it seemed so incongruent that she considered me a friend, and yet I was defending a person she despises." Gareth rested back on the sofa, running his hands over his face as he breathed out, "What the hell did he do to her?"

"I don't know. But we have to fix it."

"Can he undo it?"

"I'm sure he can. First we have to find him. But even if we can, this is his revenge and what he did to Savannah is a product of it. He wants me to pay." I choked out the last part of the sentence. Needing something to focus on, I grabbed one of the books and perused it.

Three hours later we had gone through all the books. I did a second review trying to decipher which would be the best spell. The pressure started to build as I looked at the number of colored slips peeking out from the pages. There were so many, and I didn't have the option of trial and error. It felt like a one-shot deal. If it failed, not only would Savannah see me as the enemy, but it would confirm her belief that I was some type of monster: after all, I tried to put a spell on her.

I joined Gareth and rested back on the sofa. He placed his hand on my leg and gave it a gentle squeeze. "We'll figure something out. I have the SG working on it, too. Unfortunately, with Victor there, his orders are taking precedence." Of course they would; he was the head of the Federal Supernatural Reinforcement, a federal agency equivalent to the FBI. My introduction to them hadn't occurred under favorable conditions. In fact, they were downright hostile. They'd arrested Gareth and me after I'd killed Harrah, who'd sent assassins after me. It had been a messy situation and a source of discord between Gareth and the FSR head, but eventually we'd been released. The FSR had remained a presence in the city since the attacks at the Solstice festival. Since that incident, they'd joined the Supernatural Guild in looking for the people responsible, and Victor, the head of the FSR team, had started the initiative to introduce the remaining Legacy to the world. Well, to have me do it, which left me with being tasked with finding the remaining ones.

"Have you found out anything about the attack?" I asked.

The muscles of his neck became extremely taut. His nephew, Avery, had been one of the victims. Although Gareth seemed hell-bent on making Avery's life a living hell to counter the teen's mother's extreme leniency and indulgence of his whims, he loved him and would do anything to protect him.

"No, we have no idea. It seems like Humans First has disbanded and the offshoot radical organizations that have sprung up in their place aren't considered a threat. Just a bunch of idiots screaming their dislike for supernaturals. I figure if they're ignored long enough they'll go away." He sighed heavily and looked at the clock. "It's getting late, we should get to bed."

I scoffed. *"We."*

"Yes, we." He took off his shirt and I averted my eyes with

great difficulty. Looking at Gareth, the well-formed muscles of his chest, torso, and back, and the sexy knowing smirk, made it difficult to deny him. Something he wasn't oblivious to.

"You seem to be working really hard at that," he teased, pointing out how much effort I was putting into ignoring the half-naked man standing in my living room.

He approached me and kissed me on the cheek. The second time he kissed me his tongue slipped out, tasting my skin, teasing me. I would have given in—but the smirk. Why the haughty smirk? It just pinged at my obstinance.

Stretching, once again giving me a full view of his body, he grinned when I looked, taking him in before snapping my gaze away when he noticed. "I'll just wait for you in the bedroom. I'm sure you'll be in after you finish making whatever point you're trying to make. I'm assuming you're trying to prove you're not that attracted to me and we both know that's not the case. But, please, do carry on."

A mischievous smile kinked the corners of his lips as he turned and headed for my room.

CHAPTER 3

The next day I walked into work and was subjected to several minutes of contemptuous stares from Midwest Barbie and Ken before they managed to pull their shocked gazes from my clothes to the books I was toting with me. Blu was stretched out on the sofa. Her tortoiseshell-framed glasses had hints of blue in them, like the midnight tint on the tips of her tightly curled hair. She wore a white shirt, crisp with a woven design on it, dark blue fitted jeans, and dark brown strappy heels. I looked like I was ready for a long night of research and she looked like she was holding a book for a photoshoot. Kalen made me look even more out of place. Who still wore vests? He had a dark blue one, worn with a striped shirt and dark brown slacks that complemented the colors in the shirt.

Kalen gave my outfit—an oversized white shirt, dark green jeans, blue and white Converse, and a messy high ponytail— a look of derision before allowing it to fade into a sympathetic smile. I figured he'd reminded himself of the real emergency, which had nothing to do with fashion.

Returning to his research, his gaze slipped from me to the book he was holding. He walked the length of the room, pacing with the book in his hand. His fingers moved aimlessly each time he passed me, itching to change my attire, which apparently was so egregious it was stifling his concentration.

"If you do it, you might lose a finger. Do you really want to risk that?" I teased when it looked like he was losing his fight against the urge. His massive sigh caused him to fold into himself, as he conceded that I could choose my own clothing.

He flashed me a scorned look before taking a seat in a chair near Blu.

"Okay, based on what you said Savannah is experiencing, this might be the best one." Blu didn't sound sure. I needed her to be positive, without-a-shadow-of-a-doubt sure. I didn't think I was going to get that. That was one of the complexities of magic. Location spells, cognitive manipulations done by the fae, compulsions by vampires, shifting one's body, and my ability to modify memories and implant them, use defensive magic, and build wards and protective barriers all seemed easy on the surface. Spells were never easy; there were nuances to them. Like finding the right key for a door. One might fit but it wouldn't turn. And that was the problem we were facing. Conner had modified Savannah's memories, and I could reverse it, but I had to find the right pattern to complement his. And since I didn't know everything he'd implanted, which memories had been modified, and what emotions those memories evoked, I was lost. Lost and desperate.

Later that evening Gareth and I were met at his door by a glaring and disgruntled Lucas. I'd heard the Master's reluctance when we'd discussed the plan over the phone earlier. Doubt must have overtaken him in the time it took for us to get there.

"I don't think this is a good idea," he mused, frustrated.

"We don't have a lot of options," I pointed out, my frustration mirroring his. I understood how he felt. Doing a spell while Savannah was asleep felt like an invasion, wrong on so many levels. But she wasn't likely to let me do it while awake, and I couldn't have Lucas compel her just in case it had an adverse effect on the spell. There weren't a lot of options.

After several moments of deliberation, Lucas reluctantly conceded and led us to his apartment. Savannah lay on his bed, her wealth of honey blond hair fanned out and one arm extended, exposing the open puncture wound where Lucas had fed from her. It was weeping blood. He'd purposely left it open so I could get a sample for the spell.

We moved in silence around her. I'd memorized the spell and quickly pulled out a knife and sliced my hand. I said the spell and felt strong magic pulsating through the room. It ensorcelled us and strummed through the air. I could see the kaleidoscope of colors and feel its cool breeze.

It was working. Or at least, I felt it was. I'd convinced myself that nothing that felt this strong could fail. Optimistic, but I needed to be. I needed this to work. My desperation was just as thick, heavy, and ever-present as the magic.

Savannah jumped up with a start as if she'd been shaken awake. Her normally placid gray eyes fixed on me, but the rage there was worse than it had been at the hospital. She looked savage and vengeful as she lunged at me. I grabbed her and tossed her. Her legs tangled with mine as we hit the floor. She jammed her elbow into my throat. I gasped for air. Rolling on top of me, she circled her hands around my neck. I didn't want to hurt her but I couldn't allow her to hurt me, either. I grabbed her wrist and pressed against the pressure points, trying to get her to release. She was determined, and unyielding violence wafted off of her. It was as if an assassin had been awakened, and her only goal was to kill me.

"Savannah." I said her name through a strained, tightened throat. The pressure on her points started to work and her hold loosened. I shoved her and rolled away. Assuming the defensive position, I waited for her to attack. She would have if Lucas hadn't grabbed her.

"Get your hands off of me," she demanded, beating her fists against his forearm. It probably would have deterred a human. If Lucas hadn't been looking at her, he wouldn't have been aware of how violent and aggressive her strikes were.

His voice was calm and soothing as he called Savannah's name, but she couldn't hear anything over her demands that he let her go. Thrashing wildly, she hit at his hand, demanding her release. After several more failed attempts to calm her, he released his hold. She spun away from him. Her eyes were furious, blistering as they bounced between Gareth, Lucas, and me. She reserved the most ire for me. A cloud of realization came over her face: I wasn't the only enemy in the room. Lucas and Gareth had joined the ranks. She slowly backed toward the door. When she was close enough she opened it.

"Savannah, please don't leave," Lucas pled. He started to advance toward the door, exhibiting the same vampiric ease of movement but purposely slow as if he was approaching a terrified animal. He kept saying her name over and over, a gentle melodic cadence that wasn't enough to calm her. When she fixed him with a look of betrayal, he halted.

"We're trying to help you," he entreated. "You're not well."

I wanted to do more to explain, but she wouldn't believe anything that came from me. I admitted defeat. Conner had won. Of all the things he'd done to me, the many attacks he'd executed against me, this one wounded me the most.

Lucas continued to inch toward Savannah. Since her attention was directed at him, I took that opportunity to move. I couldn't let her get out the door. Especially since she was barely dressed, wearing just a simple silk nightgown. Far too flimsy and short for a midwestern autumn night.

Before I could get to her, she was running out the door. Lucas darted after her with vampire speed.

Gareth and I followed. Lucas lived above the club he owned, Devour. Very few people seemed shocked by the scantily clad woman running through the club toward the exit. The suits, the men guarding the door, were there. They looked startled by Savannah's appearance. Not the clothing, but the fact that she was running away from Lucas. Lucas attempted to maintain his composure and offer a front of coolness despite how embarrassed he must have felt that a woman was running out of his club, barely dressed, obviously from his apartment. Savannah had been seen with him enough that people knew the two of them were involved.

"Carry on, there's nothing to see. Just a disagreement," Lucas said in a neutral voice as he attempted to de-escalate the situation to nothing more than a quarrel among lovers. He looked menacing; it was a vamp thing, he couldn't help it. His agile movements made him seem lethal despite his attempts to look innocuous.

"We have to let her go," Gareth said.

"No," Lucas and I responded in unison, exiting Devour behind Savannah. Combined with the wafer of the moon, the streetlight offered enough illumination for me to keep track of her movements. Light was something neither Lucas nor Gareth needed.

A few club visitors had edged their way out of the building, and Lucas was aware of them. His irritation with the spectators spread over the defined planes of his face.

"Savannah, you have to come back in." Concern eased into his words, and there were cracks in his composure. He seemed unsure how to handle her. That lack of assurance seemed odd on a person who epitomized self-confidence.

"You know what she is—what she's capable of—and you allowed her near me." Anger fueled Savannah's words. The moments ticked by and she stood several feet from him, looking confused. I became hopeful that maybe my spell had some late effects. Perhaps she recognized me.

I would have ignored the crowd until something whizzed in Lucas's direction. He turned and caught the stake before it hit him in the chest. That moment cost him—all of us. Strong magic moved like a cloud, covering the area and blocking the meager light available. The street became smothered and darkened. Conner was present within a fraction of time. Savannah's back pressed against his chest as he wrapped his arms around her and disappeared.

Lucas was no longer able to contain his emotions and directed them at the shooter, who was foolish enough to make another attempt. Lucas no longer hid his preternatural abilities, and with a flash of movement that seemed fast even for a vampire, the angry predator was unleashed. The car couldn't back away fast enough. Lucas was upon it, ripping open the door and yanking the shooter out of the passenger seat. The car kept moving, leaving him behind. He wore camouflage similar to that of the shooters who'd attacked at the Solstice festival and possessed the same look of defiance and hate. Seconds later, I heard Gareth call Lucas's name, demanding that he stand down. Then there was a jerk of the shooter's neck and a loud crack, and Lucas let the man slip out of his grasp. Gareth followed with a string of curse words.

"I told you to stand down!"

"I'm not under your command. I don't follow your rules," the vampire said, drily looking at the empty space where Savannah once stood.

"They aren't my goddam rules, Lucas. They're fucking laws." More curses.

As sirens broke through the noise of the crowd, some people headed for their cars, and others moved back into the club.

Within minutes, Gareth was ushering Lucas into a human police car.

"Dammit, Gareth, you can't keep arresting your friends." I was completely exasperated.

"Lucas and I aren't friends," he said in an even voice.

"Fine, you can't keep arresting vampires-that-you-have-a-strange-interaction-with-and-know-because-you-are-both-on-the-Supernatural-Council-and-date-best-friends. Is that better?"

"He didn't leave me a lot of choices. The man was disarmed. He didn't have to kill him." I couldn't detect a lie in the same manner that Gareth could, but my BS alarm was beeping like crazy. I wasn't sure the results would have been different if Gareth had gotten to him first. The only thing that might have stopped him was the hope that the shooter could have offered information on the virus.

"What will happen to him? He can't go to jail."

"Usually these things are handled quite differently." *Differently* being that Harrah would come with her kind and wholesome face and wipe away the humans' minds by just walking in the room. The next day she would be on all the networks doing a brilliant PR spin of the events. But that wasn't an option since I'd killed her and they hadn't replaced her.

"The man tried to kill him, twice," I huffed.

"I know," he pushed out through teeth tightly clenched in frustration. "This is the last thing I wanted to deal with."

As soon as Gareth dropped me off at home, I rushed into the house. Grabbing one of my knives, I slashed it over my hand in order to do another location spell, hoping Conner was too weak from traveling with Savannah to block it. I stood in anticipation over the brightly lit map, waiting for colors to light up to show his location. Once again, I was left with nothing. Savannah was scared and with Conner. *Damn.*

CHAPTER 4

*G*areth stood quietly, watching me pace back and forth in my living room.

"He wouldn't just take her without a reason. He has an agenda. I just need to know what it is," I fumed. I wasn't even pacing anymore; I was pounding on the ground, trying to release the pent-up energy and frustration directed at Conner. I didn't think I'd ever had so much rage, anger, and hate in me, and it was all for him. It had been twenty-four hours since Lucas had been arrested, and I was reluctant to ask what had happened with the situation. There was no doubt that Lucas had killed the man. However, after being shot at twice by a crossbow, was he not expected to retaliate? To not defend himself?

As if he'd read my mind, Gareth said, "Lucas was released."

"Released and not charged or released on bail?"

"No charges were filed against him."

I studied Gareth. "How many favors did you have to call in to make that happen?" His face folded into a frown before he wiped his hands over it.

It was probably safe to say that when a person had been around as long as Lucas had, they would have accumulated quite a few favors as well as connections. I was sure being Master of the city and extremely wealthy didn't hurt, either.

"It was Victor," Gareth said in a pensive voice. Before I could question him, he continued, "Victor believes there will be another attack."

"So he's sending a message by letting someone who openly killed one of the attackers go?"

"Of course not. However, a lot of people corroborated Lucas's story that it was self-defense. No one seemed to see it as an act of aggression, so there wasn't enough evidence to charge him."

Gareth came to his feet and started toward the door. I looked at him curiously. He shrugged. "Someone's at your door."

Just as he made it to the door, someone knocked. *That's not freaky at all. No, not at all.*

"Because it *was* self-defense," Lucas said, acknowledging Gareth with a nod as he entered the apartment. Did he own a pair of jeans? Or at least a pair of khakis? Once again Lucas looked unscathed by the events of the day before. Dressed in a tailored black suit and a black shirt, with the exception of the silver cufflinks that glinted in the light, he was a vision of darkness. It was an odd contrast against his parchment skin and blond hair. Lucas was usually charismatic and warm, with underlying hints of danger and eroticism. Now he seemed laden with danger.

"I can find Savannah, but I will need your help."

I wanted to find Savannah just as much as Lucas did, but right now I was apprehensive about working with the Prince of Darkness.

With hesitation, I asked, "How do you know where she is?"

He licked his lips then gripped them with his teeth. It was an impressive feat that he didn't puncture them with his fangs. When he released his lips, he allowed them to curve into a half-smile as he averted his eyes from mine. He started off slowly, considering each of his words before he spoke. "Although Savannah is different with you since the abduction—" He stopped. "With me

28

she is still the same. There are certain proclivities that she enjoys. When I take from her, she likes to do the same thing to me. She doesn't have fangs so I often—"

"I get it. No need to give me any more details. I don't need to know everything. We're good," I quickly interjected. I could feel the heat rise over my cheeks and on the bridge of my nose. I understood that when they were together, they were *together*, but I didn't want to know the specifics. I'd gone on enough trips with Savannah to various lingerie stores to get more than an eyeful and often an earful when she decided to go into detail as to why she had to purchase so much. He didn't seem to possess enough patience to undo a bra clasp and instead opted to rip them off her. Savannah had offered this information freely just to see my response. She knew I wasn't happy she was dating a vampire, but at this moment, I was so glad she was. We would be able to find her because she'd consumed his blood. Lucas stared at me, darkly amused as my face scrunched in disgust at the idea.

"I can track my blood," he said.

"Yeah, I got that. No details!" I spouted back, knowing I could never unhear what he'd said. His eyes dropped to my neck and homed in on the veins, or rather the area where the veins should be. He probably couldn't help himself. I gathered that the exchange between them coincided with sexual acts. But I imagined that wasn't enough to sustain him and he had to use other sources.

Lucas was becoming increasingly agitated as the minutes ticked by. It was safe to assume that the moment he suggested something, he expected it to be done. I didn't believe that expectation was solely driven by his feelings for her. He'd lived so long and acquired such standing in the city and among other vampires that someone not bending to his will was foreign to him.

"We should leave," he urged, impatient.

"I think it would be a good idea if we called for others to assist," Gareth suggested from behind him. Lucas glanced over his shoulder and shot Gareth a chilled look. Was it because he asked him to wait, because he was still a little upset about being arrested, or a combination of both? Since both were on the Magic Council and dealt with each other consistently, there had to be a foundation to form a friendship, or at the very least a tangible association. But the more I considered it, the more likely it seemed that they probably hadn't. They were two dominant personalities used to unwavering loyalty and unconditional power.

"I don't mind the assist if they can get there in time. But I won't wait on them," Lucas said sternly.

"The SG has access to magic, something neither one of us has."

Lucas dismissed Gareth with a wave of his hand. "You have immunity to it."

"Not his magic." Agitation laid heavily over his words. The idea of being subjugated or even influenced by magic bothered shapeshifters. Their immunity to most magic afforded them a certain level of arrogance toward others and a god complex. But Legacy and Vertu magic reduced them to mere mortals. They didn't like it, and Gareth displayed his displeasure with the heaviness of his frown.

"I'm going to get her. I just thought you'd want to know," Lucas huffed out as he headed for the door. I didn't care how much he huffed and puffed; if Savannah was behind one of Conner's wards, his self-righteous indignation and tenacity weren't going to be enough. He was going to need magic, and a great deal of it. Gareth and I both knew that, so when he headed for the door, we didn't make a move to stop him. Logic would do that.

Lucas's glower darkened his mood to match his clothing. "Levy, if Conner has her, I will need your help," he admitted quietly. Ordinarily I would have given him a hard time about his humility, but this wasn't the moment. He seemed genuinely upset that Savannah was missing, and I sympathized. He couldn't do anything about it without the assistance of others. This was something new for him and couldn't be easy for him to admit.

Being followed by Gareth and an SG officer and passing two human police cruisers didn't seem to slow Lucas down as he sped through the streets, barely adhering to any of the traffic signs and ignoring nearly all lights. The homes and buildings we passed were nothing more than blurs of color, stucco, and brick. When he finally stopped, I wasn't surprised that our trail had led us into the woods where I'd first encountered Conner. I got out of the car, Gareth easing in close behind me as we navigated through trees, thick grass, and magic-coated air. Moving at vampiric speed, Lucas was several feet ahead. We had to run several times to keep in step with him, which was difficult as he moved in flashes without giving us any warning.

Lucas finally stopped in the middle of the forest, his eyes flickering around the area. He frowned, frantically searching. Magic thrummed in the air. I tightened my grip on the twins, looking around, too, trying to get a sense of where Conner might be and hoping to follow the origin of the magic. There wasn't a pull, just strong magic lingering in the air from being used. I wondered if I'd be treated to another one of Conner's taunting messages. Gareth noticeably sucked in air and frowned.

"Her scent is here," he said, taking easy steps to survey the area.

Lucas paled. "Yes, she *was* here." Lifting his arm seemed to be an effort as he pointed to a tree. It wasn't the tree that was affecting him, but the drops of blood that stained the grass in front of it.

"Do you think it was her leaving us a clue?" one of the witches from the SG asked, easing up behind us.

I shook my head. "No, it's Conner playing games with us." I pointed to a spot to the right where I'd been left another note.

Bright gold calligraphy painted the air. I WILL BREAK YOU AND THEN I WILL KILL YOU.

I blew out a breath but it wasn't enough. My head pounded and my heart ached. I could deal with Conner and anything he threw in my direction, but I couldn't deal with him making Savannah a pawn in his sadistic game. I tried to stand up taller but instead, my heavy sigh made me sink further down. If I didn't pull myself together, I would eventually be balled up in the fetal position. I forced myself upright. I didn't sense Conner's magic near me, but if by some chance he was able to see me, I wouldn't give him the pleasure of watching me crumble piece by piece.

Reining in my erratic emotions, I took several more breaths to make sure I could talk in a steady voice. "Can you track her to any other locations?" I queried, lowering my voice until it was mild and soothing enough to calm Lucas's incipient rage. His anger was restrained, but I could see it unraveling by the moment.

"He should have been dead. Why isn't he dead?" Lucas turned his anger to Gareth, who wasn't exactly the picture of tranquility at the moment. The game of cat and mouse was frustrating.

"I mauled him, dug my claws into his chest, and did everything but rip out his heart." Gareth took a step toward Lucas. "I doubt you could survive that. I was sure he wouldn't have." It was a great explanation if we ignored the subtle threat that lingered in the first part. I held the twins tighter as I strategically eased my way between them and prepared to give Lucas and Gareth a magical bitch slap if needed. I didn't have the time or patience to play mediator when I had a psycho to deal with. I'd just let my magic do the talking and if necessary give a half-assed apology for my bad behavior later.

"He's doing this to get back at me. Don't lose focus. We need to find Savannah," I urged, maintaining my position between them. It took longer than I wanted, but after several minutes they nodded and backed away to return to their cars.

Once again, drawn to another of Conner's playgrounds, we were navigating through a crowd of trees, and I could sense the magic that entwined with the smell of oak. Lucas and Gareth inhaled, changed direction, and sped through the dense trees. Bile crept up my throat when we stopped at a tree with a bloodstained leaf pinned to its bark with a knife.

"What the fuck is wrong with him!" Lucas growled. Anger blazed in his eyes and he tensed. Gareth seemed to be holding it together but I didn't have any doubts that the game was wearing on him as well. This was the third location. Three times Conner had sent us to a false location only to reward us with a taunting message spouting his plans to break me and then kill me. My control seemed to be the only thing keeping Lucas and Gareth from losing it, but even my resolve was faltering.

"You should have killed him when you had the chance," Lucas said, pushing past us. Gareth, hands balled at his side, started toward him. I grabbed his arm before he could escalate the situation.

"He cares and he's feeling helpless. It's Lucas, can you imagine how that makes him feel?" I shrugged and worked at a smile but it was a poor effort. I was unable to commit to it and it quickly faded. Gareth placated me with a faint chuckle.

"This is so frustrating." His hands ran over his hair, mussing it.

An equally disturbing sight met us when we arrived at the fourth location. The nightgown Savannah'd had on the night before was pooled at the bottom of a tree. I was having a harder time staying strong and being the voice of reason. I wanted to hurt Conner so badly that the thirst for revenge dried my mouth. I imagined the sadistic pleasure he was deriving from tormenting us.

He's only using her to get at me; he won't really hurt her.

I really hoped I was right.

Hands shoved deep into his suit pockets, Lucas dropped his head and closed his eyes. "I don't feel anything anymore."

Because he's played his games for the day; he's done for now.

"He's using magic to block you from tracking her," I informed him softly.

"What can we do to find her?" he asked.

"For now, nothing."

CHAPTER 5

*N*early ten hours had passed, and Lucas's look of anger and hopeless resignation stayed with me. We hadn't wanted to give up the search but had nothing else to go on, and blindly canvassing the city would have left us too tired and frustrated. I'd sounded confident enough when I'd told them that Conner wasn't finished playing with me, and that had offered Lucas some assurance. It was a little disturbing how well he understood the actions of a person driven by the thirst for revenge. Most of the ride back to my home, I'd speculated whether it had to do with his understanding of how Conner would use Savannah. That would confirm my belief that Lucas had guards because of a dark past.

When I entered the Supernatural Guild's building later in the day, Lucas's past and Savannah's abduction dominated my attention, distracting me enough that I just shot my hand up to greet Beth the receptionist. Instead of taking the elevator, I used the stairs to expend more energy as I made my way up to Gareth's office. Anger and the thirst for revenge made me feel like an idling race car. Jumpy and ready to take off at the release of a brake.

Gareth and Victor, the head of the Federal Supernatural Reinforcement, stood inside the office a couple of feet apart, and the air was thick with tension. My attention bounced between the two of them and I waited in silence as Victor eventually nodded and left.

"I'm sorry, the door was open," I explained, entering.

Gareth shrugged off my interruption. "The meeting was over. In fact, it shouldn't have occurred," he rumbled.

"Are you two not playing well together? And I thought I was the only one who had that problem."

He grinned. "Well, that's not true at all, you and I play together just fine."

"Really? You can't possibly be proud of that," I retorted, giving him a disapproving look. Based on his slanted smile, he definitely was very pleased with himself.

"What's the deal with Victor?" I redirected as he closed the distance between us. He leaned down and kissed me. Then his hands slipped around my waist, pulling me closer. They moved up my back, to the twins sheathed against it.

"I can't believe they keep letting you up here with weapons," he said, exasperated.

"Maybe they don't see me as a threat. Or maybe they do and secretly want me to stab you with them." He laughed but it was too loud and self-assured, as if the very idea of me doing it was ridiculous.

"You do know that if I wanted to, I could?"

"I'm sure you could, sweetheart," he mused, giving me a light kiss on the tip of my nose. I glared at him, coaxing another devious smile from him. He was enjoying himself too much at my expense.

I was feeling a little stabby as he mocked me. He'd seen me fight too many times to think I couldn't handle myself. I smiled. It made my cheeks hurt because it required so much effort.

"That smile is scary. You look like Harley Quinn."

My mouth dropped open but I quickly snapped it shut. I was

impressed with his knowledge. Most of the time if I mentioned anything about comics, he looked at me as if I'd switched to a different language.

Resting against his desk, he folded his arms across his chest, and his lips quirked into an overly confident smile. "I'm pretty hot to you right now, aren't I?"

"Well, you were about five seconds ago. Once again it's thwarted by your humility," I snarked back and then returned to my question. "What is going on between you and Victor?"

"There was an attack at a soccer game yesterday. Three fae and a mage were hit. Victor is getting uncharacteristically nervous. Nervous people are impulsive, and that's where he is right now. He wants to start bringing in a list of people who have no firm affiliation with Humans First or any of the anti-supernatural organizations. Their only link to those groups is something as nebulous as being Facebook friends. It's not enough and if we start going that aggressively, the police and other agencies won't help. They'll consider us lawless and renegade. Their first instinct will be to protect the humans from us. We'll need their assistance on this."

I clenched my teeth so hard my jaw ached as I held back the words. Gareth always considered the political implication of things. It was his job to do so, but it made some of his decisions reactive instead of proactive. The attacks were getting out of control and eventually someone wasn't going to get to the Isles in time and would die. Then what? The supernaturals had placed their trust in the SG and the FSR, because no one had died from the attacks. I was convinced that once they did, the gloves would come off, the supernaturals would seek their own justice, and innocent people would be hurt or worse in the process.

"Are you going to say what's on your mind?" he asked wryly. I suspected he could sense that I'd sided with Victor. It was definitely not what I wanted my stance to be, but I wanted to be proactive.

Before I could address it, his office phone rang. He picked it up, and someone said a few things that sounded like angry rumblings from my position a few feet away.

"There's been another attack, in Coven Row," he growled, hanging up the phone. I wasn't going to have the conversation about Victor with him: I could see the concession in his grimace as he rushed out of the room. I allowed myself to get lost in the crowd of agents streaming out the front door; I needed to remain out of Gareth's sight because I didn't want him to ask me not to go. There was no way I was going to stay away.

Coven Row wasn't nearly as deserted as I'd expected it to be after the Solstice festival attack. Supernaturals still attended clubs but seemed reluctant to hang out in obvious places like Coven Row, which catered to humans who enjoyed buying spells, partaking of herba terrae—witch's weed, something they had in common with supernaturals—and experiencing the magical escapes on offer.

Humans might continue to visit Coven Row, but they'd probably be met with the same CLOSED signs that were visible now. Whoever was responsible for the attacks might not have gotten rid of the supernaturals but they had instilled fear. It might not be their ultimate goal, but it was a result. There was a cure for the virus but it was in limited supply, especially since Savannah wasn't easily accessible to assist.

I looked around and found an arrow that had missed its target. Standing over it, I examined its location and tried to figure out where the shot had originated. There were no buildings tall enough for the assailant to have remained unseen, which meant they'd had to be lower, maybe in a car—a drive-by like at Devour—or located in the parking garage. Either way, the various cameras would've caught them. Gareth was preoccupied with evaluating the area, speaking with store owners, and questioning witnesses. I went to the parking garage. The parking space closest to the stores, which would've given the best access, was vacant. It could have been coincidence but it was highly unlikely. This had to be the spot the shooter had used.

Conner's familiar magic laced around me, yanked me back. The moment it released me, I spun, twins in hand, shoving them into the open space. His deep, goading laugh wisped out of the depths of the garage. Running, I followed the sound, but the area it had come from was empty.

He was there, I knew he was. "How long do you plan to play this game?" I yelled into the darkness.

"Until it no longer entertains me, and then I'll kill you," he drawled. Ice coated his words.

Sai still in hand, I searched the garage and found him tucked away at the far end, watching me. Something I was sure he'd been doing the entire time I searched for him. His lips lifted at one corner into a half-smirk as he moved closer. I stood in a vacant parking space, and he kept one car between us.

"Return Savannah. You don't have a problem with her. It's me you want to hurt—not her."

"True. I don't want to hurt her, but I will for no other reason than to get back at you. You left me for dead, after I saved you." His voice dropped low, and his last words quivered. I wasn't sure if it was from sorrow or anger or a combination of both.

"You were going to keep me there."

"So? With me is where you belonged. This…" His gaze swept over the garage and then settled on the view outside of it. While he was distracted, I considered attacking him. As if he knew my intentions, his eyes snapped back to me. Frowning, he continued, "This…this isn't a world for us. We deserve better, and you're too foolish and complacent with it to even consider obtaining more. They've made you ashamed of who you are. We are the most powerful beings that exist—we should not be ashamed. We should be feared and revered." The crisp coolness had returned to his voice and made its way to his eyes as if he blamed me personally for the absence of the nirvana he'd never experience.

"This paradise you speak of could've only been achieved by killing others. That's why I stopped you. Don't make me the villain in your delusional story." I quickly relaxed my clenched jaw. Guilt rose and settled heavily on me. I wouldn't be able to live with myself if he took his anger with me out on Savannah.

"In a war there are always casualties," he said softly and too casually for a discussion about murder.

"It's a war of your creation. There doesn't have to be one. If you do another Cleanse, a new chapter in history is added, and once again we are the antagonists. Our children will deal with the same things we have to now. They'll be viewed the same way people view us—as monsters," I pointed out. Reasoning with Conner didn't work and I wasn't sure why I continued doing it.

Remaining silent, he studied me. His eyes were deep, penetrating, and dark, and reading them was difficult. Gripping my sai, I prepared to react if necessary.

"If you had stayed longer, I do believe I would have convinced you."

"Return Savannah's memories and let her go home and I'll go with you. We can talk then, see if we can come to a mutual agreement," I offered. Spending more time with Conner, hearing his inane spiel about a paradise where Vertu and Legacy lived, with only a few allies living outside of our separate world, mingling with the humans and ensuring they wouldn't rise again, was less appealing than gouging my eyes out with my sai, but to save Savannah, I would do it.

Feeling the weight of his penetrating gaze, I tensed. He shook his head. "No. Now you are lost beyond redemption. Your commitment to them can't be broken." He disappeared.

"Conner!" I kept calling his name. For several long minutes I waited for him to return, although I knew he wouldn't. He hated me and wanted to make me suffer in a way he felt I deserved for my alleged betrayal. It was written all over his face and hard to deny.

CHAPTER 6

*I*t took me hours to fall asleep because I couldn't stop thinking about my interaction with Conner. Consequently, I wasn't in a good mood when Kalen called me at five in the morning to tell me he needed to talk and was on his way to my apartment.

Less than five minutes after I hung up the phone, there was a knock at the door. I opened it, rubbing my eyes before widening them to try to wake up. Gareth was as alert as if he'd been awake for hours. I hated people who could just spring out of bed and leap into action, and that was exactly what he was. He'd pulled on his pants and was standing near the door by the time I had put on my clothes.

Blu and Kalen were more casually dressed than I ever thought I would see. She had on a simple tank top, yoga pants, and a hooded sweatshirt, and her hair was pulled back in a braid. Kalen wore what he considered casual wear, a pair of pants and a V-neck t-shirt that conformed to his thin, toned physique. They looked slightly disheveled—or their version of it—and I guessed that they'd pulled an all-nighter doing research. His eyes were alight with excitement, a feeling that Blu clearly didn't share.

"I have a really great idea," he said excitedly.

Blu frowned. "I wouldn't say it's a good idea. It has a very high success rate but is extremely dangerous." Then she directed her attention to Kalen and gave him a sharp look. "So you can't say it's a good idea if she could possibly die."

He gave her a quelling look in an effort to silence her and she made it quite apparent that wasn't going to happen. As they entered the apartment, the frown she'd directed at him eased. When he reached for her hand, she moved away from him. She *definitely* wasn't on board with whatever he was about to offer.

He leaned into her. "The other spell failed. When they get her back, Levy has to make sure this one doesn't," he whispered.

Blu's deep brown eyes were on me and I could see the concern in them. "Desperation makes people fools. Fools often die quickly," she warned.

It was something I often said myself. Fear was another problematic emotion because it made people irrational. I wasn't afraid but I was definitely desperate. "I agree. But if it'll help Savannah, I have to try. I'm the reason she's in this mess."

She nodded in assent, and Kalen took that as a cue to proceed. "You know how Savannah is an *ignesco*, she can indiscriminately enhance anyone's magic?" he started.

I nodded.

"*Roboro* works the same way. It's a magic booster. It's a spell that will boost any magic or any subsequent spells you do after it is invoked. I don't think the spell you performed was the wrong one, it just wasn't strong enough to undo Conner's. If he's as powerful as you say, you need to be twice as strong as he is to reverse anything he does. The *roboro* will fix that."

I didn't want to be too optimistic because I could see the pained look on Blu's face. Her eyes narrowed on Kalen and she allowed them to travel up and down him. By the uncomfortable way he looked, I could tell he knew she was doing it. "Go ahead and tell her about the ingredients needed for the spell," she said in a fake dulcet voice.

"You need the bloom of a *Culded*," he said, his voice significantly lower than before as if he was whispering a secret. His tone had lost all enthusiasm. Instead it was heavy, laden with apprehension.

"Go ahead and tell her where she can find it," Blu interjected again, in an acerbic huff.

He inhaled and held the breath for a long time, and just as he was about to speak, Blu said, "It's on Menta Island."

Kalen made a face and then rolled his eyes away from her. "Why don't you go ahead and finish telling her, darling?" he rebutted in a saccharine tone that matched hers—his passive-aggressive way of showing his irritation. With an exaggerated gesture, he bowed and stepped back, giving her room to move in front of him and finish.

His dramatics weren't lost on her and she fixed him with a look but continued. "Menta Island is located near the Virgin Islands, and its occupants choose to stay as far away from us as we want to stay away from them. It's a good rule to live by. A rule that keeps us alive." I assumed that her concern for me had made her overzealous and dramatic until Gareth sucked in a sharp breath.

She gave him a knowing half-smile as if they were bonded by apprehension.

"I'm good at protecting myself," I told her. Not because I was arrogant but because she seemed to need the assurance. Obviously Kalen hadn't truly expressed the dangers of going to the island.

Blu sighed. "I know you are. We want Savannah back just as much as you do." I didn't just *want* Savannah back; the city needed her as well. With a combination of my blood and Savannah's they were able to treat those stricken by the virus delivered during the Solstice attacks. I assume they had saved some of the concoction, but magic couldn't be duplicated the same way an antiviral could. Once they ran out, they were out.

She started to pace the room, and for the first time Kalen seemed to share her concern. "I think you've been given a crappy deal. Half of your life you had to hide and pretend to be something you're not. People try to kill you because of their bigotry and hold you responsible for something you had nothing to do with, and yet you found it in yourself to actually help us when we needed you. No one can do anything to help you now that you need it. It's not fair," she said.

Long ago I'd realized that life just wasn't fair. Once I'd accepted that, things had become a little easier to handle. "You're helping me now. You've helped me countless times."

Nothing I said was going to soothe her worries. After several moments of consideration, her frown faded. "It's not easy to get there, either," she informed me.

"If she decides she wants to go, I'll get her there," Gareth said. His lack of enthusiasm was starting to worry me as well, but with full disclosure about the island made, Kalen had regained a look of muted excitement. He was confident in the spell and my ability to obtain the necessary ingredients for it.

"Well, if you can get the *Culded* the rest will be easy."

"*Easy.* I can't get near Savannah without her screaming or trying to attack me."

"I can do the spell if she won't let you near her," Blu offered. Then her gaze slipped in Kalen's direction. "I think we should go with you."

"No," both Gareth and I responded. Kalen looked relieved. He was a great employer and had become a wonderful friend, but he wasn't likely to run in the direction of danger.

"I think it will be best if you two stay here." It wasn't what Gareth said that bothered me, it was what he hadn't. I could hear the doubt in his words, as if he was saying he needed them to remain in case we didn't come back.

How dangerous was Menta Island?

Blu nodded and Kalen expelled the breath he'd been holding since she'd volunteered them. They agreed to acquire everything else needed for the spell. By the time they left, we still hadn't decided on a day to go. Gareth wasn't optimistic about setting one, which set off all types of alarms for me.

Once the door closed behind Blu and Kalen, I turned to face him.

"Tell me about Menta Island." The fact that I'd never heard of it whetted my curiosity. "Why does the idea of going there scare Blu so much?" She didn't strike me as the type of person who was easily driven to fear, and she was definitely afraid for me.

He was just about to take a seat, but suddenly rushed past me to my bedroom. I followed close behind. Before his phone stopped buzzing, he picked it up off the dresser and answered. The fact that he could hear his phone vibrating hundreds of feet away was another display of his preternatural abilities. There were a few quick exchanges, which consisted of him asking: "Where?" "When?" "How many supernaturals were involved?" During the conversation he'd started to put on his shoes. His anger and frustration were noticeable, along with the slight flicker of his shifter ring, which had brightened.

"What's the matter?" I asked after he hung up.

"Another attack, in Forest Township." This was where most shifters resided. "They have the shooter and are waiting for me to talk to him. This one seems to know something."

"He's talking?" I asked. Most of the people they'd caught didn't know anything. The few who had information made it very clear they weren't sharing. It was only with the help of the fae that they revealed what little they had. Whoever was behind this went to great lengths to hide his identity.

"No, but he seems like he has something to withhold." I realized that Gareth was trying to get there before the police intervened. Usually the lines between the human and supernatural

45

authorities were well defined. The Supernatural Guild handled crimes that supernaturals committed, and the police handled those by humans. The rules became more nebulous and ill-defined when a crime included a human and a supernatural. When a human committed a crime against a supernatural, there were organizations that petitioned to try to let it be handled by the police instead of the SG because they assumed the perpetrator would be treated more harshly by nonhumans. Most of the time, a human was sent to the police department. When I'd been charged with murdering a fae, a shapeshifter, and a mage, no one had petitioned for me to be sent over to the human courts—but I'd been suspected of being not completely human although I'd been living as one. It probably hadn't helped that the crime had been considered egregious.

"Do you think they'll want him released to the police?"

"Things have been strained. The supernaturals aren't as trusting now that there's someone with the ability to kill them slowly with a simple virus. And the humans are more suspicious now that things aren't being covered up as well as they once were. We need to replace Harrah." He blew out a rough breath. I wondered whether this hypothetical replacement would be as powerful or strategic as Harrah. There had been something ruthless and scary about her, and seeing the results of her absence, I wondered if those qualities were necessary to do her job.

I will not feel guilty. It was easier said than done. Harrah had deserved the ending she'd received. Whether I owned the guilt or not, I had irreparably changed things. She'd provided an invaluable service. Being a powerful fae who could nearly erase a person's memory by just walking into a room had made her a force most couldn't contend with. She'd protected the image of the supernatural community—ruthlessly. If she'd suspected a person was a problem for it, they would eventually be eliminated. I was a problem, and she'd attempted to get rid of me.

"How many shifters were injured?" I asked before he could exit.

"Ten." I was trying to keep up with the number of victims. Eventually they would run out of the cure. We had to find Savannah and get her memory back, or at least locate another *ignesco*.

I hadn't been able to go back to sleep after Gareth left. Instead I spent my time looking up information on Menta Island on the web. After two extensive hours of searching, I understood Blu's concerns; I shared them but for different reasons. There wasn't any information about the island anywhere. Not even an errant article from suspicious sources. Nothing. How did a place exist without someone posting about it? Blu, Kalen, and Gareth knew about it. Was it folklore passed down from generation to generation by word of mouth? For a brief moment, I questioned whether it even existed. It could possibly be a story of a mystical place that was pure fantasy—but behind every fantastical story was a little truth. It wasn't beyond reason that a "Harrah job" had been performed, someone strategically wiping away any evidence of its existence, but I found it hard to believe given the level of detail it would have taken.

My research did reveal articles about small islands that people never returned from and tales of boats disappearing, but there wasn't a specific mention of Menta. Tales of the Bermuda Triangle came to mind.

In need of a break, I took a shower. Steam filled the small bathroom and gave me clarity, or maybe the heat just relaxed me enough to clear my head. I prioritized things. I would find Savannah and then assess her mental state before I considered traveling to an island people were afraid to even document under the cloak of Internet anonymity. Meanwhile, Savannah could stay with Lucas—*wait*. It wasn't unreasonable to think Conner would remove all her memories and implant more false ones to make her think we were all her enemies. Lucas having allowed us to attempt the spell earlier would rationally support the latter. There was no way Savannah was going to be okay with hanging with Lucas.

Back up the bus. I couldn't find Savannah because Conner kept blocking my location spells. I needed the *Culded* to make my magic stronger, break the wards, and find my friend. *Crap, need to go to Menta first.*

Where are you, Conner? I thought as I pulled my towel-dried dark brown hair into a loose bun on top of my head. I examined the roots for any signs of red, my natural Legacy color. Odd persimmon hair was a giveaway and concealing it had become a habit for me, even though it didn't matter as much now. We were going to come out publicly soon and would no longer be reduced to ominous tales and speculations. I wasn't looking forward to it. The questions. The fear. A new crop of anti-supernatural groups whose sole purpose was to make our lives a living hell. It was bad enough we had to deal with the Trackers.

I'd just sat down with a plate of bacon, three donuts, and a bagel with a generous helping of Nutella spread over it when the image of Savannah looking at my plate with disapproval popped into my head. She always managed to scold me for my food choices while posed in one of her advanced yoga positions. A frown didn't look any friendlier in downward dog and looked hostile in warrior.

A knock at the door interrupted my breakfast. Assuming it was Gareth, I opened the door and was surprised by the lively greenish-brown eyes and oddly familiar persimmon red hair of the extremely attractive man standing there. His height, which I estimated at nearly six-eight, was more overwhelming than his overly defined features. A long aquiline nose was complemented by a razor-sharp jawline and broad cheeks. The shadow of a beard covered his face. Even his lips, which were curled into a faint smile, were thin and edged. Tall and slim, he still seemed intrusive as he blocked the entryway.

After we'd stood and looked at each other in a way that could be described by no other term than *weird*, I finally spoke. "Hello."

"Hello," he responded in a deep, raspy voice.

Oh, come on. "This is the part where you tell me why you are standing at my door," I urged.

"May I come in?"

"Probably. But it definitely won't be before you tell me who you are and why you're here."

He smiled. It was forced and strained. "I'm Elijah, and you are Olivia, correct?" Since he hadn't bothered to change the color of his hair, I assumed he wasn't using an alias.

I nodded and waited patiently for him to elaborate. He didn't.

"Seriously, this is like pulling teeth. Elijah, why are you here?"

"You've been looking for me, right?" His intrigued gaze tracked me as I shifted back and forth, anticipating a reason why a stranger was standing at my door. Shoving his hands into his jean pockets, he remained silent.

I exhaled a deep breath, hoping it would calm my nerves, which were being tried by the new visitor. "Let's start again. Hello, stranger who showed up at my door uninvited, what brings you to my home at the lovely hour of eight a.m.? And please feel free to provide as much detail as possible because that will be the difference between me slamming the door in your face and calling the Supernatural Guild, and something worse."

"The Supernatural Guild sent me," he explained, extending his arms to stop me from closing the door. "Tina...Tina Merkle sent me." I quickly realized that he was being just as cautious as I was. He probably had a long history of people hunting him down, too. And Tina being the head of the SG in a neighboring city probably wasn't enough of an incentive to trust me.

"Okay," I said slowly, using those moments to try to figure out what to do. "Give me a moment. I need to make a call." He lowered his arm and I closed the door and locked it. I wasn't sure why I even bothered. If he were a Legacy, a locked door wouldn't stop him. I considered erecting a ward, but I'd run into the same problem: he'd be able to break that as well. Or could he? Was I stronger than him? Maybe as a Legacy, but definitely not if he was a Vertu.

After meeting Conner I'd realized the limitations of my skill with magic. It wasn't wise to think this guy had the same ones I had. Quickly I made my way to my bedroom, grabbed my phone, and called Gareth. It took several rings before he picked up and he sounded rushed and distracted when he spoke. "Yes, Levy?"

"Do you know anything about Tina sending a Legacy to me?"

He cursed under his breath. "Did you not get my text? I tried to call, too, but I've been busy here." I looked at my messages. I had a missed text from him. It was succinct and only requested I call him; he might know a Legacy who could help.

"How does she know him?"

"He was brought in after he had a run-in with Trackers. Tina called me because she suspected this situation was similar to yours and since we're supposed to be finding other Legacy she sent him here."

"Run-in?"

"Yeah, *run-in*, like the one you had a couple of weeks ago." That incident had led to me killing three of those who had ambushed me. I wondered if Elijah's situation had ended similarly. I was reluctant to ask.

"Where is he?" Gareth asked.

"I left him outside to call you."

"Is something wrong with him? Is he odd?"

"Well, I don't see him winning any awards for being particularly normal." Grinning, I added, "And you must be really secure sending random hot guys to my door."

"I have no idea what he looks like. But she seemed to trust him and I trust her. If he possesses as much magic as you do, he could be of use in helping us find Savannah."

He'd beaten me to the suggestion. But if Elijah was as cynical as I was, would he be willing to help me—a stranger? It gave me hope that just on Tina's instruction he'd come to meet me. "I need to talk to him. I'll call you later."

Gareth called my name before I could hang up. "And yes, I *am* that secure."

"And truly humble as well," I mumbled to the dead air.

Quickly, I made my way back to the front door and opened it. "Please, come in."

Giving me an appraising look, he hesitated and then stepped over the threshold.

"I hear you had an incident with Trackers."

"They came up to me and I killed them." He didn't mince words. I wondered if he did it by combat or magic. "I was under the impression that they weren't a problem anymore," he added.

How did he know that Conner had retaliated against several of them after taking them from SG custody?

Before I could ask, Elijah crossed his arms over his chest, gave the room a quick once-over, and returned his attention to me. "Everyone knows about it, but you never know what's truth and what's creative spin to protect the supernatural community." He started to stroll throughout the living room, examining everything in it as if he was trying to get a sense of who I was based on its contents. "Rumor has it that they were part of a hate group— and were killed while the SG was trying to apprehend them. It never rang true to me."

After several moments of looking around the room, he returned to a position in front of me, directing all of his curiosity back to me. We stood several feet apart, and he seemed to be appraising me as much as I was appraising him.

"Is this the first time they've come after you?" I asked.

"No. The other times ended more favorably for the Trackers. I modified their thoughts and made them think they'd killed me. I thought that would stop them."

I gave him a wry smile of understanding because I thought I'd done the same. "You don't change your hair to disguise yourself?" If he was going around with his hair that color, he was a walking target.

He ran his fingers through it, changing it to dark brown, which was more pleasing since the red clashed with his fair skin. "Since I was coming to see another Legacy, I changed it."

Am I the only one who can't do that? "How do you do that?"

Blocking his hand as it came toward me, I stepped back out of his reach.

"Your hair," he pointed out. "It's brown."

"I know, I saw it this morning when I got dressed."

Smiling, he requested, "Change it."

"I don't know how," I admitted softly. For the first time, I was embarrassed by my limitation.

"It's easy enough." Moving forward, he touched a strand of it, a warm tingle moved over my head, and when his smile widened I knew it was our natural color.

"Do you know how to do a protection spell?"

I nodded.

"Can you move objects with your magic?"

Again, I nodded.

"Then you can do it." His face contorted to the side; I figured he was trying to think of a way to show me how to do it. He took my hand, and magic coursed over it. Prickled, moved along my arm, curled around it, and then unfolded in a multitude of directions. It felt like a unique brand of offensive magic and my body responded accordingly to protect me. Heat and energy moved through me, different than anything I'd tried before.

"Think of a color as you move your fingers through your hair and change it."

I should have thought of the color I had before instead of blue.

When I looked in the mirror, I was shocked to see I had electric blue hair with brown ends. I ran my fingers through again, pulling the magic. It seemed so simple with the right directions—as opposed to winging it—and I left it persimmon red and turned from the mirror to Elijah.

"It fits you."

I wasn't going to lie to him; he looked better with brown hair.

"Can you transport?" I asked.

He nodded. Now that he'd edged himself even closer, I became more aware of the undeniable strength of his magic. Was he a Legacy or a Vertu? The idea of him being the latter bothered me. I realized they weren't all the same, but it was a struggle not to consider him an egomaniac whose goal was to start the Cleanse again. Responding to my change in mood, he noticeably stiffened and took a step back.

He looked around the apartment, giving me the impression he was trying to figure me out in the same manner. "It's harder than it looks. Not everyone can do it. My mother can, but my father can't."

"Are you a Legacy?"

He shook his head.

"Thank you for showing me this." I pointed to my hair.

He moved closer to me. He might not have been odd—I was still on the fence about that—but he had difficulty with boundaries and personal space. Despite my doubts, there was something about him I liked. Perhaps it was just the desire to befriend another person like me.

When I offered him breakfast, he was polite enough to accept the donut but turned his nose up at the bacon and Nutella-covered bagel. Maybe I didn't want to be friends with this guy. *He hates bacon and Nutella, clearly there is something wrong with him.*

Three donuts and a cup of coffee later, Elijah had relaxed and was resting back on the sofa.

"How many times have you been tracked?"

Inching his brows together, he considered my question. "Two that I'm sure of, and I believe another was following me for a while but then he disappeared." I wondered if the last one had been called away to help apprehend Conner, never to return.

"I move a lot. My parents have been in the same city for years unnoticed."

It was ridiculous to be envious of something like that, but I was. His parents were alive. The silence between us wasn't uncomfortable but it wasn't cordial, either. Caution, pragmatism, and skepticism seemed to rule us.

"Are you really trying to spearhead the campaign to find and reveal Legacy?" There was a hint of interest and cynicism in his question.

Spearheading made it seem so important and planned, as if it were a well-orchestrated campaign as opposed to me falling into the situation. Instead of pointing that out, I nodded. There were more bouts of strained silence than actual conversation and I was relieved when Gareth called. I excused myself to my room for privacy.

"What do you think?" Gareth asked as soon as I answered the phone.

"About the hot guy you sent to my home?"

"Yeah, you already mentioned that. Besides ogling him, what do you think of him?"

"You know he killed a Tracker. I suspect more."

"And you've killed at least three. Three that I know about, and your point?"

When you say it that way it sounds pretty damn bad.

"He's cautious and I understand why. His magic is strong, really strong. He's a Vertu."

If Gareth was surprised, he didn't let on. "Tina said his magic felt strong. I'm sure he has a mark to mask his just like you do. Do you think he can help find Savannah?"

"I haven't gotten to that part. I wasn't going to introduce

54

myself, offer him a donut, and then ask him to help me track down an egomaniac with plans of world domination. Give me some time."

"Levy, we don't have a lot of time." Getting Savannah back wasn't just for my benefit but for his as well. They'd need her if the attacks continued. "The longer she's with Conner, the more I fear things will end up worse than we can imagine."

I couldn't blame Elijah for the dark looks he shot in my direction. His narrowed eyes told how audacious he considered me. I'd known him all of three hours and was now asking him to do a spell with me to track down Conner. But not before I'd told him everything Conner had done, his plans, and his seeking retribution. And that Conner had been mauled by Gareth and still lived.

"Did you pierce the heart?" He looked over his shoulder and asked Gareth, who was staring at us, his attention going to my hair, which I'd kept red. Briefly, I wondered if it bothered him. He'd made the comment that he'd asked me to keep my natural color and I'd refused, but hadn't refused Elijah. Was Gareth capable of jealousy? He didn't seem to be, despite Elijah commanding a great deal of his attention.

"I don't know, but I went deep enough that I should have."

"Piercing the heart would have done it," he informed us.

"So we die like vampires? You have to pierce the heart with a stake or behead us?" I asked.

Incredulous, Elijah said, "Everyone dies without a head, Olivia." Setting back on task, he said the first few words of the locating spell. Refocused, I positioned the knife to draw blood from me first and then Elijah. It would be the second time we'd done it. Even with our combined magic, our first attempt hadn't been able to break the ward that protected Conner's location. The flicker of color had illuminated but faded before we could get a clear direction.

Cutting my hand, I started the location spell. Elijah shot a look over at Lucas, who was leaning against the wall. My new comrade kept his cool, relaxed demeanor, but kept his eyes on the vampire, who looked particularly hostile dressed in all black again. Gone was his typical suave manner, replaced by tension and barely restrained anger. Although we knew it wasn't directed at us, it was still uncomfortable.

The knife slipped over Elijah's palm and blood welled. He did a location spell, I followed, and we alternated, getting flashes of the location. It flickered and faded, but doing the spell in succession finally gave us a firm location. My hand was sore from being opened so many times, and Elijah looked as if the idea of us becoming friends wasn't an option. I couldn't blame him. After everything I'd told him, perhaps keeping his distance was the smart thing to do.

CHAPTER 7

I squinted at the bright sun that blazed through the thick branches, unable to enjoy it the same way because I was in the woods again, and not on my own terms. Woods and forests had lost their appeal. I wished Conner was a madman with a caffeine or sugar addiction so I could hunt him down in a coffeehouse or bakery. At this point, I'd prefer a park or golf course. Anywhere but another woodland. But he was a creature of habit.

Thick trees crowded the area and their earthy oaky smell consumed the air but didn't mask the magic. I'd have preferred Elijah to come with us, but he'd politely declined. I didn't blame him. Knowing everything he did of Conner, it was a smart choice. He'd promised he would stay in town for a couple of days, but I had a feeling that being around us wasn't on his to-do list. His life was less chaotic than mine and he seemed quite happy to go back to it. He was uneasy about the Legacy coming out; even after the debate where I'd presented the pros of doing so, he'd seemed hesitant.

"Announcing our existence won't automatically garner acceptance," he'd stated several times during our discussion earlier.

Despite his objections his eyes had looked hopeful. I knew he wasn't willing to be too optimistic about the possibilities because he was right, coming out didn't automatically mean we would be accepted or safer.

Dismissing thoughts of Elijah, I continued through the thick mass of trees, tall grass, and dirt trails. There was a sudden rumbling noise, and Gareth reacted first, heading in the direction from which it came. It didn't take enhanced hearing to find the location. An odd, massive creature was coiled around a sleeping Savannah; its three animal heads bobbed, alert and ready to strike. I'd met Conner's pet—a grotesque combination of feline, wolf, and snake—before. I remembered its sinewy movements and powerful strikes. The serpent's head was the part of the creature I despised the most. It moved too freely, making it the one to watch at all times. Its tongue slithered out at our approach. The animal stayed in position, unbothered by my presence, which made the situation seem more ominous. Why was it so calm?

Conner's magic brushed over me and even though I couldn't see him, I felt his foreboding presence. He wouldn't deny himself the pleasure of seeing me fight his little pet. It was doubtful that he cared that I had a shapeshifter and a vampire with me.

"Savannah?" Lucas called out, his voice loud and soothing. Before I could call her name, Lucas lifted a hand to stop me.

Right, she hates me. The pain it caused just wouldn't go away. I realized it was illogical to be hurt by it, but that didn't make it sting any less.

The serpent head stretched its neck the range of its reach until it was just inches from my face, exposing its fangs before recoiling. Were they poisonous? What would they do to Savannah if used on her? Tightening my grip on my sai, I continued to advance.

"Conner, your issue is with me, so take it out on me!" I yelled. Lucas shot me a sharp look. My patience with the vampire was growing thin.

Conner's cruel laughter carried with the wind, floating in the air, bouncing off the trees, creating a menacing echoing sound. I snapped around, surveying the area, trying to isolate the location and find him. Although there were twinges of rationality behind his cruelty, he seemed to have only a tenuous grasp on his sanity and was driven by revenge. That was harder to work with because it wasn't rooted in something tangible like logic, but something as imperceptible as emotions.

Sword in hand, Lucas moved quickly toward the creature in a blur of a movement and was thrown back by a purplish lucent wall that had just sprung up. Returning to his feet, he charged again. Waves of color sparked and powerful magic flowed over the area, but the wall remained.

"I'll have to get her. He wants me," I said, coolly. "He'll block anyone but me."

"It's a trap." Gareth's voice rumbled with anger.

"Of course it is." I inhaled, letting the oaky smell calm me. I'd taken on his pet twice and neither time had been easy. I wondered if things would be harder now that Conner didn't care about my life.

Slowly I approached the wall. It held. "Move back." When the wall remained up, I looked over my shoulder; Gareth and Lucas had only moved inches away, maybe a full foot.

"Gareth."

Reluctantly, he nodded at Lucas, and they kept retreating. Every so often I looked over my shoulder to see how much distance they'd gathered. It must have been an acceptable amount because the wall dropped, the animal uncurled from Savannah, and the snake lurched, mouth open, ready to plunge its fangs into me. Dropping to the ground, I felt it graze the top of my head. I shoved my sai up, piercing the body but missing the throat I'd been aiming for. Blood gushed as I positioned my second sai to strike my intended target. The creature wrapped its body around me. It plucked me up and slung me. Grabbing the end of the embedded sai, I used the force of the toss to rip it out as I crashed to the ground. I rolled to my feet the moment I landed and crouched low, waiting for it to attack again. The serpent's mouth opened, and I leaped, turned out the handle of the sai, and hit the fangs with enough force to break them off. It shrieked and retreated. Twirling the sai, I positioned it with the blade up and waited for another strike. The snake recoiled and made a hissing sound.

A growl reverberated from the wolf's mouth, loud enough that it should have woken Savannah, but it didn't. Conner must've sedated her with a spell. The wolf furled back its lips and growled again. It drew back to slice me with a paw. Distracted, I missed the snake's head, which butted me with such force I lost my footing. The creature used that to its advantage and raked its claws against my stomach. Pain seared through me. Damn, I remembered that feeling from our first encounter and I could go many more years without feeling it again. I heard another roar, but not from the creature. A cave lion's massive body thrashed into the magical wall, trying to break it.

Conner chortled but I refused to try to identify the location of the sound. "I want him to watch you die."

"I've encountered your freaks before and managed to live."

"Because they were instructed to let you live. No such restraints have been imposed this time." Magic slammed into my back; I careened into the animal but was able to roll out of the way before it could take a bite out of me. Once again claws dug into my flesh. I wailed in pain and tears sprang to my eyes. Conner's mocking laughter made me adamant that I wouldn't shed any more. When the claws came at me again, I jammed one of the sai into it and then the other. I yanked the first out and continued through a cycle of four strikes. I was covered in blood as the monstrosity lumbered back. I drew in magic and sent it thrashing through my sai. A pained howl rang in the air and the thing retreated even further. I kept calling up the magic, stronger, fueled by my survival instincts as much as by anger. I dropped one of the twins and pulled magic into me, feeling the summation of it, and coiled it into a massive force and lobbed it at the wall. The barrier held for longer than I expected but eventually it gave. A blur of movement, and Lucas had Savannah in his arms, rushing away from us. The cave lion loped toward the creature. They both made powerful leaps, crashing together in midair. Gareth's commanding feline mass overtook the creature and it fell back. He quickly answered the question of whether the creature could live with one of its heads missing. It was moving despite the sliced-off serpent's head.

The creature had mass on Gareth, but the dead weight was a disadvantage as it lunged again. The cave lion jumped out of its path and clawed its side. It roared. Gareth made another attempt at an attack but was met with claws digging into his own flesh. The monster retreated and bared the teeth of the two remaining heads. On the offensive, the creature watched Gareth's every move, turning as he rounded it, looking for an advantage. Too distracted by Gareth, it wasn't able to react when I attacked from the rear. Leaping onto it, I embedded my sai into its back. The conflation of the two wailing sounds of pain—one from a lion, the other from a wolf—filled the air. The creature bucked like a bull trying to throw me. When it lifted its body to toss me off, it exposed its vulnerable necks and chest to Gareth. He lunged and tore the wolf's neck with his teeth. Conner's pet immediately collapsed. I pulled out the sai and kept stabbing until it stopped moving.

When it was undeniably dead, I snatched out the twins and dismounted. I wiped off my weapons on my pants. Gareth stayed in animal form as we both surveyed the area. We were met with silence, but I could feel Conner's magic—it was tumultuous.

"Conner, your pet's dead." I kept my voice level and even. I wasn't trying to taunt him. "This will not end well for you. You have an issue with me, take it up with me. Leave Savannah out of this. Don't come near her again."

My words were met with more silence. Waves of magic filled the air and twirled around. It was as if Conner was trying to speak to me in magical code. I continued, "I know you're here. Reveal yourself."

A powerful gust of magic slammed into Gareth and me, sending us several feet into the air. We landed, hard, on the ground. Another blast hit Gareth, and then another. Each one sent him farther away from me. I started to roll to my feet and found myself enclosed in a diaphanous shell, with Conner standing over me. I tried to stand but with a wave of his hand, my legs collapsed under me and I hit the ground.

"Stay down." His voice was rough and cruel. A huge contrast to the eloquent and alluring way he'd spoken before. He'd been charismatic and kind, but at that time, he'd been trying to seduce me into his world, to convince me to see things his way and eventually to be with him so I could bear his children.

I didn't like being on my knees looking up at him, especially since he looked like he wanted to take my head off. My eyes widened at his appearance. He was unmarred, as if he'd never felt the claws of a cave lion and been left for dead.

I made another attempt to stand, and once again my legs were swiped from under me. I tightened my grip on my sai and prepared to engage. "I'm not going to stay down," I hissed angrily.

"You'll stay where I put you," he bit back with so much fiery anger it sent shivers down my arms.

I narrowed my eyes on him and looked at him with defiance. Lifting the twins, I lowered my gaze to his crotch. "Are you sure you want me down here? It gives me perfect access. You know I won't have a problem using these."

Oddly, that brought a smile to his face. "Anya, it's your wit that leaves me torn between wanting to taste your lips"—his voice dropped to a sultry purr—"and ripping out your tongue."

"Do I get a vote? Because I'm going for the tongue-ripping option as opposed to kissing you," I sniped back.

His throaty laugh filled the small space. It stopped abruptly as he looked at Gareth, who was beating against the barrier. Conner rolled his eyes. "Your cat annoys me."

More than just annoyance reverberated in his voice; there was a tinge of hate as well. Conner didn't stop me when I came to my feet. Standing face to face, we gave each other matching assessing looks. Conner shot a quick look over his shoulder as Gareth continued to try to break the barrier.

"I plan to kill Gareth," he said matter-of-factly. His emotionless, level tone scared me more than anything. "But not before making his life a living hell. He will rue the day he ever challenged me."

"'Rue the day'? Are you fucking kidding me? Why don't you just wear a cape and dramatically wrap it around you as you disappear into a cloud of smoke? That has supervillain written all over it. 'Rue the day.' Oh. Come. On."

My words were cut short when I was swept up in a cyclone of magic and then tossed against the luminescent barrier. "I will not be mocked by you."

No, but you will be killed by me. Sai in hand, I lunged at him, and was met with air. I whipped around to find him standing behind me. He wasn't angry anymore; he looked bored. I was treated to another of his assessing gazes. His voice had dropped to a chilly timbre. "You ruined it all," he accused. "You're a fighter, a true warrior. We could've had something great. We would have achieved greatness together. Superior to anything anyone could have imagined."

Oh no, he's starting to monologue. Why do they always monologue?

"You're naïve. You think you are going to reveal us without consequences. Harrah knew what you were. How did that work out for you?" He was upon me so quickly magic had to be involved. As he leaned into me, I could see into the opening of his shirt: He hadn't been left unscathed from Gareth's attack. Light rake marks ran along his chest.

"Conner, remove the spell from Savannah and go away. You lost."

"I only lose if you come out of this alive." His voice was laced with ire and ice. The shell shattered and he disappeared. Gareth was upon me in seconds, his eyes running over me as he looked for injuries.

Satisfied that I wasn't hurt, he pressed his palm lightly against my cheek as he exhaled a sigh of relief. He kissed me lightly on the other cheek and then on the lips. With effort I pulled away, aware that his kiss was a distraction—one we didn't need.

Gareth and I looked around for Lucas, but he was gone. I hadn't expected him to stay and I wasn't very confident that he would let me see Savannah, but I was going to try.

CHAPTER 8

"*J*'m in here!" I snapped at Gareth as he eased himself into the shower. I'd assumed he would use another once we'd entered his home and he'd directed me to the shower in his room, which reminded me of the waterfall he had in his pool.

"I need a shower, too," he said, a small miscreant smile curling his lips.

I wiped the water off of my face. Multiheaded showers had their advantages, but I felt like I was being pummeled from all directions.

"Oh I'm sorry, I thought the four other bedrooms would have showers as well. It's a pity that you have a five-bedroom house and just one shower. Must be hell when you have guests," I retorted.

"Well, this is my favorite one," he said, nestling in closer to me and letting the water spill over him to wash away the grime and blood from our run-in with Conner. He eased me out of the way and squeezed earthy sandalwood-scented bodywash onto a cloth and lathered. I averted my eyes as he ran the washcloth slowly over the hard muscles of his chest, abs, and back. Stepping back to give him room, I smiled.

"Look at that. I'm getting a shower and a show," I teased.

"If you have a problem with what you see, close your eyes." He grinned and inched closer to me. I could feel the warmth of his body and the steam of the water as he leaned down and kissed me. His tongue explored my mouth while his hands did the same to my body. The distraction wasn't enough. "Conner's insane," I said.

Gareth nodded, the water beating against us as his fingers trailed along the lines of my body. "He was always crazy, now he's just unhinged. Revenge makes people a little more impulsive. The desire for it overrides logic."

"He's not impulsive. His behavior today was calculated. What he did to Savannah was a well-thought-out plan. He may be emotional and unhinged, but his behavior isn't." Inhaling the various scents that coursed through the room, I leaned into Gareth. His arms circled me, pulling me closer. His head brushed against my hair, and when I looked up at him he kissed me. "We are going to fix Savannah."

Whether or not we could do that wasn't the real question: How many things would we have to deal with before we could get to Menta Island? He brought his fingers to my chin and lifted it so my eyes met his. Giving me a reassuring smile, he said, "Trust me, we will fix this." His lips covered mine, gentle and warm. Breaking the kiss, he pulled away, enough to look me in the eyes again. I nodded.

Commanding hands ran along the curves of my body, kneading my skin. The lingering warmth of the shower was replaced by the heat of his lips. I eased into the languid pleasure as he explored my body with his mouth and tongue, coaxing a shudder from me. He kissed my lips again, fevered and rapacious. Pressing me against the wall, he curled his fingers into my thighs as he secured my legs around him. He coaxed a moan of desire from me as he sheathed himself in me. The weight of his body secured me to the wall, my legs wrapped around his. Our kisses became more passionate and the need for more blazed in me. I nipped at his lips and entwined my fingers into his hair.

Smiling, he pulled out, teasing me. Shifting forward, I felt him again, hard and ready against me, delighting in my frustration. He chuckled lightly.

"Gareth." My breath wisped against his lips as I breathed out his name in a beseeching pant, needing more. I was treated to light, feathery kisses against my jaw and cheek and neck before he sheathed himself in me again. We moved in a steady rhythm until it wasn't enough to slake the growing desire. My back hit the tile of the shower in a constant beat as Gareth's thrusting became more intense. Our kisses were as fiery and frenetic as our movements as we achieved the peak of pleasure. Gareth felt like a blanket of warmth as he rested against me. For several minutes we stayed entwined and connected to each other.

I slept longer than I expected and awoke to find Gareth dressed, sitting on the living room sofa with his computer.

"Did you enjoy your nap?" Amusement and arrogance coiled over his words.

"I took a nap because I was tired. I haven't slept in days," I asserted. His aloof arrogance forced me to be more belligerent with my protest.

The smug smile would not disappear. "Yeah *that's* the reason."

This guy.

I frowned at his lingering assessment of me that moved over my uncombed hair, his shirt that I'd borrowed since mine was bloodstained beyond repair, and my bare legs. He didn't share what he found so amusing and simply returned his attention to his computer.

On my way to the living room, alluring smells from the kitchen stopped me in my tracks. Not only was I tired, I was hungry, too. I needed to decide where to go first: the kitchen for food or the living room for Gareth.

"You might want to refuel first," he said, noticing my dilemma. "Leslie made lunch. It's in the refrigerator. She also baked you some bread." Apparently, she believed that I had an appetite like a farmer, and I'm sure she held that opinion because of Gareth. When I entered the kitchen and opened the fridge, I found two sandwiches, a large salad that I had no plans to eat, and a pasta salad. There were several bags of chips on the counter, along with a loaf of sourdough bread and a cheese and olive tray. Quickly finishing off one of the sandwiches, I grabbed a bag of chips, a few slices of bread, and a small stack of cheese and took a seat next to Gareth.

He moved his eyes from the screen to me and then to my purse, placed on an accent chair. "Your phone's been vibrating for over two hours, you have a message."

I grabbed it quickly hoping it was a message from Savannah, which I knew was unlikely, but at the very least it could be Lucas. There were three messages from Elijah asking me if I'd found my friend. Instead of texting him back, I called in the hope that I could gauge his plans. I wanted him to stay, not only because of the magic he could teach me, but because the idea of having another Legacy, or rather Vertu, close was comforting. For too many years I'd distanced myself from them, and now we were going to let ourselves be known by more than just the SG and I didn't want to do it alone.

As the phone rang, I wondered if I was being selfish, expecting so much from a stranger.

Elijah answered on the first ring. "Levy, are you okay?"

"Yes."

"Is your friend safe?"

She was away from Conner but as long as her memories were compromised and he knew he could use her as a pawn in his games, she wouldn't be safe until he was gone. I hesitated too long before I spoke. Elijah repeated his question.

"She's safe."

"But still the same as before?" he inquired.

"I don't know. She's with a friend and was asleep when we retrieved her."

"You haven't called her?" he asked with strained incredulity. I'd called Lucas on the way to Gareth's and he'd informed us she was still asleep. Reluctant to wake her, he'd asked for a couple of hours to see what happened. His voice had been tight, anxious. I knew he didn't want me there when she awoke.

"Then I doubt he did anything else to her memory. That's good, less to be undone."

"You wouldn't know how to undo it, would you?"

"Unfortunately, I don't. Cognitive manipulation on that level is difficult and requires a surgical touch. So much can go wrong, it's frowned upon." From the heaviness of his voice and the tight delivery of each word, he didn't have a high opinion of anyone who would do it. "I do hope you can help her. All magic that can be done, can be undone. Even the Cleanse was stopped."

Yes, but that was because of the death of the initiators, who'd had an active spell in progress. Contrary to what the fairy tales would have people believe, all magic wasn't undone once the conjurer was dead. Even if that was the case, I wasn't a fool to think that killing Conner was going to be easy. If a big-ass lion mauling him in the chest hadn't, what could?

"What are you looking for?" I asked after ending the call, returning my attention to Gareth.

"Based on where the island is located, we'll have to take a plane as well as a boat."

"How did you find the coordinates? I spent hours researching it. I was starting to think it was a rumor."

"Most people know about it; it's just not advertised."

"I'm most people and I didn't know anything about it."

Gareth flashed a grin. "There are benefits to my position." Finding me unamused, he let his smile falter briefly. "Think about it as Area 51. People know about it—not too many people have the privilege of visiting it. The same with Menta Island. We don't want people visiting, and the location is guarded."

"Why?"

"That island has existed for hundreds of years. It's where many of the original supernaturals decided to live when the human population exceeded ours. They prefer not to be around humans, and because of that they are the purest form of magic because they never mixed with humans."

It was similar to what the Legacy and Vertu had done. We'd lived in our world. Since I hadn't read or been taught of a Great War that involved the Mentas, I assumed they were satisfied with seclusion and had no intention of world domination. They just wanted to live away from the humans and other supernaturals who had been tainted by humans. And now we were planning to go to their island to find a plant. *Great.*

"How close can we get with a commercial flight?" I asked, leaning in to look at his screen.

"We aren't going to take a commercial flight, we'll use my family's plane. They'll be able to get us here." He pointed to a spot on the map. "Menta Island doesn't have a place to land a plane. We'll have to take a ship and crew."

I was stuck on the fact that his family had a plane. "Do you even have to work?"

"Of course, what else would I do with my time?" he offered breezily, dismissing my question.

His job was dangerous. Why would someone like him take a job where he had to risk his life constantly? Was he some type of adrenaline junkie? He relaxed back on the sofa. "What's on your mind?" he asked softly.

"Nothing."

"Do I have to go over the heart rate, breathing thing again?"

"Stop listening to my private information. It's invasive."

"Reading your openly available vitals is invasive?"

"When it can be used against me, then yes, it is," I shot back. I didn't want to discuss his family or whether he was an adrenaline junkie. He was trying to help Savannah and that was all that mattered. "Thank you." I kissed him on the cheek. His brow furrowed with confusion.

"What are you thanking me for?" he asked.

"For this." I waved my hand at the computer and the little notepad he had next to him with ideas of how to get to the island.

"Levy, you don't have to thank me. I want to do this for you. I want to help Savannah." Giving me a coy smile, he said, "I kind of miss her. After everything that happened today I kept expecting her to call and tell me how disappointed she was, what I did wrong, and the next time something like that happened I'd have hell to pay. You know, the typical Savannah drill."

I laughed. Sadly, it was something she would have done. I fondly recalled his first dealings with Savannah when she'd shown up at the Supernatural Guild ready to launch a one-woman protest to get me out of the Haven, where I was being held after being accused of murder. Savannah was daring and stubborn. She possessed a lot of courage—too much for a human. And she didn't possess a healthy dose of fear. I didn't want her to be a coward, just demonstrate a functioning fight or flight response.

"Should I call Lucas again?" I frowned at the idea of Lucas being an intermediary between Savannah and me because she saw me as her enemy. Whether it was one day or ten I doubted the hurt feelings would lessen.

Pulling out his phone, he scrolled through his contacts and then handed it to me.

"Just the person I was about to call," Lucas said, his voice sounding hard and strained. I wasn't sure if vampires could actually become fatigued but there was a weariness to his voice.

"You were going to call me?" I asked.

He made a sound. "I thought you were Gareth. I need to speak with him."

"About Savannah?"

"Yes," he said tersely. There were several beats of silence as I waited for an explanation that never came.

"What about her?" I probed. Anything that had to do with Savannah needed to be shared. "Did she not wake up?" It had just dawned on me that she was under a spell or maybe drugged; there had been enough activity going on around her that she should have woken up. Her being spelled into sleep wasn't the worst idea. At least we wouldn't have to worry about her running again.

"I must speak with Gareth," Lucas asserted with the same cool, withdrawn voice. I quickly realized it wasn't fatigue in his voice but irritation. Who was he irritated with?

"Go ahead and talk to Levy, I can hear," Gareth said from his position next to me. I knew I wouldn't have to relay the information because Lucas heard him as well. That was something I'd undoubtedly never get used to.

Lucas didn't need to breathe, so his sigh of annoyance was for my benefit. "Savannah came to, and let's just say she wasn't very happy with my involvement with you trying to spell her. She left."

"You let her!"

"What exactly would you have liked me to do? I wasn't going to hold her against her will."

"Compel her," I snapped and immediately felt a wave of filth wash over me as if I'd been wading in mud or slime. What I was suggesting wasn't just morally wrong, it was illegal, although I wasn't convinced vampires had stopped doing it. They'd just become savvier about it. But in this case, I wanted Savannah safe and was willing to take extreme measures to make her so.

"Do you know where she went?"

"Yes, to the Shapeshifter Council's office. They won't let me see her, because she's requested protection from us—from *me*." The last words were laced with a mixture of sorrow and the anger of a person who wasn't often denied. Lucas's voiced changed, becoming more assertive. "Gareth, I need you to change that. Talk to them. I want Savannah back here with me."

Oh, that's not going to work. Have you two met? Gareth, Lucas. Lucas, Gareth.

That captured Gareth's undivided attention. Abruptly he stopped searching his laptop to look at the phone. He gave it the same dismissive look I was sure he would have given Lucas if he was present. Gareth's lips tightened into a thin line.

I muted the phone. "Play nice. You miss Savannah; you think he doesn't?" This was such a peculiar situation. Savannah, my annoyingly bubbly, clean-eating, neat freak of a friend had apparently managed to wiggle her way so firmly into Lucas's heart that he'd forgotten himself. By the look Gareth was giving the phone, he was about to be quickly reminded of it.

I waited a few more minutes, giving Gareth time to get some semblance of composure after being delegated duties by Lucas.

Not in a million years would I have thought I'd have to give the head of the Supernatural Guild and the Master of the city each a timeout. When Lucas spoke again his voice was velvety smooth and even. "Is there any way you can get them to at least allow me to speak with her? I went there and they said that she'd asked for sanctuary."

That sounded serious and it was confirmed when Gareth sucked in a sharp breath and frowned.

"They won't let anyone see her if she's requested sanctuary, and any violation will have dire consequences. Shapeshifters take that very seriously."

"Maybe she didn't know the gravity of it. Maybe they need to understand that." This time, there was pain. It weighed so heavily on my chest, I was having trouble breathing.

"If we get the *Culded*, how can we undo the spell if we can't get to her?"

I wondered if Gareth was thinking the same thing because he

grimaced and dropped back against the chair with his fingers clasped behind his head, concentrating. "I'll see what I can do," he offered after several moments of contemplation. There was uncertainty in his words, and if I heard it, I knew Lucas did as well.

"Very well." Lucas's tone was curt as he hung up. Gareth took the phone from me and called him again.

As soon as he answered, Gareth spoke, in a cool professional voice. "Despite your desires, you will need to let me handle it. At least I have a chance of reasoning with them. If you go, it will not end well." There was a long pause, "I do mean not well for *you*. A request for sanctuary is taken as a very serious responsibility. Do not challenge them on it. I am asking you to let me handle it."

Lucas seemed to have gotten past his bruised ego. "I will. I just ask that you keep me informed of all matters."

Gareth ended the call, fell back onto the sofa, and let out a long string of curses. He even became creative with them, and dropped so many fucks he wasn't going to have many more to give.

"I don't think she knew the seriousness of what she was asking."

"No, she did. That's the thing they let a shifter know once they join the Council. It is drilled into all that it's not to be asked lightly. She's afraid, and we have no idea what Conner has put in her head so we can't even determine if it's unwarranted." His lips lifted in a mirthless half-smile. "You saw the way she reacted to you. There is a real fear of you."

"Can you at least check on her?" I could imagine her waking up with Lucas, Gareth, and me over her, after I'd performed a spell while she'd been sleeping. I understood why she was afraid of us. I didn't understand why she would request refuge from people who were virtually strangers. I hadn't realized how much it was affecting me until I felt the solitary tear course down my cheek.

Gareth leaned over and placed his hand over mine. "We should at least talk to them."

I couldn't meet the shapeshifters in Gareth's clothes, so we had to stop by my apartment for me to get dressed. I put on clothes and then sheathed the sai on my back.

Gareth gave me a disapproving look. "Do you think you're going to have to fight your way out of the place?" Incredulity and amusement twined over his words.

"If I have to," I shot back with a lot more confidence than I felt. Especially after getting a look at how entertained he was by his comment.

The corners of his lips lifted into a rueful smile, and once again I was under his assessing gaze. He took in my casual attire of jeans, a peach shirt that was a gift from Savannah and her effort to "find the woman under the plaid," and brown flats. I was sure I looked odd with a sheath on my back.

"Where's your bag?"

My brows inched together. "Bag?" I asked.

"Yes, bag. We had the discussion less than twenty minutes ago so I can't imagine you have forgotten already. Remember, I suggested you leave some clothes at my house so we won't have to make stops like this." He was unsuccessful at hiding his irritation. Packing a bag had been heavily debated on the drive to my apartment and I couldn't help but smile at his frustration with me. Gareth wasn't a person used to having to debate his requests, and I had a strong feeling based on his reaction that I may have been the first woman to ever decline an invitation to keep clothing at his house.

Perhaps it wasn't a big deal to him—and it shouldn't have been to me—but I hadn't fully relaxed into a life where I didn't have to be prepared to leave at a moment's notice, move somewhere different, or lie low for a while. Gareth was foolishly optimistic about the smooth transition of the Legacy and Vertu into society. It would be easy to possess such positivity if you hadn't lived through or lost anyone in the Cleanse.

"I will. Later."

"Why put off something for later that you can do today?" His attention shifted to the hallway.

Did he just use that pitiful platitude?

I stood up taller, squared my shoulders, and fixed him with a hard stare. A display of determination that was wasted on a person who was the head of the Supernatural Guild and dealt with surly supernaturals on a regular basis. I was a novice trying out for a professional league.

Gareth laughed when I blew out a breath so hard it made my lips rumble a little. It was a valid suggestion, and if I weren't so stubborn, it probably wouldn't have been such an issue. It didn't take me long to fill an overnight bag with clothes, and I tossed in a toothbrush and a stack of graphic novels as well. I was putting in the latter when Gareth commented from behind me, "If you're staying at my house do you really think you'll have time for those? I'm betting that you won't." There was no need to turn around to witness the flourish of his smug and wicked grin; I could hear it in his voice.

Keeping my back to him, I shrugged. "We make time for the things we love. Sometimes I might want to cuddle up with Wolverine, Rogue, Kitty Pride, and…" I turned, swooning. "I can't forget Remy Etienne LeBeau."

"Gambit," he offered. Baring his teeth in a wide smile, he licked his lips. "I'm more interesting than him, aren't I?"

"Your humility is so sexy. It's taking everything I have not to rip your clothes off and take you right now," I quipped back.

He cleared the distance between us, grabbed my bag for me, and headed out the door. "Let's pretend that was a joke." His deep, rumbly laugh drifted down the hallway. "I can hear your eyes rolling," he teased.

Good.

Sanctuary. I didn't expect Savannah to be hidden away in a bunker or something that extreme, but when we had to give our names as well as show ID to the person manning the front gate before they would grant us entry, I realized it might be more like a secure fortress. For several minutes we were under the scrutiny of the shifter at the gate. He gave Gareth a quick once-over, but I garnered a great deal of his attention. The shifter ring danced around his eyes as he examined me. It was apparent that what he saw wasn't quite impressive. I wondered if he knew what I was, had heard the rumors, and had expected someone bigger than life. Perhaps it was a look of pity because he was aware of the reason for our visit and knew it would be unsuccessful.

The long driveway led us to a three-level French provincial home. A steep conical roof, complete with a spire, made the grand, ostentatious house look more like a castle than a home in the suburbs. Perhaps estate was more fitting, given the thick flourish of bushes that formed a verdant barrier around the building. The wooden doors, although intricately decorated, looked very thick and probably heavy. The windows on the first floor were uncovered and double paned. They distorted objects and made it difficult to see what was inside, though I suspected occupants could probably see out. Then Gareth rang the doorbell, and within seconds a dusk-colored man answered the door. His smile was warm and welcoming but it didn't extend to his chilly, chestnut-colored eyes.

"Gareth," he said, extending his hand in a greeting. Gareth took it and gave it a firm shake before the man moved aside to allow us to step in. He possessed a quiet strength and also, based on the way he moved, a smooth agility that he used to his advantage. He had Gareth's six-five height by an inch or two.

"Michael," Gareth greeted him with the same warm tone. They

were full of it. The nicety was just a display of dominance. Mine is bigger than yours so I can be cool and collected about it. *Shifters.*

With Gareth to my right and the other shifter in front of me, I felt towered over. I didn't like the feeling and moved a couple of inches away from them. The shifter gave me a sharp and hostile look, which made me glad I'd left the twins in the car. If simply moving agitated him, bringing a weapon into the house might be tantamount to an act of aggression.

"I suspect your visit is about Savannah. I figured once Lucas was denied, he'd send his attack cat. No offense." Michael bared his teeth.

It doesn't work that way. You don't say super offensive things and think it's okay because you add "no offense," you jackass. No offense.

Michael's attention came back to me as he gave me a long, evaluating look. "This is her?"

"Her" has a name, jackass. Once again, no offense.

"Levy, I'm her best friend and roommate," I said, working hard to keep my annoyance out of my voice.

He nodded his head slowly. Gareth lifted a brow and his gaze traveled up the top of the stairs to the right. I followed it in time to see a whirl of blond hair as Savannah moved out of sight, probably into one of the numerous rooms on the top floor. I wondered if there was a little keep where she was housed.

"She's had magic used on her and her memory has been distorted. She requested sanctuary based on false memories," Gareth informed him.

Michael made a sound of dissent. "You all didn't come to a place where she thought she was sleeping safely and attempt to perform a spell on her?" he asked with cool reproach.

The silence swelled along with the animosity between the three of us. "I was trying to help her," I explained.

"By betraying her trust, which was already fragile. That's an approach."

His sardonic response snapped my patience. "What exactly did you expect us to do? We didn't have a lot of options." My retort was fire-laced and definitely wasn't helping the situation. Taking several calming breaths, I forced my voice to soften. "What options did we have?"

Under his appraising look, I felt the flames of my irritation light once again. "Legacy," he said as if he were tasting the word. A long drawl with a definite air of curiosity and disdain. "Is it true that you are one?"

There was a list of things I'd rather do than play this game, but I needed to be amiable. He was the person standing between me helping Savannah if we got the *Culded*.

"Yes."

His lips lifted into a small smile as his eyes sharpened on me. "Your magic can work against us—against shapeshifters."

I nodded.

The same morbid intrigue and fear I'd seen on Gareth's features the first time I'd used magic against him spread over Michael's face.

"Show me."

He didn't have to ask twice. I was more than happy to accommodate him. A surge of magic came from my body, inching toward my finger, and vibrant colors danced along my fingertips. Gathering the magic into a ball, I held it. He eyed it as I eyed him. Curiosity skated along the sharp planes of his face.

"Are you ready?" I asked.

He nodded, and the ball struck him. Not with as much force as I usually exerted, but he let out an audible gasp when it crashed into his chest and pushed him back several feet. He stood, straightened, and squared his shoulders. After several minutes, he was able to pull his rigid lips into a humorless smile. "Impressive," he admitted in a flat, even tone. Despite his voice, I could see a tinge of aversion and poorly suppressed anger.

Shapeshifters had warranted arrogance about magic because of their immunity to most of it. Their vulnerability to the Legacy was a reason there were so many shifters among Trackers. They wanted to rid the world of the only people who could use magic against them. Several long moments passed before he directed his attention to Gareth.

"I understand *her* desire to help her friend, but Gareth, wouldn't your time be better spent finding out who is responsible for the attack at the Solstice celebration? Lives could have been lost."

Gareth's difficulty with diplomacy was noticeable. "I have an entire agency at my disposal, and the FSR is assisting us in the matter. But Levy and Savannah are the reason we had no casualties from the attack. Despite what you think, Levy's motives aren't entirely selfish. We have no idea what has been implanted in Savannah's mind and whether she is willing to help if we call on her in the future. If she doesn't, people will die if there is another attack."

Michael shook his head in consideration and remained quiet for several minutes. "I won't violate her trust and allow you to do a spell on her without her permission, but I will do what I can to persuade her to see you." He addressed me. "But anything she does will be of her own volition. You will not come here while she sleeps and do any spells on her no matter how confident you are that they will work. We don't operate like that."

Gareth nodded in agreement. He didn't look apprehensive or doubtful. He trusted the guy, which made me feel more comfortable.

Before we could leave, Michael said, "Please let Lucas know that the same rules apply to him. I will talk to her on his behalf, but if she chooses not to see him, so be it. You might want to educate him that his power and influence don't extend this far. I'd rather you tell him than me having to show him."

Well, that's the politest threat I've ever heard.

I waited until we were in the car and driving away from the house before I made a comment. "He's rather intense, isn't he?"

Michael was dangerous—there wasn't any denying that—but so was Gareth. At the forefront of my mind was how he'd dealt with his cousin, who was still a Tracker and the person he suspected was a traitor in the Supernatural Guild. He never went into detail, but the dark cast that moved over his face when he discussed it indicated it wasn't anything good.

"He's actually one of the most reasonable heads they've had"—he flashed a grin—"since my tenure."

"Never miss a chance to toot your own horn, do you?"

"I thought you would value honesty, but apparently you don't. Fine." He shrugged. "Michael can be persuasive when necessary. We'll work on finding the ingredients for the spell and worry about getting to Savannah later. Hopefully we won't have any problems. But we will get to her."

CHAPTER 9

*E*lijah was already seated and drinking his coffee when I entered the café. It had been two days since he opted out of going with us to get Savannah. Appreciative of the help he offered in order to find her, I felt I'd asked enough of him and wasn't in a position to ask for more. I took a seat across from him, but he continued to eye the door.

"Are you waiting for someone else?"

"Your shifter friend," he said, his attention still on the door.

"He's not coming; did you want him to?"

He shrugged. "I just thought he'd be curious."

"About our meeting?"

"No, about me," he said, smiling as he took another sip.

I wasn't sure how to take that. Was it a statement of arrogance or general curiosity about Gareth's intentions?

"I piqued your interest when we met; I figured that would bother him."

"I'm sorry, you can't do that."

His brows inched together as he waited for me to continue.

"The position is filled. I already have one arrogant Vertu in my life, I don't have an opening for another. But once he's gone, I'll make sure to let you know of the vacancy."

Chuckling, he took another sip from his cup. "It's not arrogance, it's self-preservation. I figured your shifter would be concerned about you meeting another of your kind. There are so few of us, I know at some point you had to think about how we would preserve our species. That has to be among your considerations and reasons for us coming out."

I looked at the coffee bar.

"Do you need a drink?" He stood to go to the counter to get me one.

"Yes, but if we're going to continue this conversation, I need something stronger than coffee. Too bad this isn't one of the cafés that serve wine, too."

"I've upset you. Why?" he asked softly, returning to his seat. The earnestness in his voice made it clear that he was concerned —concerned about me.

Sighing, I smiled—it was forced and mirthless but the best I could muster at the moment. "I'm not thinking about our lineage, increasing our numbers, or any of those things. My efforts to come out are nothing more than me no longer wanting to hide who I am. I no longer want to be the face of this horrible crime against humanity. My only goal is to have a normal life. I'm sorry, it's not deeper than that. I'm not trying to start a Legacy and Vertu make-a-baby-campaign or dating site where we meet and procreate. My motives are simple. I don't want to hide or be hated," I confessed, exasperated. Why were people making things more complicated than they had to be?

A smile slowly curved his lips. "Simple is good." He looked at the bar again. "Do you want to stay here, or have drinks?"

"Since it's ten o'clock in the morning, maybe we should stick with coffee."

I settled back into my seat after getting my drink, and Elijah occupied his time by looking around the café. The shifter ring gave away the two shifters in the corner. A waft of earthy magic that drifted over the room identified witches in the far-right corner, and a warm humming of it unmasked the mages just a few tables away. Elijah's gaze roved over every customer, spending more time on the humans interspersed between the supernaturals.

"We're stronger than anyone in here," he said thoughtfully. He did another sweep of the occupants of the room. My eyes trailed his, taking in the people.

"Probably."

"No 'probably.'" He was barely audible even to me, sitting next to him. "We ran and hid from them for years. Were hunted and demonized."

No, he cannot be as bad as Conner. Please don't be like Conner. Pulling his gaze from the patrons, he settled it on me. His voice was level, but held an edge: "Do you think it was wrong for us to want to live apart from them?"

"No. I think it was wrong to try to kill everyone who wasn't one of us," I offered, keeping my voice just as even as his so it wouldn't reveal my feelings. I needed him to feel free to express himself. This would determine his position in my life: friend or foe.

He smiled. "That *was* cruel and shortsighted," he said, relaxing back in his chair.

Maybe ten in the morning isn't too early to drink. "Shortsighted?"

Elijah's head barely moved into his nod. "If history has taught us nothing, numbers matter. Although we had great magic, we didn't have the numbers. Defeat was inevitable. Conner is short-sighted and foolish as well."

It was hard to remain casual and indifferent. "You've met Conner?"

Chuckling, he attempted an unsuccessful eye roll. "He's one of the most powerful wielders of magic I've seen. His motivation is awe-inspiring. And his drive and desire for a fantastical world where we can exist together, away from everyone else, free to be who we are without limitations or judgment, make him sound like a ranting crazy person. These people don't bother me. I like being around them. I can't imagine a world where we live apart. I don't want to, which is why I came to meet you."

"Me?"

"You. Tina spoke so highly of you, and your vision seemed more than just the ranting of a person with a superiority complex. It's well-thought-out."

Sure, it's so well thought out. I'd rolled out of bed and had this crapfest fall in my lap while fighting a supervillain who had a propensity to monologue. I didn't say anything that would change Elijah's impression of me and my plight. Maybe one day I'd look at this as being wrong, but at the moment, I had no problem with him thinking I was a woman with a vision.

Coffee with Elijah had left me feeling emboldened. If I ignored that part about him making me consider day drinking or our brief discussion about breeding, something I was sure no one should ever discuss on their second meeting, he made me feel that coming out wasn't going to be as bad. And if it was, I had someone who was like me. I knew I had Kalen and Savannah—old Savannah who would support and stand behind me—but it was good to have someone who would be affected as well, if things went poorly.

Before heading to work, where I expected to face Kalen's version of "Oh, so you still work here?" I stopped by the Supernatural Guild to talk to Gareth since the café where I'd met Elijah was just a few blocks away. I wasn't sure if I'd chosen that café for my benefit or Gareth's. I wanted to talk to him after my meeting with Elijah.

When I arrived at Gareth's office he reminded me of a

confined animal as he paced, his large stride devouring most of the space with just a few steps. Shapeshifters could sense emotions, feel changes in others' behavior, and use physiological signs to determine a person's mindset. I didn't need any of it to determine how he was feeling. He was wound so tightly he was just a bundle of frustration and anger, which forced me to be calmer than I actually felt to neutralize the situation.

"This is getting ridiculous. First HF, now this new group. I'd rather have Humans First anytime over these new guys. HF was all talk and rhetoric. They just wanted the Cleanse," he barked, glancing at the monitor on his desk. I assumed there'd been another attack.

"Just?" I asked skeptically.

He stopped pacing and gave me an icy look that would have been better directed at the assailants.

"Yes, *just*. Performing a Cleanse isn't an easy job. It requires strong magic, your magic. Not just any damn person off the street can do it, and it needs to be a well-orchestrated action. Best case they acquire objects necessary to do it, like the Necro-spear. Worst case they collude with someone like Conner, but even he needed more magic than his own to do it. These new asses are trying to pick us off one by one." He pushed the last part out through clenched teeth. "How long before they go into our homes, restaurants, bars, and clubs?" So far, all the attacks had been outdoors, but it was just a matter of time before the attackers became bolder. He shook his head. "Whoever is behind this is good. The shooters never know anything about the person who supplied them. The person doesn't even give a name and never uses the same point of contact."

"Who would follow someone so blindly, especially at the risk of getting caught?" I wondered aloud.

"People who don't like the fact that we live among them," Victor said as he entered through the slightly ajar door. "They never change. I'm sure they are the same people who were part of

HF. The manner in which the group was disbanded probably made recruitment easier." He gave me an accusatory look as if I was responsible for it.

Maybe Conner was behind this. Or someone who had dealt with him. It could very well be that Conner's antics had incited this, but his obsession with me wasn't my fault. The inner workings of the mind of a sociopath couldn't be made my responsibility.

Giving me a wry smile, Victor continued, "I don't blame you, Ms. Michaels."

Great—another vitals-reading freak. I'd felt my pulse quicken quite a bit at the implication that I had something to do with the rising violence against supernaturals.

Victor didn't wear his frustration well. Squared shoulders made him look rigid and uncompromising in his dark blue suit. Golden brown eyes glinted under the fluorescent light. His lithe, sinuous gait made it apparent that he was a shifter, but I still hadn't figured out which type. Nothing about his broad build gave any hints. He was just an inch or two shorter than Gareth but had a similar commanding presence. It looked like each of them was fighting for his share of space in the massive room.

The fae behind him decided not to share in the struggle and stayed just outside of the room. Behind his striking azure eyes was a quiet strength, and his lean body made me think of Kalen. He didn't look like he belonged in a job where conformity was necessary. While Gareth wore dark slacks and a white shirt, and Victor a dark suit, the fae had opted for a hunter green vest, brown slacks, and a white shirt. A brightly colored woven handkerchief peeked from the pocket of the vest. After he ushered a tight crooked smile onto his face, I realized I'd been staring. He seemed to take it as interest in him. His features found a comfortable place between handsome and striking. It was doubtful I was the first person who'd stared. His gaze shot in Gareth's direction and back to me, and his brows rose slightly in inquiry. A silent questioning of my status with Gareth. Anyone who spent any time in the SG had an idea that something was going on with Gareth and me. Discretion wasn't something they even pretended to have when it came to gossip. I was the talk of the building and heard the hushed voices anytime I walked past a group.

Gareth's head was tilted to the side. "Answer his question, Ms. Michaels," he coaxed as staunch amusement skated over his words. Crossing his arms over his chest, he waited, looking at the fae's questioning expression.

"Answer what question?" *Yeah, I'm going to play naïve.*

"He wants to know if the rumors are true. Are you single?"

I so do not want to do this in front of an audience. It didn't help that even Victor, who often behaved like he couldn't dislodge the stick crammed up his hindquarters, found a modicum of humor in the situation.

Gareth should have been trying to keep our relationship under wraps. There had to be a rule about this kind of impropriety. Thou shalt not date the person who's a Legacy but is out and now helping the SG, or something like that. The taunting smile that tugged at Gareth's lips made every part of me crave to wipe it off.

"I like your handkerchief, which is why I was staring, *but* I'm sure you're used to women staring at you for other reasons. Sorry, I'm not that woman, I'm crushing on your hanky."

Ha, solved that. The fae didn't look disappointed, although he made a show of pretending he was. Gareth's smile quickly twisted into a scowl. Switching back to business. "Let me guess, you weren't able to get anything."

"Same as before. They met with their contact. No names were exchanged, and even when I compelled them to truth, their descriptions are rather lackluster. No distinguishing marks and the general features are the same. Sometimes the color of the hair changes. I wonder if it *is* the same person? We have a name, but it's a generic one that I doubt will be of any help."

"What's the name?" Gareth asked.

"Jonathan."

Ordinarily I would have said it was coincidental that the person had the same name as the mage who'd been on the Magic Council and had betrayed them to team up with Conner and Humans First to do another Cleanse. It very well could be chance that the name came up again in an effort to get rid of supernaturals. The strategy of using the virus was different than the Cleanse and wasn't as efficient. The end results would be the same: the supernaturals would be dead, with the exception of the Legacy and Vertu who were immune to it.

"Are you sure *that* Jonathan is dead? Did you see a body?" Victor asked. That might have seemed like a ridiculous question before the situation with Conner. Now, anything was possible.

"He's definitely dead," Gareth replied.

"Could it be someone seeking revenge on his behalf?" the handsome fae asked, his right leg crossed over his left as he leaned against the doorframe as if he'd lost interest in standing. He wasn't a typical SG agent. Most of them stood at attention when dealing with Gareth.

Gareth considered the question for a long time. "We should look into it. He left behind a sister and a girlfriend. Perhaps they had similar views." Frowning at the assumption, I cast a look in his direction. People had assumed I was a certain way because of my lineage. The idea of someone else being treated in the same manner bothered me.

"It's an investigation, every avenue has to be explored," Gareth offered in explanation.

I knew the reason; it still didn't make it any better.

CHAPTER 10

The dark Gothic exterior of the home of Calista, Jonathan's sister, wasn't doing anything to exonerate her. The gray bricks had small cracks that looked intentional. Gargoyle statues perched on the posts at the foot of the stairs leading up to the house. Black wrought iron fenced in the home. Heavy, ornate gates opened at our arrival and closed immediately after we entered. They could have been motion activated, but I couldn't help but wonder what type of person didn't have a problem with random people entering her estate.

Scanning the area, I didn't see any cameras. "There aren't any," Gareth said to me as we walked up the stairs.

"What, you can read minds, too?" I muttered, slightly irritated.

"No, just yours. You're very skeptical."

"Skepticism has kept me alive this long," I said pointedly. Frustration, fear, and dread of the unknown were starting to affect me and cause me to be short with Gareth. I had a feeling he was having the same problem because he was being curt with me, Victor, and Mason—the attractive fae, who'd offered his name once he'd realized I would be tagging along on the trip. Being a Legacy had some advantages, but being precluded on a trip to visit a mage, who might want revenge for her brother's death, wasn't one of them. If the SG thought they were going to need a great deal of magic, they didn't mind ignoring the rules about bringing a civilian. For the most part it didn't bother me, but I had no idea what we were dealing with. Mages were direct descendants of Legacy with just a bit less magical ability. They were a force to be reckoned with. Mages possessed the closest form of magic to ours.

Victor knocked on the door, hard. Nothing. He knocked a second time and it opened on its own.

"Do we go in?" Mason asked.

"Mr. Reynolds, I suspected I would see you soon," said a honey-sweet, light voice that floated in the air. The whimsical, welcoming sound didn't match the stern features of the woman who eventually revealed herself. Walnut-colored hair was piled on top of her head with small ringlets falling from the pile. Her wide bowed lips strained at a smile, exposing deep dimples in a narrow face. Amber eyes shone with disdain and sparkled under the recessed lights.

The gothic theme continued in the home, with gargoyles on stands in each corner of the room. Clay ceremonial masks lined the burgundy walls. Bronze and tan furniture darkened the room even more. Had it always been like this, or had she redecorated in response to her brother's death? There was something about her that felt wrong. Perhaps it was the string of brightly colored beads that dangled midway down her long, black gossamer dress. If it weren't for the dark coloring, the dress would have had an angelic appearance. The flowing fabric moved in a steady rhythm as she approached us.

Grief drifted off her like a fragrance. If it was apparent to me, it had to be apparent to the others.

"Calista," Gareth breathed out her name in a low voice. "How are you?"

"How do you think I am?" she asked, eyes narrowing on him.

"You know why I'm here?" Gareth asked.

"I suspect you think I share my brother's obsession with power." She continued to move along the room, eyeing each of her creepy gargoyles. "Our views might have been different, but that doesn't change my love for him." Sorrow trembled in her voice.

My opinion quickly changed: She was grief-stricken but she was ominous and creepy as hell, too.

Victor watched her carefully as she roamed through her room, looking even more like pictures I'd seen of the weeping woman walking along the river, withdrawn so far into her grief that she appeared to be a revenant.

"There have been attacks on supernaturals. Bad attacks." She pointed out matter-of-factly, "We're going to die." Stark decisiveness made her words seem as if they were a prophecy. No, it wasn't prophetic, it was a desire. That made her even more dangerous: She didn't care whether she lived or died, which meant she probably didn't care whether others did.

"Do you know anything about it?" Mason asked. Calista's attention moved from his face to his hand where magic sparked from his fingers as if he were waiting for her to make a move. Giving him a look of inconsequence, she continued walking. It didn't go unnoticed that she was closing the distance between her and us.

"Yes, it's a quite powerful drug. Humans are resourceful and resilient when they feel they are under attack. You know they wouldn't have cared about the Cleanse except for that small percentage of those identified as humans who had enough supernatural in them to fall victim to it. They would have been content to let us die—except they didn't know which of their forefathers had a liaison with which creature that may have linked them to the supernatural world. That's why they cared. What they are doing now is better, cleverer. It's more discriminating." Wiping her hand along her dress in one sweeping move, she produced seven little arrows that hovered in the air by magic, directed at Victor, Gareth, and Mason.

"You know I'm not going to let that happen," I asserted, infusing steel into my voice to discourage her.

"Of course not, Anya. You won't let it happen, which is why you will need to be stopped."

The moment I felt Conner's presence I turned, thrusting magic at him, but he disappeared before it made contact. A firm casing of magic wrapped around my waist and yanked me back against him. When I jammed the heel of my boot into the top of his shoe, he groaned and tightened his hold around me, digging his fingers into my stomach with such intensity if felt like he had talons. He didn't. There was nothing but vengeance and hate behind his touch. Clawing at his hands, I pulled at his skin, but he was relentless.

Aware that he was about to take me, I gave up trying to stop him and pushed a wave of magic from me. It smashed into Calista, unbalancing her. The arrows flew, but I was gone before I could see if they'd hit their intended targets. The moment my feet were on solid ground, Conner tossed me away from him.

Reflexively, I went for the sai that were usually sheathed to my back. When I came up empty, I remembered I'd left them in Gareth's car. Conner kept his distance from me; anger marred his face with a twisted, merciless smile.

"You don't give up, do you?" I asked, splitting my attention between him and my surroundings. It wasn't anywhere he'd taken me before. When he was making an effort to woo me, he'd brought me to beautiful places with fragrant air, magically enhanced beautiful trees, lush grass, exotic plants, and the promise of a life of nothing but beauty and pleasure. The honeymoon was over. This place was dank. The overpowering smell of something rotting lingered in the air. The surrounding trees were dead; dark leaves wept from their branches, waiting for a big enough wind to blow them away. Brown grass covered the ground, and clouds overshadowed the sun. It was dreary, desolate, and discomforting. Was he planning to leave me here? What was his end game?

Keeping his distance, he watched me with acute interest, a conflicting smile that was both cruel and enchanting playing at his lips. Raising a brow, he said, "Do you wonder what happened to the cat? Did your intervention help anything, or is he now struggling to stay alive?" Self-satisfaction danced along the planes of his face. "Here you are, one half of any chance he has to survive if the arrow didn't miss. What a quandary to find yourself in."

He walked with leisurely, graceful steps, enjoying every moment. Splitting my attention between him and my environment, I tried to find the border of the ward while listening to everything around me. I paid close attention, listening for the sounds of padding steps to make sure one of his creatures wasn't around. Nothing. It was just the two of us.

"What do you want?" I asked, venom lacing my words. I couldn't indulge him. One on one, I knew I wouldn't be able to best him with magic. He was stronger and more experienced and wore the knowledge with arrogance. He started to inch closer to me.

"You've opened the way for more Legacy to come forward. You think that will work to your advantage—it won't." Cruel confidence inched over his face, kindled by my irritation. "The odd thing about magic and science: It's peculiar how they interact. Who would have thought that a virus the humans had been working on for years could be cured with the blood of a Legacy and an *ignesco*? Savannah, how eager she is to help. I felt it when I was there in her mind. She's a sweet woman; I see why you like her. She's rather enthusiastic, isn't she?"

The mention of Savannah's name and the mocking reminder of what he'd done to her ignited anger in me that wasn't easily controlled. Magic shot from me like a cannon and he went back several feet. The edges of the ward wavered, and I saw where that world ended. Before he could come to his feet, I hit him with another blast of magic. I went on the offense and attacked, forcing him to focus his energy on me and not on maintaining the ward. Sparks of magic twirled around my hands, electric, prickling at my fingertips; it shot from me and wrapped around him in a cocoon of vibrant colors. I concentrated, holding the binding around him, moving farther away from him toward the ward, waiting for it to waver and fall. I kept my magic trained on him, refusing to divert any of it to break the ward.

"You get out of here, and then what, Anya? You try to reverse what I did to Savannah? It's highly unlikely that you can. You are a murderer to her. Her hate stems from her memories of your brutality and cruelty. Visions of you ruthlessly and needlessly killing the people I loved, while making me watch. And now she's sought safety from you. The shifters won't let you near her. She's afraid, and your attempt to undo what I did failed. She's more afraid of the things you've done than any memories I could give her. She doesn't trust you, Lucas, or Gareth. Do you think she will be so willing to help now? With all the attacks, I'm sure there isn't much of the antidote left."

My yanking at the magical threads around him pulled a yelp from him. "I'll undo whatever you've done to her." My assertion had more confidence than I felt. The tighter the binding wrapped around him, the more confident I became.

"Oh Anya, you fight so diligently, for what? The humans have turned on you. We might not have the Cleanse, but they've started a purge. They'll start with the obvious supernaturals and then go after those humans who have any magical DNA. The only ones left will be us—the way it should be."

"Who's behind it? You know, don't you?"

I cringed at the sound of his ominous, dark chuckle. He'd always been misguided, but now he seemed excessively cruel, calculated, and heartless. Or perhaps he was always that way and the person he'd formerly presented had given me the impression he could be reasoned with.

"After I healed from your cat's attack, I made it my mission to find out who it is. The odd thing about humans and radicals is that they will work with those they despise if it furthers their agenda. All I had to do was make sure they wouldn't fail again. I suspect the next attack won't have a plucky little blonde and her Legacy partner making an effort to save the supernatural world. You'll never get her to help. The poor woman is just wracked with nightmares and memories of all the cruel acts of the Legacy, you especially. She won't go near one, and the way I left her the last time has her terrified of all other supernaturals except shapeshifters. If Gareth is alive, how will he make the ones harboring her comply? Force? The Shifter Council is a force to be reckoned with. Shall he use the Supernatural Guild's magic wielders to get them to drop their vow to protect her? Of course, their magic doesn't work on them, only ours." Conner's eyes danced with satisfaction.

I let the threads fall and punched a ball of magic into his chest. He expelled a sharp, short breath. His cough mutated into a dark crow of laughter.

Curling into himself, he guarded his chest against my magic. After several moments he spoke, his eyes still alight with anger and spite, and the emptiness of a man who had nothing to lose. "Would being with me be so bad? Bad enough to warrant what you have now? Does it warrant having me as an enemy?"

"You have me as one, too. If the past is any indicator of what is to come then you know how things will turn out. I kicked your ass before and I have no problem doing it again."

Gray eyes clouded with anger as he came to his feet, shooting magic I hadn't been prepared for. Hit hard, I went back several feet and crashed on my butt. He was standing over me before I could get up. His foot came down hard on my ankle and I howled in pain. I rolled out of the way before he could do it again. When his magic hit me from that close, it was excruciating. A rainbow of colors flashed before me. I blinked several times and when my vision cleared, I lurched up. Or at least I tried. I was pinned to the ground, Conner standing over me. He *was* magic; it wafted off him like heat from the sun, intense and unrestrained.

"Let me go," I said, struggling against the hold.

"You do realize in the end, if you're not dead, I will have you. But you will be pursuing me. What do you think will happen when all the supernaturals are gone and the only ones left are the Legacy and Vertu? They will wonder about their fate, too, and those who remain will be looking for a way for preservation. I will be the answer." He leaned in even closer, his lips inches from mine, and I vowed to bite them off if he touched me. My thoughts must have shown on my face because he inched back just a smidge.

"You won't last very long," he growled before he disappeared. Able to move again, I got to my feet and walked to the edge to the vast area. I knew he was near, observing me in the space of his design. Darker than what it was on the other side, or what it had been when I'd left. I had no idea how long I'd been in his little world. Quickly, I moved toward the edge of the wavering ward and pushed my finger into it. Colors of pink, blue, and teal came off it. It seemed so innocuous, but I was sure it was anything but. Concentrating, I called in a great deal of magic, afraid to use so much that I'd be too fatigued to defend myself against Conner if he showed up again. I weighed the pros and cons. I needed to get out of there and make sure Gareth was okay, and if he wasn't I'd have to somehow convince Michael to get Savannah to the hospital.

I pushed, and it wavered, extending to its limit and then rebounding with a snap. I called on more magic, stronger, more virulent. It was like using dynamite when a sledgehammer would do, and I felt like something was detonating in me. My body hummed and warmed and I yelled in pain as the magic ripped from me. The ward fell with such a powerful force it rebounded into me. I hit a tree a couple of feet away.

"Good luck," Conner's jovial voice whispered in the air as I ran. I looked around the area and had no idea where I was. I hated when he did that. My phone had survived the fall and I pulled it out of my back pocket and started to call Gareth. *Hang on, give it a few minutes.* Five minutes became ten. After several calls to his phone went straight to voicemail, I gave up on reaching him and accepted that the arrow hadn't missed. My next impulse was to call Savannah. Exhaling a breath of resolve, I called Kalen instead. It took him thirty minutes to get the location that my phone indicated as my whereabouts.

Blu was with him. She was always with him. One chance meeting and they were now joined at the hip. "I'm so glad you are okay," she said, opening the door.

Giving her a tight smile, I slipped into the backseat of the work SUV, which didn't look like the type of vehicle anyone would use to haul most of the junk we found. It was functional but far from utilitarian—Kalen considered a fully loaded luxury SUV a "work" vehicle.

"Have you heard from Gareth?" I asked hopefully. He and Blu were friends and he'd introduced me to her.

Her thick, coarse ringlets were pulled away from her face with a decorative silk scarf, giving me an unobstructed view of her face. I could see her jaw tense and her eyes close. "He, Mason, and Victor are at the Isles, along with nine other people who were attacked on the street in Forest Park," she said softly. Blu's voice, which was usually wispy and light, was now heavy and strained. It took several moments for her tense scowl to melt.

"Chaos and discord," Kalen said quietly, focusing on the street.

"Discord?"

"People are afraid. Rumors about the Legacy are surfacing. There's talk that the SG isn't able to control the supernaturals and with Harrah's..." Blu's voice drifted off. The tension that tore through the silence swelled. The heaviness of guilt was getting the best of me. I was to blame for some of the things that had occurred. I should have let Harrah live; she could have fixed this mess. Sometimes deals with the devil had to be made. That was also what Conner was doing, and he was kicking my ass.

"Can you take me to the Isles?" I asked.

Kalen made a noise of disapproval. "I think your first stop should be the Shapeshifter Council to try to convince Michael to bring Savannah to the hospital. They don't have enough serum to treat everyone, and the shapeshifters are being...well, shifters. They've built their wall of protection and no one is able to get through to them."

"And you think I can? I don't have the best negotiation skills"— I looked around the SUV—"and I don't have my 'play nice' sticks."

"I don't think your sai are going to help you as much as your magic."

Kalen had the look of a betrayer and I had a feeling that the person he'd betrayed was himself. It cast a dark shadow over his face. He was suggesting that I take Savannah by force if necessary. My eyes met his in the rearview mirror.

Flashes of my interactions with Savannah ran through my head, and I tried to cling to them for the levity they evoked because things were going to take a turn—a bad turn—if I had to use force to get her. Even though I'd fought a shifter Tracker and won, I wasn't so sure how I'd fare against a group of them.

"I'd like my sai," I said softly. They were probably at the SG building. Or at least I hoped they were.

Sai sheathed to my back, we went through the same security check Gareth and I'd experienced at the gate of the castle-like home. Michael and his welcoming party, a group of ten shifters, met me outside. Giving the small pack a quick once-over, I gathered I was working with a bear, a couple of felines, and definitely some wolves. *Great.* The moment I got out of the car, some of the guesswork was solved for me. Several had shifted to animals in the short time it took to approach them. There was a leopard, a cheetah, two wolves, and a badger. I wasn't expecting the waiflike redheaded man to shift into what was essentially a stocky weasel with anger issues.

At their not so subtle display of aggression, Kalen and Blu started to get out of the car. "Stay, I have this," I advised them over my shoulder.

Haughtiness flitted across Michael's features and his brows arched in dissention. "Really." His eyes immediately went to the pack of people and animals next to him.

"I didn't come here for a fight," I said softly. *Diplomacy, Levy, you can do it. If you can practice it with a sociopathic megalomaniac, you can do it with a few well-intentioned jackasses.* But they were wearing that jackassery with special pride, as if there was an award involved or something. I felt like I was in a nightclub with the various glows of shifter rings in front of me.

"Believe it or not, I'm helping Savannah. If she comes out of this and knows that people died because of her, she'll never forgive herself. She's not in her right mind. I respect the promise you made to protect her and I don't want to cause you to violate it, but you have to talk some sense into her. Explain to her that people will die. If nothing else, that will change her mind."

Michael emerged from the jackass assembly, maintaining an air of arrogance and staunch confidence that annoyed me in the same manner it had when I'd first met Gareth.

"Her fear of you is odd, Ms. Michaels. I can't figure out how a woman who once lived with you has such an extreme fear of and hate for you. I've never seen anything like this. I consider myself a person who can hate with a passion like no other."

Is he actually bragging about being a master of hating people? Who brags about that?

"It's magic and I'm trying to figure out a way to reverse it, but I'm pleading with you to get her to the Isles to give blood." I sucked in a breath, pulling a lot of my pride in with it, too. "Michael, I have a feeling that if anyone can convince her to do it, you can."

Groveling didn't taste like chicken—more like rolled-up mud that had been sautéed with sewage. I wasn't a fool; threatening to kick their asses wouldn't help. Plus, I doubted I could. The angry, fat, bushy-tailed weasel looked like he was itching for a fight. All Michael had to do was give the signal and the feisty rodent would probably attack the hell out of my ankle. I had to use my words to convince them to find the goodwill to help.

CHAPTER 11

The Isles was exactly how I'd expected it to be when I walked in. Panic, worry, and poorly suppressed anger coursed over the faces of most of the staff. Dr. Patterson, the physician we'd met after the attack at the Solstice festival and whose name I had to find out because referring to him as Dr. Condescension seemed rude, was waiting at the entrance. I hadn't had a chance to change or clean myself up and purposely avoided the mirror. I could feel the bruising on my arm and a hurried brush of my hand over my hair was all I needed to know it was a mess. Looking presentable was the least of my worries. There were so many bigger priorities than grooming. Get to Menta Island, find the *Culded* plant, stroke Michael's ego enough to convince him to let me cast a spell on Savannah, deal with Conner, and find the people responsible for the virus. The latter was probably going to be handled by the SG and the FSR but I wanted to see the person who was behind it. That was a total lie. I really wanted to see what they looked like after I smashed their face into the ground. So, looking presentable to offer blood to save people wasn't anywhere on the list.

Dr. Patterson waved at me absently as he kept his eyes on the entrance door, probably waiting on Savannah. I suspected he remembered we were friends and thought we'd arrive together. Frustration lay heavily over his features. It had to be difficult to be a defenseless mage. Between his magic and medicine, he probably always had answers, and now his options were reduced to depending on the assistance of two random people. One from a group reviled and thought to be extinct and the other a peculiar woman with an obtuse magical ability. An ability I was sure he'd had to research based on the look he'd given Savannah when she'd told him what she was when we'd worked to heal victims of the Solstice festival attacks. When a look of reproach fluttered along the lines of his face, I wondered if he was thinking about his last encounter with the vivacious blonde who was just short of doing her "I told you so" dance but had forced some modicum of decorum for his benefit.

"She's coming," I said, sprightly, thankful he wasn't a shifter. Unfortunately, the woman next to him was, and she shot me a look of censure. I wasn't going to modify my statement. Hope was all I had, and it was placed on a stranger: Michael.

"Follow me, at least I can get your offerings."

My brows rose at his suggestion. *Who speaks like that? It's okay to say, "Let me take your blood," Dr. Highfalutin'.*

Highfalutin' or not, he was obviously grateful for my "offerings" and spent most of the time he drew blood thanking me. Something he likely didn't do often. I was a special case. The idea to tell him that Elijah was in town and could help popped into my head, but he really couldn't help without Savannah. *Ignesco.* It was a matter of time before they were on the "hot new supernaturals" list. A magical booster—a talent that I viewed as laughable at best—just seemed so innocuous. She couldn't perform magic, borrow it from others, or do anything other than help those with magic. How was that even a thing? But it was, and her ability had saved a lot of lives. My heart clenched. There had to be a time when thinking about Savannah and her absence from my life wouldn't cause such heaviness in my heart. This was dangerous—I'd always believed that if necessary, I could leave. Go AWOL and start over without a second thought, and maybe a couple of years ago that would have been the case. Now I wasn't so sure.

I was thinking about that and the list of things I had to do—make sure Gareth was okay, find a cure for Savannah, find out who was responsible for the attacks, locate more Legacy and Vertu—as I navigated through the hospital to find the room where they had Gareth. My emotions rolled off me so strongly that Gareth frowned when I walked into his room.

Based on the scowl, he was running on pure anger. "Who pissed you off?" he asked, making an attempt at a half-smile. He failed. It didn't quite make it to his eyes.

"Just the situation."

"Is Conner…"

"He's still very much alive. I really want to remedy that."

For a person who could die soon, Gareth was calm. Perhaps he had more faith in Michael than I had. He watched me from his position at the window. "Michael is very persuasive, as any person would have to be to lead the Shifter Council."

"Despite what Conner did to Savannah, he didn't remove her tenacity," I offered softly. I'd lived with Savannah long enough to know she might be more recalcitrant than any shifter. Stubbornness and fear were a terrible combination. Keeping that thought to myself, I forced myself to appear as relaxed as Gareth was. His mood didn't make me feel any calmer. It only made me irritated that he could die and all he could do was look at the window as if he was waiting for a pizza to be delivered; I was about to point it out.

"Worrying or being upset is counterproductive. It will only make you more anxious." He must have figured out what I was thinking, or at least seen it on my face.

"I hate feeling like my hands are tied and relying on someone I don't know and I'm not confident I can trust." I breathed, trying to subdue my emotions enough to make my voice neutral.

He eased his way toward me and pressed his lips firmly against mine. He pulled away and licked his lips. "Do you need a distraction?"

"You can*not* be serious about this!"

"Well, if you're going to say no, then I'm not serious." He grinned.

Recalling how quickly his nephew's health had declined when he'd been shot with the virus, I knew it had to have cost Gareth a great deal of effort to stand in front of me displaying confidence that probably wasn't there, for my benefit. Or maybe it was for his.

I kissed him lightly on the cheek and then hugged him. He wrapped his arms around me, and we remained like that for several moments.

"Why don't you have a seat?" I suggested, attempting to give him permission to be ill, to be concerned, to feel overwhelmed. He didn't need to protect me.

"I feel better standing," he said quietly as he backed up to the wall and rested against it. Color left his face and he looked pallid. His breathing had changed noticeably, becoming ragged and sharp. His attention kept going to his hand; I figured he was feeling an abnormal sensation.

Michael, please be as good as Gareth thinks you are.

"What happened to Calista?" I asked, hoping the discussion would be a good distraction.

"She made an attempt to keep us there." His tone was cold, but weak. "It didn't go well for her. We were able to call into headquarters on our way here. She's been apprehended." He made a face, his voice softening as he continued, "It's easy to forget about the family." Frowning, he turned to look out the window again. "She's not cruel, just mourning."

"Then she should handle it like the rest of us and shed a damn tear rather than align herself with the likes of Conner and whoever else is involved with this." Finding the silver lining in the situation, I asked, "Have they questioned her? Do they have any idea who's behind this?"

He shook his head. "No. Whoever it is, they are quite clever. She got the virus from Conner. He knows who's behind this—I'd love to question him." Based on his anger-infused words he, like me, wanted to do more than just question him. He wanted revenge. But even Conner might not have been allowed to meet the mastermind. He could be just as useless as the others.

I stopped questioning Gareth; it wasn't going to distract him from what was going on with his body. Within minutes sweat formed along his brow. He slipped into the visitor's chair, next to the window. Closing his eyes, he sank back into it.

"I'm fine," he said when I crouched next to him and rested my head against his shoulder, blinking back tears. "Levy, I'm just tired."

"I know," I whispered. It was all I could say without my voice starting to shake. My frustration and anger weren't enough to ward off the overwhelming feeling of hopelessness.

"They're here," Gareth announced weakly. It was none too soon. His hands were cool and clammy under mine.

I hurried out of his room to see an influx of shifters forming a human circle around a petite blond head—Savannah. I moved back a little to make sure she didn't see me and get spooked away as her histrionic entourage led her down the hall.

"Shifters are dramatic," I said, flashing a grin. "Present company *included*," I teased. "Who offers to 'distract' someone in the hospital? You should be ashamed of yourself."

It took a great deal of effort but he shot back, "You were worried and in need of a distraction to take your mind off of things. That's what I did. I'm your handler."

I rolled my eyes at the title he'd given me when I'd agreed to help find all the Legacy only if I could work with him. Officially, he was my handler, but I hated the title, which meant he enjoyed it a little too much. "Are we back on that? I said I'd work with you to find other Legacy. You aren't *handling* me."

"Clearly."

Ignoring the innuendo, I breathed out a sigh of relief. He was going to be okay.

CHAPTER 12

*G*areth had a quick recovery, along with the others, and I was thankful for that. He and I had a hotly contended debate over whether to go to Menta Island or stay and try to find out who was behind the attacks. We'd decided to leave finding the assailants to the FSR and the SG while we helped Savannah. If the attacks continued, we'd need Savannah in her right state of mind anyway.

Two days later we were at the airport. Gareth refused to hand over his bags to the person who met us at the car when we parked at the tarmac near the airplane. I felt a little guilty because I'd probably made too many smartass comments about him owning a plane. Each time he'd corrected me and pointed out that it was his family's plane, as if that made it different. It was pretty much like saying, "I don't own an island, my family owns an island."

"I'm dating Batman," I mumbled, taking the large leather seat next to him.

"No, you aren't. Batman is a billionaire and by day he runs Wayne Enterprises; he has a butler, and people signal him using an insignia," he said brusquely.

"Fine. Your mother has a corporation that I don't doubt for

one minute you'll eventually run. Instead of an Alfred, you have a Leslie. Very progressive of you, but your car is kind of the Gareth-mobile."

Sighing, he relaxed back into his seat in silence. I focused on the pre-flight details, but once we were in the air, I was faced with the overwhelming reality of what Gareth had done.

Unfastening my seatbelt, I leaned over and kissed him on the cheek. It was more than just an apology, it was appreciation for making this happen so quickly. "Thank you. I really mean it."

Giving me a half-smile, he said, "You don't have to thank me for this, Levy. I wanted to do this for you." He laid his palm against my cheek, and his lips were just inches from mine. "But if you *want* to thank me..." I had no idea what he was about to request. "No more Batman comparisons, or Ironman, or Captain Beatty or whatever."

"I can definitely assure you I'll never call you Captain Beatty because there isn't a person by that name in the Marvel or DC universe. In fact, I'm pretty sure there isn't a person by that name in any superhero franchise." Before I could begin naming those who were, he pressed his lips against mine. His tongue was gentle and coaxing. As I laced my fingers through Gareth's hair, he pulled me over the chair and into his lap. His hands slipped under my shirt and caressed my back then started to roam up to the edge of my bra. They would have progressed if it wasn't for someone clearing their throat behind me. Embarrassed, I shifted to return to my seat, but Gareth wrapped his arm around me, keeping me in place.

"She needs to turn around. I have to go over emergency instructions. It won't take long," the flight attendant said in an even voice. I turned in Gareth's lap to find the man devoid of any surprise or disgust at our display. I figured he'd seen worse and was used to people trying to get inducted into the mile-high club.

Gareth's warm lips eased against my ear. "You're fine, he's seen far worse than this," he confirmed.

"Don't brag," I shot back, giving him a look.

"I'm not talking about me. I'm talking about my parents." He made a face and shuddered. "They can't keep their hands off of each other."

Laughing, I focused on the attendant as he went over his instructions and waited until I'd moved to my seat, buckled my seatbelt, and acknowledged that I understood everything. Gareth and I declined food when it was offered but settled on a few drinks. I chose cognac, something I would nurse the entire flight. Gareth could drink several of them and be unaffected, one of the benefits of being a shifter, but it was a nine-hour flight and the boat ride to the island added another two hours; I didn't want to be hindered in any manner. Flashes of Blu's concerned face in my mind made me more determined than ever to be on my A-game when we arrived.

Once we were airborne, the drink had relaxed me enough that I accepted Gareth's offer to take a nap in the plane's bedroom. An expansive king-size bed was placed in the middle of the room, a shower to the left, and two large, comfortable-looking leather chairs were positioned in front of a small television that was mounted to the wall.

Gareth's lips angled into a devilish smirk as he followed me into the room. "It must be killing you that you can't say something snarky. Poor Levy, she has to keep all her little comments to herself." He kissed me again. His lips trailed from mine to the curve of my neck until he came to the V of my t-shirt, moving away just long enough to ease it off. His touch was gentle and fluid as it roved over me. Deft fingers slid along my back to unclasp my bra. He discarded it on the floor next to my shirt. My pants quickly joined them. He lifted me and my legs encircled his waist. Depositing me on the bed, he broke from me to slip his shirt off. Cords of defined muscles along his stomach and chest tightened with each movement. I hated his arrogance but it wasn't without merit. I inhaled his earthy scent as he lay over me. Kissing me again, he nestled between my legs and took no time to settle himself in me. This time the sex wasn't wild and heated as it usually was but in contrast grew into a steady, easy, sensual movement. His kisses were as languid as our movements together. His fingers glided over my body with a newfound interest as if he was seeing it for the first time. Our culmination came after hours of unhurried lovemaking. It was different, a change I enjoyed.

Gareth pulled me closer until my back was molded to his chest and I was settled into him, as if we were one. His hold tightened and he kissed me lightly on my shoulder. "I'm sure you'll sleep well." A light purred chuckle filled the room.

Okay, Mr. Arrogance. "I wonder if your parents just used this bed to sleep the last time they were on this plane," I said, smiling as his body noticeably tensed for a second before relaxing.

"Thanks for that image." I could hear the scowl in his voice.

"You're welcome," I said, kissing him lightly on the chin.

My lips remained pursed tightly together when we boarded the "boat" Gareth had chartered. I'd been expecting a cabin cruiser, not a midsize vessel and crew. Yes, an actual crew. Gareth explained it was a trawler boat, better to handle any unexpected water conditions.

Before I could comment, he cut his eyes in my direction, a reminder of my promise not to call him Batman or any variation of rich superhero. With great effort I kept that promise as we sailed toward the island. On the deck, I admired the open, azure sky and inhaled the crisp air. The weather was perfect and the motion of the boat was barely noticeable.

"It won't be like this the closer we get," one of the burly crew members said. His resting face was severe, his brown hair cut short. A black t-shirt stretched over his solidly well-defined body. The edges of the sleeves obscured the upper half of his sleeve tattoos. Clearly a man who could handle himself, and his eyes were filled with solicitude. His concern for the trip seemed to be the source of his sullen mood.

"Have you been to this location before?" I asked.

He nodded. "Three times—" He stopped abruptly, censoring his words.

"Continue," Gareth urged, quietly.

"Each time we returned with just the crew."

Gareth moved closer to me when I sucked in a ragged breath. If I died, I wouldn't need the bloom anyway. But that wasn't the truth. It was needed because Savannah couldn't live in a heightened state of anxiety about supernaturals, especially since to a lesser extent she was one. How long would she require sanctuary?

The closer we got to the island, the denser the air became. Gareth felt it, too, but our human companions didn't. Magic breezed through the air, flickering over my skin and burning my nose. Strong. As the boat continued to drift toward a landmass, the waves became more turbulent, rocking the boat so hard it unbalanced me, sending me into Gareth. He held me close, assessing me. I knew he was doing it because he scrutinized me and then frowned. "We can turn around and try to find another way."

I shook my head. "I doubt we have another." Elijah might have been able to show me a few spells including changing my hair color, but he'd been just as lost as everyone else when it came to finding a way to undo Conner's mind manipulation. I pulled away from Gareth, which I knew wouldn't help hide my reaction. He could probably hear and feel the desire for revenge—it was palpable.

"I can go alone if you want," I suggested, peering out at the barely visible island that was ominously dark despite the sunlight.

He gave me a look as if I'd asked him to cut off his arm and give it to me as a birthday gift. "I could never do that. We go together and we come back together. We fix Savannah and then find that son of a bitch who's responsible for the attacks on super-naturals."

"Well, if for some reason we can't get off this island, Blu and Kalen promised to come for us."

Gareth choked out a laugh. "That's backup I don't want to put my faith in."

It was wrong to laugh at them; their intentions were in the right place and I was sure they would make every effort, but I suspected they were better at theoretical practice and non-life-threatening jobs.

"They'd waste a day trying to choose the best rescue outfits and matching footwear." He continued to laugh, a deep sound that carried in the wind and lifted my mood. My levity didn't last long. Moments later the boat rocked so hard it sent Gareth and me to the other side of the deck. The captain began to make commands, and a burly tattooed man ushered us below to the cabin.

After about half an hour, the waves settled, but the air was so heavily drenched with magic, I knew the waves hadn't been natural. They were a warning. One that we had every intention of ignoring. We reached the shore, and for the second time I stood face to face with the white-haired captain. He squinted past me, looking at the horizon. As planned, we got there just at the height of the sun. Warmth licked at the skin on the back of my neck, which was exposed because I'd placed my hair in a high ponytail. A teal long-sleeved shirt kept my arms from being exposed, but I'd still slathered on sunscreen just in case. I would hate to survive my visit only to fall victim to the weather. Cargo pants wouldn't keep me as cool as a pair of shorts, but they had ample pockets where I'd stored knives, zip ties, and two spells Blu had made for me. One was a *sopor* spell that would render anyone within twenty feet of the mint-colored dust a sleeping beauty. I was convinced that it was nothing more than a heavy dose of witch's weed. On too many occasions I'd seen patrons at their shops slumped back in their chairs after indulging in it. She assured me it was much stronger. The second one was a *carcer* spell similar to the protective barriers that I erected. Instead it would keep anyone or thing from advancing, if they weren't a shapeshifter.

The captain guided us off the boat. "Good luck, but as per our agreement we will only stay until an hour before the sun sets. Then we must leave. I wish I could offer you more, but that is our policy." Again he looked out at the island and sighed. "I have no idea why anyone would come out here, but I'm sure you have your reasons."

"We do," Gareth confirmed.

"Remember, they don't play by the same rules we do. They don't have any that I've heard of, which is the reason they live here. They like the old ways, without restrictions. Don't trust your eyes; glamours might be used. Be careful of shifters: they are far more aggressive than anything you've encountered. And you might even encounter one you've never seen before."

"I fought a three-headed nightmare. There aren't too many things that would shock me now," I countered, giving him a reassuring smile. But I had experience with being attacked by something even more monstrous just when I'd thought something couldn't be topped. Regretting my statement, I wished I could take it back. I didn't want to tempt the fates.

"Vampires won't extend the same courtesy that they do in the States. They can compel with impunity and killing their donors isn't unacceptable here."

I nodded. "I get it, they are in their natural state without societal constraints."

Walking ahead of Gareth as we disembarked, I tried not to lose my courage. My vitals were probably sending out too many panic signals and I didn't want Gareth to suggest we abandon the mission—I wasn't confident I wouldn't.

He was dressed in a long-sleeved shirt and khakis. Instead of sai, he had a saber sheathed to his back and enough knives and blades strapped to him to take on a small army.

Pale sand, clear blue waters, and flowering trees that willowed out made the place look less ominous than it had when we were approaching.

Trudging through the sand, I assessed the area and then took a drink of water. "It doesn't seem that bad. With the exception of the sun." The longer we walked, the brighter it seemed to beam. I slipped on my sunglasses. Gareth's heightened vision had to make dealing with the sun more difficult.

"I assume you didn't hear that?" he whispered.

I shook my head, afraid to speak.

"Footsteps," he mouthed. Touching my arm, he gave me a signal to halt. I didn't hear anything. He inhaled and frowned. Waiting made me even more anxious. Several minutes passed before he finally waved me forward. Moving single file, we followed a path between the crowd of palm trees, which led us to something unexpected. A city. It was a city—rows of brightly colored restaurants, buildings, and homes.

"Maybe the people who came here weren't injured but decided to stay," I suggested, looking over the city. Were the stories embellishments to keep others away in order to maintain the purity of their island without outsiders asserting rules over them? Magic pulsed through the air, and I wondered if this was an illusory glamour like those that Conner did. Who had the ability to do that? A fae could present something this deceptively beautiful.

We stood at the edge of the precipice trying to decide whether or not to proceed. There was a lot of magic. So much that I couldn't attribute it to a particular supernatural.

Slowly moving out of the cover of the trees, we approached the city. There was a flash of movement, and a body whizzed past us, moving at a speed that made deciphering its appearance difficult.

"What the hell was that?" Gareth asked.

I shook my head and stilled, pulling out my sai and preparing to defend myself. Vampires didn't move that fast. Shifters moved quickly, but not as fast as a vampire. It zipped by again, Gareth groaned, and I quickly found out why when claws sliced into my arm. The scratches weren't deep, it wasn't to injure—more like a warning. The claws were sharp enough that if it had wanted to do real damage, it could have. With my back to Gareth, I erected a diaphanous wall around us. It was shattered immediately. Another whip of movement from another direction. Magic thickened in the air, and I was struck again. Deeper and in the other arm.

Reaching for the ingredients for the *carcer* spell, I waited for the thing to buzz by us again. It didn't take long. Another flash of movement, claws skated across my skin, and blood leaked from the cut. Before it could move again, I evoked the spell. It flitted away and slammed into the lucent enclosure around it. There was a lot I needed to learn about magic, and with the help of Blu and Elijah, I planned on learning all of it. The creature bounced back and forth around the enclosure; it was like watching a trapped fly. Eventually it wore itself out and sat resting against the magical prison wall, and I could tell it wasn't an "it" but a "he." With precise movements, his claws moved lightly over the front of his face, removing the shaggy mass of ash-blond hair that had fallen over his pale brown eyes that had such deep yellow undertones, they gave his eyes a daffodil tint. The shifter ring glowed around his eyes.

I expected to see anger or at the very least menace, but instead, he flashed us a miscreant grin.

Inching close to the barrier, I assessed the assailant. "How old are you, twelve?" He wasn't twelve, but I wasn't off by many years. Being generous with my assessment, I'd put him in his early twenties. Very early twenties.

Unfolding from his bent position on the ground, he stood and stretched, elongating his tall, lanky frame.

"I'm twenty," he growled with an unusual pride about the number of years he'd been in existence. In a wisp of movement, he'd bounded across the magical prison, until it was the only thing keeping us from being face-to-face.

He slid his claws against the barrier; vibrant colors sparked, but it held. He made a show of retracting his claws. Then he bashed his fist into the prison wall. When it didn't falter, he hissed, "Let me out. I was just playing with you."

I rotated my arm and gave him a full view of the slashes he'd inflicted. "This is 'playing' to you?" As he made a show of retracting his claws, I made one of healing the cuts in front of him.

A derisive snort emanated from his narrow nose. His delicate, angular features hardened, and he narrowed his eyes on me. Magic swept through the air.

"Are you doing that?" I asked suspiciously.

"Why?"

Because shifters can't perform magic. At least, in our world, but here things could be different. An assailant with magical ability made me think of all the possible scenarios that could result from supernaturals crossbreeding. Shifters were immune to all magic with the exception of mine and that of Vertu. Would a shifter/Legacy offspring produce a shapeshifter magic wielder?

The magic wasn't coming from him. Gareth scanned the area, looking for the source. He closed his eyes for a few seconds to focus on the sounds. Except for the waves of the distant ocean and the bustling activity coming from the city, I couldn't detect any more.

"I'll let you go if you tell me where I can find *Culded*," I offered, infusing my voice with enough steel to let him know I wasn't about to negotiate.

He grinned, backed away with the grace of a shifter, and sat. "Of course." His smile widened, exposing canines that looked awfully close to vampire fangs. "When the sun goes down, I'll take you anywhere you want to go."

I had no idea what the hell happened on that little island of misfit supernaturals at night but I had no plans of finding out. He rested against the wall of his magical prison as if he had no place to be.

"Angel, have you gotten yourself into trouble, again?" asked a honey-sweet voice a few feet away. Gareth looked as shocked as I was by the presence of the visitor. His shock eventually faltered into a scowl. It was apparent he didn't like being in a place that made him feel human—his senses unable to give him the upper hand.

My miscreant captive was all smiles as the newcomer with the gentle voice approached him.

Angel? I really hoped that was a term of endearment and not his actual name. Either way it seemed like a misnomer since there wasn't anything angelic about him.

Tilting her head, she studied him. "It would be to your advantage to let him go." Maintaining the same enchanting lilt, she'd effortlessly managed to convey a hint of warning.

"He attacked us," Gareth informed her, unsuccessfully keeping the threat out of his voice.

She tossed a glance over her shoulder to get a look at Gareth and smiled before repeating her suggestion to let "Angel" go.

I took just a few seconds to debate it. It was too early to start making enemies. As soon as the walls fell around him, Angel zipped away, leaving an endearing smile on the woman's face. She looked too young to be his mother but there was something similar in their delicate and honed angular features.

Giving us her full attention, she moved closer. Too close. Uncomfortably close. Gareth garnered a great deal of attention from the dark-haired woman. Apparently, clothing was optional on the island, or maybe the rule was they had to make sure their naughty bits were hidden. Hers were barely concealed behind a beige shirt that consisted of a fragile string around her neck and an even thinner one that held what could very well have been a handkerchief around her breasts. It was straining to perform the job with efficiency. It left her warm sienna skin exposed. The matching fabric that covered her lower half was connected by beads but didn't completely circle her waist, offering two very long slits on either side of it. It allowed her to move freely and gave an adequate view of her body to anyone who cared to look.

"You seem lost, may I help you?"

I wasn't sure what it was about her, but I erected my mental guards and quickly went on high alert.

Not getting a response fast enough, she smiled, exposing fangs. When she repeated her question, her eyes danced over me and then fell on Gareth, who respectfully averted his eyes. Smiling at his efforts, she moved closer to him.

"May I help you?" Her velvet voice made it quite clear she didn't want to assist but to help herself to our necks. With sweeping, agile movements she moved between us. Her magic slithered around me, warm and comforting, and she mentally pulled me to her. Just a gentle nudge into complicity, coaxing me out of my high alert. I felt it but couldn't reject it. My shields dropped and I was rewarded with another fanged smile. I knew I should shield myself from her, but desire kept me from doing it.

I moved toward the outstretched hand. Her lips parted. I ignored Gareth calling me and focused on her. Chocolate eyes were a river that I was swimming in, and soon I was adrift, the easy waves carrying me away—to her. Gareth yanked me to him, pulling me out of her thrall. He positioned himself between us, a wide roadblock that I definitely needed. I understood why it was illegal for vampires to compel people. I felt violated and sullied, my will having been hijacked. Inclining her head and shifting, she tried to make eye contact with me again. I closed my eyes and took a deep breath, inhaling hints of fruit and berries and an overwhelming amount of magic that wafted through the air.

"You don't want to look at me?" she asked softly. "Have I offended you in some way?"

"Not at all. I tend to get on edge when people strip me of my will. I'm peculiar that way."

A smile edged at her lips. "You didn't seem to mind"—her sharp gaze landed on Gareth—"but he did." She wasn't very happy with his intrusion and made it known with her icy stare.

Her irritation seemed to bring Gareth an absurd deal of satisfaction.

"I'm Gareth," he said with a polite smile. Keeping his position between the vampire and me, he offered her his hand in introduction. Her lips pressed into a stringent line, and reluctantly she took it. "Shifter," she purred, her gaze roving over him slowly. "You'll see that the shifters here prefer their various forms."

Various forms? I hadn't realized there were more forms than animal and not an animal. It hadn't been an hour and I was ready to get off the island of Dr. Moreau where shifters were able to take on more than one form. Was it a genetic disorder or actually evolution? The useless residual magic that came from the magic she'd used to compel me repelled off of him like rain off an umbrella.

Annoyed, she moved her gaze from us to the vast stretch of the city.

"I'm Vanessa," she finally offered. "I assume you aren't here for pleasure. How can we serve you?"

Gareth's lips pinched together as he scrutinized the intent behind her words in the same manner that I had. There was something about the wording that unnerved me and made me wary. The aggressive way her magic pushed against my mental shields wasn't helping. Feeling my resistance, she smiled.

"You didn't come here to visit or play. Why are you here?"

"We need *Culded*; can you direct us to where it can be found?"

"I'd love to be of service to you." Bystepping Gareth, she moved toward me. "Please, allow me to be of service to you."

I stared at her extended hand as if it were a viper ready to strike. "Why do I feel like I'm dealing with a troll at a bridge?"

Her light, airy laugh drifted throughout the immediate area, and if it weren't for the ominous undertones, it would have been a beautiful, melodious sound.

"Troll at a bridge." She laughed again. "I like you."

"I gathered that from your magical seduction and your attempt to make me your next meal. It's all fun and games until someone loses some blood, right?"

Maintaining the gentleness she'd had before appeared to take more effort.

"Why are you wording it that way? Allow me to be of service— what's with that?" I asked.

"It's polite," she responded tersely. Again, she treated me to a congenial smile that was laced with so much venom I felt like I needed antivenin.

"You pay for services here. And for a vampire/mage hybrid, believe me, the debt would be steep and heavily enforced," offered a baritone voice that had the same musical notes as Vanessa's. Expecting to see another vampire, I was surprised when we were joined by a half man, half horse. I assumed he was a shifter in half form, but he could've been a centaur. I had no idea what to expect on this island.

It was comforting that I'd almost been bested by a magical hybrid and not allured by *just* a vampire. It didn't make it any easier to deal with, but at least it didn't make me feel like a magical failure. If she was a high mage, I was dealing with a worthy magical adversary. I wondered if we had such hybrids in the States. If we did, I'm sure they kept their genealogy carefully guarded for fear it would incur more restrictive laws and regulations.

Shifting my focus from Vanessa, I gave my attention to the shifter.

If he was a shifter, it didn't seem like being in a state of half shift bothered him: He seemed to enjoy that I was gawking at him. I couldn't help it. His top half was a medium build, toned human

121

male, with ash-colored hair long enough that he needed to tuck it behind his ears. Hewed features lacked the definition for me to consider him handsome, but he wasn't unattractive and definitely didn't look like a horse. Shifters usually seemed to take on some of the characteristics of their animal. The silky sand-colored coat of his lower half shimmered as the light hit it and was several shades lighter than his skin. He was an Akhal-Teke horse. Horse-shifter's amusement with my interest crept into his words as he spoke. "Do you need help?" he asked. "No payment necessary."

While Vanessa seemed to have enjoyed bantering with us until becoming increasingly irritated by my questioning, Mr. Horse-shifter appeared rushed, as if he couldn't help us fast enough to get us off the island.

"Vanessa, I'll help them. Enjoy your day."

She pouted in a manner that was only adorable when done by a child. Apparently Mr. Horse-shifter found it appealing. "Did I ruin your day, Vanessa?"

"You gather so much fun in spoiling my day. We get so few visitors, let me enjoy it." She moved fluidly toward him until they stood close as if they were going to kiss. Several beats later, they were. Their lips brushed briefly before Vanessa slipped away.

"Why are you here?" he asked coarsely as soon as Vanessa had left. His cordial smile disappeared and he glanced at Gareth, then his eyes narrowed to slits as he studied me with interest. "You're not a witch or mage, are you?"

I shook my head.

"What are you?" He inhaled, his nose flaring briefly. I quickly recanted my prior assessment: He was very horsey at the moment. "Ancient magic," he whispered. His eyes widened with disbelief. "Legacy?"

It took several moments before I answered; as a shifter he would have known if I'd lied. I nodded.

Gareth stood taller, returning the hard look that the horse-shifter had directed at me. Even the denizens of an island that didn't have much to do with the outside world seemed to know about our role in the Cleanse. It was likely some of them were killed by it before it was stopped.

"We need to find *Culded*," Gareth informed him, breaking off the silence.

"What do you need it for?"

"A spell?" I offered and was treated to another cold look as if he expected me to do something nefarious with it.

The truth might have been the best option, but I had a feeling telling him I needed to undo a spell by a Vertu wasn't going to improve his opinion of me and my kind. So I went with a variation of it. "My friend had a spell cast on her. I'm not skilled enough to remove it and I need to undo it."

Nodding slowly, he started to walk away. Gareth and I looked at each other before following the man of few words. Once we'd caught up, he said, "I suggest you don't accept service from anyone on this island. I find the trickery distasteful but I'm not in a position to stop it." He continued to walk and talk, as if he were taking us on a sightseeing excursion, going through the island and down the stone-paved streets, where we received the same looks any stranger would get in a strange land. People were familiar with and greeted Dorian, our guide, who apparently had decided that providing a name wasn't necessary.

Navigating through rows of homes and shops, he increased his speed, which caused Gareth and me to trot behind him as the blazing sun beat down on us. The buildings dwindled and then gradually melted into more stretches of sandy land. Dorian covered his eyes to block out the sun and pointed to another, smaller, island. He slowed as he traipsed to the shore.

"The garden where the flower can be found is there." I looked around for a boat but then realized I'd have to swim. I worried I wouldn't be able to keep the bloom dry and wondered if it would be of any use wet. Sensing my concerns Dorian said, "Anything you acquire off this island will serve its purpose. The magic is strong and untainted. Water will do nothing to hinder it."

He started to trot away as we inched toward the water. His voice was light and whimsical, too affable for his words: "If the sun sets while you are on the island, it will be where you stay and eventually die. Your body will become part of the beautiful boundary that makes up this island."

"Isn't that something you should have told us earlier?"

"Would it have stopped you? I sensed your desperation. Whether I told you then or now, this is where you would have ended up."

"Is there a guide who will show us where the *Culded* is?"

"You won't need one, it will be easily found." Without another word, he was gone, trotting away, taking on full form. His beautiful, metallic coat quickly disappeared from sight.

CHAPTER 13

*T*he water was clear azure, making it hard to believe it might be anything other than water. What spell or curse could have caused such a thing? Colorful fish swam there, their fins whipping about as they moved throughout the water. We wouldn't become water, we'd become part of the ocean life. How many of them were humans? I edged closer to study the fish.

"You can stay here," I offered to Gareth. "I'll go and—"

"Don't you even finish that sentence. We go together and we return together." He continued walking toward the water until he was submerged before he swam toward the smaller island. I debated whether or not to leave the sai sheathed to my back behind and decided I wanted them with me. Knives were fine, but the sai were my weapons of choice and in an odd way, my security blanket—or security blades.

The cool water was refreshing, but the sounds of the water were calming. So much that it felt as if they were lulling me to sleep. I swam faster, jolted by the memory of the Mors, the assassin that had been sent to kill me after its hypnotic sounds had debilitated me. I hoped this wasn't doing the same thing. Ignoring the mesmerizing sounds, I pushed against the gentle waves until I made it to land. Gareth waited for me at the edge of the water, his expression indecipherable. He had to be as disturbed as I was that we weren't wet. We were as dry as we'd been before we'd swum over.

"Should we start freaking out now?" I asked, with a faint laugh. It was forced, an effort to calm my jitters. The dark, bleak island wasn't anything like the island we'd left, which made it harder to determine if the sun was setting. It looked as if it already had. The only indication to the contrary came from looking at the other island and Gareth's watch.

Stiffening, I examined the new island. Sand and trees were the only things that populated it. The fragrant smell of flowers inundated the air, lightly masking the smell of magic that I felt crawling up my arms.

"The magic here is stronger." I pointed out the obvious, another nervous reaction. I didn't like this place. It was too pretty and too serene. Conner had made me skeptical of beautiful and serene places. They could give a false sense of security and lure a person into letting down their defenses.

Gareth and I started to walk past trees, some palm and others that reminded me of weeping willows, long viney branches moving oddly with the gentle breeze. Too animated, as if they could possibly come alive; I wasn't putting anything past this place.

"Watch out for the trees," I warned and expected the look Gareth gave me. It sounded ridiculous.

His brows arched. "Of course," he joked. "They look dangerous." He pointed to one large one with limp branches that appeared to be struggling to live. "Especially that one. I bet it's the most dangerous of them all."

"Okay, when you get tree-slapped, don't be upset that I have no sympathy for you. And I'm not above telling you 'I told you so.'"

"I never thought you were above that. Not one time since I met you did I *ever* think that." He stretched his arm out to stop my advance. "Do you hear that?"

I shook my head. He pulled out the knife sheathed at his leg and I followed suit, taking out the twins. We continued to slowly pad toward the center of the island until we came to an illuminated area surrounded by the willowing trees we'd seen before, but instead of the refreshing sweet redolence, the area gave off the powerful and odd scent of cinnamon and cloves. The willows' long, limp branches spilled over into the large garden. There was only one type of flower, and based on Blu's description it had to be the one we were after. Harmless-looking, with delicate, pale yellow petals that reminded me of night-blooming cereus—except for the hints of crimson in the middle.

I shrugged off my sheath and took out the bags I'd stored in my pockets. Before I could move any farther, there was a whipping sound. The vine-like branches from one of the trees wrapped around Gareth's waist and tossed him back several feet. Another branch wrapped around my neck, tightening. I clawed at it. Yanking out the knife I had at my waist, I slashed at it until it released me. I darted out of the way when another branch snapped toward me. I crashed to the ground and landed on a lump. I cursed under my breath when whatever I had hit awoke. After seeing Dorian's centaur-like form, and Conner's creatures, I was prepared for anything.

It unsettled the dirt with its movements. I could have easily missed the creature since its skin matched the dark soil that it emerged from. It was another of the oddities on this island: Like Dorian, she was half human and half animal. Her reptilian form stopped at the waist. Nearly twenty feet of her body was visible, and there were still parts that weren't unearthed. Her upper half was quite human. Spiraling sienna curls spilled over her chest and were the only thing covering the front of her body. Her gentle, welcoming smile was so innocuous it sent off alerts. She possessed a magnetism that reminded me of Vanessa's, and I stepped back, instantly suspicious. Her attention skipped over me and landed on Gareth.

"Hello," she greeted him in a light, melodious voice that matched her appearance. Despite the sharp lines of her jaw and cheeks, her face seemed gentle. Too gentle.

Cautiously, Gareth returned the greeting. Again, he garnered a great deal of her attention.

"Why are you standing so far away?" she asked.

I don't know. Maybe because you are half naked woman, half super-long snake.

She reared back, using her reptilian body to give her extra height, and towered over us by several feet.

"I enjoy visitors, come closer," she urged. Gareth and I maintained our distance. With a quick, sinuous movement she lowered herself, and a ripple in the earth moved, giving us some idea of the length of her remaining body. She controlled the length we could see with ease, which supported my belief that she was dangerous.

Her brown eyes dimmed and a dark cast spread over her face, sharpening her features like knives. "Now!" Her previously harmonious voice now cut through the air, and magic pulled at us —at me. Gareth stayed rooted in the same spot. Sai in hand, I dug my heels in, aimed one of my blades at her, and countered with similar magical force. She gasped at the retaliation and hissed. Her tongue, which had been human before, was now long and split at the end like an actual serpent's.

She regained her composure, and her mood softened as she moved in a slow, rhythmic motion from side to side. I watched for a few minutes but taking a cue from Gareth directed my attention behind her. There was something entrancing and beguiling about her, making it difficult to ignore her even for a few seconds. Slinking back and forth, she shifted her body until she was just inches from my face.

"You've come to visit me," she said in a low, sultry voice, seemingly uninterested in Gareth now that she realized her magic was ineffective on him.

"We came to the garden to get *Culded.*"

Making a whimpering sound as if she'd been personally hurt by my assertion, she said, "No one ever comes to visit me, but just to come take from my land. You can't imagine how hurtful that is." Again, she extended her hands to a small section near her. "Please, sit and visit me for a while. I really enjoy visitors."

Squashing my apprehension, I moved toward the area with Gareth close beside me and took a seat, keeping hold of my sai.

"Oh, put those away, silly woman." Her eyes flickered in the direction of a small wooded area, darker than the rest of the island, where a crowd of trees hid the bodies of innumerable glowing eyes. "If I had intentions of hurting you, surely I have the means to." A snout peeked out from the darkness and then a mouth full of dagger-sharp fangs. "No harm will befall you while you are here with me."

The specifics of her wording didn't escape me. I was nice and safe as long as I was with her. I could only imagine what would happen to us when we were no longer in her sight.

"Will you be so kind as to tell me what it would be used for?" the woman asked.

I didn't want to be so kind, but I was positive that being amenable to her request would ensure we got off the island without any further incidents. With the passing moments, her gaze drifted to Gareth—a wanting gaze.

You're half snake, woman. What exactly do you plan to do with him?

"Are you here only to help her with her mission?" she asked, now just inches from Gareth. He handled it with more diplomacy than I would have.

Shifting his gaze at me, he smiled. "Yes, wherever she goes, so do I. I'd like to think she feels the same."

"So if I can convince her to stay, will you?" she asked.

Go ahead. You're just as likely to convince me to give up chocolate—

and that's never going to happen. But have at it, Ms. Snaky. Give it your best.

"Perhaps I can convince you." A twirl of her fingers, and a lovely small house appeared just a few feet away, and trees bearing tropical fruit sprouted from the ground. The scents of water, fruit, and fresh earth were quite welcoming. A less skeptical person might have been drawn to it. I looked at it with pure cynicism. Why was she on the island alone? Was she banished from the other one? Was there a reason people didn't want her there? Was she the reason people came to the island and never returned?

"It's beautiful and I'd love to stay, but I have a friend who needs the *Culded* to help her. She needs my help."

Genuinely hurt by my rejection, she frowned and nodded slowly. "If it weren't for that, would you stay?" she asked wistfully.

Sure. Why not? Me lying about it won't hurt anything. I nodded and looked around the darkening island. "Of course, it's beautiful."

Gareth quickly jumped up, showing me his watch. What had seemed like minutes speaking with her was actually nearly two hours. *How the hell did she do that?*

"We have to go. May I?" he asked politely, pointing at the flowers. Shifting out of the way, she watched him with purpose as he plucked several of them from their stems and dug a few others out from the root.

Storing the *Culded* in a bag, he moved away from the garden and increased the distance between the host and us.

"I do hope you reconsider. Will you stay longer, perhaps until the morning? One night here and maybe you'll reconsider." Her genteel, pleading voice was hard to hear; we had no plans to stay and nothing she could do would change that.

"Sorry. We have to go; we can't be here when the sun sets," Gareth pointed out.

Scoffing, she rolled her eyes and waved a hand in dismissal. "Are they still telling those tales? Nothing will happen if you stay longer. Did they also say that you'd become part of the water?

They do have fun with the guests with their obscene stories." I listened to her but watched Gareth's face. His eyes narrowed on her just a bit and his ears lifted ever so slightly to hear the changes in her speech pattern, heart rate, and respiration. There was a subtle change in his disposition. She was lying.

"I figured that, but our transportation will be here. We have to go." Following Gareth's lead, I backed away.

When we were out of earshot, he leaned into me. "Be careful. She's lying through her teeth." Scanning the area, he pulled out his knife, closed his eyes, and listened for a few minutes. He shoved the bag with the flowers into another thicker one that he'd brought, and we headed toward the water. The snake-tress slithered around us, moving rhythmically to music that no one else heard.

"What is your friend's name? I can send someone to help her and you two can stay longer," she suggested, her voice a soothing, melancholy cadence.

Still trying to be polite, I smiled. "That is quite kind of you, but I would like to do it myself."

"Please, I will help her. My gift to you. All you have to do is stay as you said you would. You said your friend's safety is all that is of concern. I can give that to you in exchange for what you offered."

"No, I have to do it myself, but thank you anyway."

I felt bad as she whimpered, looking genuinely hurt and deflated by the rejection. Her mood turned sullen as her eyes glistened with unshed tears. Surely she'd been rejected before, but she behaved as if it were the first time she'd experienced it. Head bowed, she slithered away, her shoulders lowering like her mood.

Gareth looked as confused and shocked by her response as I was. *Let's get the hell out of here,"* he mouthed.

I couldn't agree more. We quickly made our way to the edge of the island.

A few feet from the shore, the ground rumbled. A tail punched up, slinked around me, and pulled me into the sand. Sand spilled onto my face as I clawed my way up. The tail yanked again, and I was pulled deeper into the sand tunnel.

Gareth exerted the same force, tugging me toward him. She had snaked around my lower body and had a positional advantage. He leaned forward to keep hold of me and prevent her from pulling me away. He used his other hand to scoop away sand until he could grab the twins. He yanked one of the sai out of the sheath and moved from my sight. Within moments, the snake-tress was wailing, her hold loosening. Gareth returned and pulled me up. I yanked out the sai embedded in the sand and the snake-tress and started running at top speed toward the water. Wails of pain echoed throughout the island; we could still hear them as we swam. Dorian met us on the other side, glaring, a scowl firmly fixed on his face.

"What did you do to her?" he spat angrily. His brow furrowed, and although he was in mid-form, his nose flared as if he were a horse. He pawed at the ground, kicking up sand, his aggression apparent.

I pulled out my sai and pointed them at him. "She attacked us. It was unprovoked."

"She asked you to stay?" he asked softly.

I nodded.

"And you denied her." He was getting angrier with each word. I suspected he knew we would be asked but hadn't been prepared for us to decline. I wondered if it was the first invitation, or the first to be declined. Sorrow moved along his features as he looked over at the island, the sounds of anguish filling the air. It was hard not to feel guilty for causing such mournful sounds. Quickly I reminded myself of all the things that were incredibly wrong with the island. It helped that the taste of sand still lingered on my palate, a reminder that she hadn't taken no for an answer.

"Get off my island. You are never to come back, and if you do, you won't be allowed to leave." He'd barely gotten out his request before we were running toward the boat, nearly forty feet away now that the sun had set. Without breaking stride, we dove into the water and swam toward it. Increasingly harsh waves made it more difficult to stay the course toward our ride. A large wave smashed into us; Gareth went under and stayed under for several minutes. By the time I'd made it to him, he'd emerged. Treading water, I craned my head to look back. Joining Dorian were two other people—a man and a woman—and I was willing to bet they were responsible for the change in the ocean, responding to the sorrowful sounds of the snake-tress in the air. My arms were tiring from trying to swim against the turbulent current. One of the crew members tossed us a life buoy, which would help if we could get to it.

Weakened to the point that I was using everything I had to stay afloat, I was resting, treading water, then attempting to get to the boat. The tumultuous waves stopped when I no longer heard the snake-tress's gentle cries. Unsure whether it was permanent or just a reprieve, I swam as fast as I could to the buoy. The crew helped us onto the deck, where we lay to catch our breath. Gareth was lying faceup next to me.

"That was a hell of a disinvite," he panted out.

"Do all women interested in you react like that when you deny them? If so, we can't see each other anymore."

He barked out a laugh and then coughed up water. "Not usually, but she seemed to be equally interested in us. I guess we are quite the pair."

After several moments we came to our feet. The wailing started again—gut-wrenching, a disconsolate cry. Sadness pulled at my heart, along with guilt. Turbulent winds followed and rough waves shifted the boat off course. Chaotic gales and volatile swells that almost flipped the large boat continued until we were nearly an hour away.

"Seems like you two made someone very angry," the captain observed, coming down to the cabin area where we were in clean, dry clothes. Still shivering from the cold water, I inched closer to Gareth, taking in his warmth. He wrapped his arm around me, enveloping me in heat. Gareth ran hot; I supposed it was a shifter thing, although he assured me he was "just hot." The innuendo train could never pass without him boarding it.

"I have no idea what happened," I admitted.

The captain's eyes showed a wealth of experience, and he still seemed shocked by the situation. "Was it a banshee?" he asked with childlike hopefulness.

"Do banshees exist?" I inquired and immediately wished I could recant. I was starting to accept Gareth's belief that nothing was a tale and most things we thought were extinct weren't.

"I sail for a living; sirens and banshees are all you hear of. The wailing women, the sirens that call to the captain and crew and lead to accidents and ships going missing."

"No, it was just a misguided snake. Half woman, half snake," I told him. I still couldn't help but wonder if she made her docile offer frequently and if she didn't, what about us had made her want to extend such a peculiar proposal.

"Blonde or brunette?" the captain inquired, becoming serious.

"Brunette," we answered simultaneously. I moved out from under Gareth's arm where I'd snuggled in.

"Hmmm. It appears you all are the first to survive an encounter with the supernatural they call the Naga." The man tried to push a smile onto his face, but it wouldn't relax from his rigid mask. "Then you all are luckier than I thought. And if folk-lore is even the faintest bit accurate, you would have been condemned to spend eternity with her. Of course, no tale is complete without someone assuming she's a god of some sort." Head tilted, he gave us an appraising look of disbelief, perhaps trying to see what was so enticing about the two of us that would warrant an offer from the Naga.

I suspected it was an ambiguous name given by the person who had first told the tale. She wasn't a god, but had exceptional magical ability. After considering all the possibilities I concluded she was either a mage/shapeshifter or a witch/shifter hybrid, which would explain her magic and her ability to shift. Or maybe she had fae in her genealogy, since she seemed to have the ability to glamour, too.

"We need to get you back to your plane," the captain said with a newfound urgency as he started to leave. There was something he hadn't chosen to share behind his expressionless face.

"Do you think there's more to the Naga?" I asked Gareth.

He shrugged and frowned, grabbing his phone. He searched and then read the information he found on the Naga. The description of her was nothing like what we'd experienced. The depths of the magical ability weren't really explored. The Google version of the Naga made her out to be nothing more than a beautiful, hospitable deity. To prove his point about how limited Internet search was, he pulled up Legacy and there wasn't any mention of Vertu. "What makes someone like Conner dangerous is that the world isn't aware that he exists."

"The Trackers are."

"No, they know of Legacy. Vertu are like Legacy on steroids. History has the facts wrong—I suspect it was the Vertu who orchestrated the Cleanse. Legacy participation doesn't make them any better—perhaps it's just semantics. It seems like it should be a point of distinction." He pulled me back against him, and a welcome warmth wrapped around me.

We were in calming waters and I had the *Culded*; nothing else seemed important, even being banned from Menta Island.

CHAPTER 14

*T*he rest of our journey home was uneventful. We returned to Gareth's house, showered, and spent several hours sleeping, ignoring the incidents on the island. We ate an early dinner or late lunch, we hadn't decided, and afterward, I sat next to him on the sofa. I placed the wineglass I'd been sipping from on the coffee table, drew my legs up, and lay next to him. He was doing what he'd been doing for the past few minutes: staring at the *Culded*.

He shrugged. "This is so powerful that it can undo Conner's spell?" After several more beats of silence, he relaxed his back against the arm of the sofa and pulled me to him. "I don't like magic. It's too nebulous."

I twisted to look at him. Smiling, I agreed, "I'm with you on that. Will you call Michael tomorrow?"

He nodded, tension playing along his features. I couldn't quite blame him for it. He'd have to convince Michael to allow us to do a spell on Savannah, and as persuasive as Michael believed he was, Savannah hadn't stopped being Savannah. If she didn't want to do something, it wasn't going to happen. She'd wanted to save the lives of the supernaturals, which was the only reason she had come to the hospital.

"We have to find out who is behind the attacks on the supernaturals," Gareth breathed out after he glanced at his phone. I assumed there must have been another one.

"Has anyone spoken to Gordon Lands?" The former mayor had taken over Humans First after his friend, Daniel, the founder of HF, was killed.

"He's been questioned repeatedly and even agreed to do it with a fae. It's not him. He's appalled by it. His beliefs haven't changed regarding supernaturals; he wants us segregated but doesn't want it achieved this way—by violence."

I'd become too cynical for my own good. "Do you think a supernatural could be behind this, too? The person responsible has to have some knowledge of magic, and this could possibly lead to a war between humans and supernaturals."

"I think that person is Conner. We've underestimated—"

"Not me! I haven't!" I pointed out. "I said he was a freaking super villain." Now he was unhinged and pushed to the point that he only cared about chaos and destruction—oh, and making me pay for ruining his plans.

"Then we need to bring him in. Do you think you can do that?"

"No," I responded honestly. There were a number of reasons, but the most pressing was that I wanted Conner dead. It was a need so deep that it made my bones ache. Although I knew with effort I could put my desires aside for the greater good, I believed he'd rather die than be apprehended. His life would end with him knowing that he was leaving behind chaos and possibly the beginnings of a war. "I'm sure Elijah can help."

"The hot guy I sent to your house?" Gareth teased, kissing me on the forehead.

"Yep. What were you thinking?"

"I'm confident enough to not allow something like that to bother me."

He didn't have to tell me he didn't have a problem with confidence. It was humility he didn't seem to be acquainted with.

The next day, as Gareth and I stood at the door of the house where the shifters were keeping Savannah, I'd concluded that humility and low self-esteem weren't things that shifters possessed. Or perhaps anyone in a position of power had to exude overconfidence to command compliance and trust in those they led. It was what I chose to believe as opposed to thinking Michael was an arrogant ass. An air of superiority and haughtiness curled around his lips, skated over his features, and made its way to his eyes. The shifter ring had more than just a light glow; it shimmered.

"I told you I can be quite persuasive when necessary," he informed me, moving aside to let us in. I was still wearing the look of shock and disbelief I'd donned when I learned he'd persuaded Savannah to see me in less than an hour after Gareth's call.

"Thank you, Your Majesty. If I ever doubt your gifts of persuasion may I be taken out back and given fifty lashes with a wet noodle," I mumbled. I knew when I lifted my eyes I wasn't going to like what I saw. I didn't. A group of shifters' sharp, unamused gazes were fixed on me, and the weasel with the bad attitude—I mean badger—looked as if he was going to *make* me apologize. I wished I had a magazine to whack him on his flaring nostrils. Michael had come through, though, and I really shouldn't have been snarky.

"I'm sorry. I have a terrible sense of humor."

Michael's deep laughter diffused the situation. "I think you are amusing." Condescension dripped off his words. We'd settled in a comfortable place of dislike.

Savannah hesitated at the top of the stairs before slowly

descending, keeping a careful eye on me the entire time. Once at the landing, she eased herself back, allowing the shifters to be human barriers between us. Her eyes still shone with fear and disdain as they stayed on me. It made holding eye contact difficult.

"I lived with you?" she asked.

I nodded.

"If we lived together, you couldn't have done all those things I remember. I wouldn't live with anyone like that, would I? You didn't kill one of Conner's friends in front of him, did you? Or attack him after he saved your life? And his pet?" she whispered. "You didn't kill his pet, did you?" Her focus dropped to the ground. I could see the struggle vividly on her face, her fight to reconcile all the images in her mind; her gut was probably telling her they couldn't be true.

She lifted her head. "You didn't do any of that, did you?" she asked, hopeful. Her eyes were wide and expectant. I was having a difficult time trying to resolve the many emotions and quandaries that went through my mind. I wouldn't lie to her, but Conner had implanted a colorful spin on the stories, and I could only imagine what type of monster she believed me to be. I could see it. I stepped toward her, and the shifters formed a bastion, blocking me from advancing. Focusing on her through the allotted space, I searched her eyes.

"Yes and no. The stories have been distorted by magic. They're Conner's embellished versions. Will you let me undo it? I promise after I perform the spell, if you want me to go away, I will."

She nodded but didn't move past the shifters. When I stepped closer to Savannah, they tightened their circle around her, exhibiting a careful protectiveness. It was annoying, but I found comfort in the fact that the shifters, out of obligation, felt the need to enforce Savannah's request for sanctuary even if it was from me.

"I want her to do the spell," she said softly. As quickly as she made the request, they moved out of the way. She approached me with caution, eyes honed on me as if she was trying to make sense out of everything. It was as if a thousand-piece puzzle was placed in front of her, and she was piecing things together to get the true picture.

Michael led us to another room where there was more space, but it was still limited with four shifters and Gareth in it. I knew they weren't going to leave. The spell didn't require space, just Savannah's and my blood. She hesitated before extending her hand to me.

"After you get a blood offering, what happens?"

"We both offer blood to this"—I lifted the bowl of herbs and the flower to her—"and then I perform the spell."

She nodded. I started to chant the invocation, and her hand took hold of mine. She smiled gently. "Just to make sure we have enough magic to make it work." Looking at the bowl again, she added, "The benefits of being an *ignesco*." I cut my hand first, and then hers, finding more discomfort in her pain than mine.

I was strong enough to do it, but I didn't mind her pitching in. It felt familiar and friendly. I started the spell, slowly reciting the words. Suddenly, Savannah began reciting words of her own and grabbed my cut hand. A dark cast came over her eyes as her words became louder. A strong burst of magic wrapped around me, and I sucked in a breath before the rest were ripped from me. I felt like someone had punched me in the chest. A pearly illumination haloed over her as she gripped my hand tighter to keep me from wrenching out of her hold. Savannah could perform magic.

I was faced with a distasteful choice—I had to defend myself against Savannah. I gathered the magic was borrowed from me and would be quickly depleted, but I had to stop her. I broke her hold and thrust powerful magic into her. She went back—hard, crashing into one of the shifters. Before she could fully recover and regain her feet, I hit her again with enough force that she smashed into another shifter, bringing him to the ground with her. I kept her and the shifter pressed against the ground, fighting off the anger of betrayal by reminding myself that she wasn't acting on her own. This was Conner. All Conner. When I finally had a chance to see him again, I wouldn't show him any mercy.

Keeping my magic and eyes on the secured pair, I grabbed the bowl and started toward her. "Savannah," I said softly. "You don't want to hurt me. The memories you have, the feeling of hate, aren't yours. They are manufactured. You can't fight me on this if you want your life back. Because I will continue to do what I can to make you the way you were. I can't let you be like this."

"Or will your spell distort the real ones," Conner retorted, popping up behind her. I cursed under my breath. I hated that he could do that. Strong magic floated through the air as he pulled away my hold on her, keeping the shifter against the ground until he had cleared enough distance. Erecting a diaphanous wall, he protected himself and Savannah from the shifters who were moving in toward her.

"She sees between your lies. She knows the truth. Don't take that from her," he accused venomously. Astonished by how he spewed lies with such ease and conviction, I stared at him.

I didn't want him to leave with her, so I inched slowly toward the magical barrier. The disturbing image of her back pressed close to his chest as she found comfort and safety in him just fueled my distress.

Ignoring him, I concentrated on Savannah as I spoke. "Savannah, Conner is not the good guy here. Whatever you think of me, it is far from the truth. I give you my word. Please think about it logically. Could you be friends or even live with the person you imagine me to be? You know Gareth—he would never do that. What are your memories of Lucas? Remember them. He would never hurt you nor allow you to be around anyone who would bring you harm. Savannah."

Confused, glassy eyes stared back at me, and I could tell she was sorting through her mind. My heart ached for how difficult it had to be to try to navigate memories, wondering which were real and which were false. She kept her position close to Conner. She trusted him. It was a hard pill to swallow when just days ago she'd have been packing up her quest bag ready to follow me anywhere to help me kick his butt.

"You have a quest bag. I make fun of it. But you take it every time you think we're going to have an adventure. You had it with you the first time I took you to Blu and she discovered what you were. Remember?" I asked hopefully, blinking back tears that were forming as she continued her wide-eyed owl look.

"Do you remember Kalen?" I asked. Again she was searching for the memories—there was something there. A light. It wasn't just blank anymore. "I taught you how to fight. Remember?" I pulled out the sai—my "sticky things," she had called them on more than one occasion. I gently suggested memories that I thought might not have been distorted. I hoped they were vivid enough to make her question the ones that didn't fit. I needed her to doubt them. At least that would put me in a better position. I smiled. "You did a protest at the Supernatural Guild—just you—when I was arrested for a crime I hadn't committed. You yelled at Gareth. Do you remember?"

Another light. She smiled. I kept inching closer, hoping Conner was paying more attention to my words than my movement. She blinked several times. "Gareth said he was going to arrest me," she said softly.

"He threatens to arrest everyone. It's his thing. I'm working on it." I smiled.

As she switched her eyes to Gareth, the smile that emerged settled in. I'd take it. I kept talking. Conner stood confident in his success, arrogance his biggest flaw. I shattered his wall with so much force he and Savannah were blown back. Within a blink, Michael had Conner hoisted against the wall by his neck.

Gareth had Savannah next to him, and in one sweeping move the others were in front of him, blocking Conner from Savannah.

Vertu magic could be used against them, but since Conner was probably more concerned about trying to breathe than performing magic, I felt confident I didn't have anything to worry about.

With her reluctance gone, Savannah willingly gave me her hand again and I cut both our palms again. I quickly did the spell, watching it spiral to life in a dense lavender and crimson fog that swept in Savannah's direction and then covered her. Stepping back, I was awestruck by its animated movement, coiling around, meshing and unmeshing as if it were grabbing every memory and cleansing the magically enhanced ones. Savannah was frozen as the magic moved around her. Nothing distracted me, not even the commotion to the right where Michael and Conner were. I'd deal with him later. Savannah was my priority, and I kept a magical ball sparked in my hand ready for Conner if he attempted to stop the spell.

Michael's string of curses warned me that Conner had gotten away. I kept my magic readied to engage with Conner. If he'd gotten away, it was only a matter of time before he resurfaced. On edge, I waited for his appearance as the spell continued to work on Savannah. Gareth caught her as she started to collapse to the ground.

"Did it work?" Michael asked, concerned, as he inched in, wearing his anger in his frown. Savannah was in a deep sleep. Or at least I hoped she was sleeping.

"Savannah." Gareth whispered her name. Unresponsive, she continued to breathe heavily, which was oddly comforting. It was a restless sleep, because her eyes moved frenetically under her eyelids.

Four hours later, it could have been a scene from *Snow White*, except instead of seven dwarfs there were five hulking shifters circling her. We weren't dealing with the antics of an old witch, rather those of a magical, psychotic asshole. And there wasn't anything charming about the blond vampire prince who'd spent the last three hours since his arrival glaring at me.

Savannah's situation was nothing like Snow White's, but the mental acrobatics it took to try to see the similarities served as a good distraction. She stirred and Prince Fang pushed up from the wall to get a better look. Moments later, she sat up with a start and stared around the room. I took it as a good sign that she didn't look surprised. Her eyes finally landed on me. The heaviness that had burdened me over the hours lifted with the light familiar smile she gave me.

"Hi." She beamed.

My voice was raw. "Hi," I muttered.

"Thank you, Levy." She jumped off the bed and hugged me. I blinked back tears, refusing to break down in a room full of strangers. Lucas moved to my side, and she switched to him, giving him a hug but keeping one hand on my arm.

CHAPTER 15

The day after I'd removed the spell from Savannah, seeing her pink yoga pants–covered ass hiked in the air as she assumed the downward dog position was a welcome sight. At my approach she jumped up, her face bright, eyes as emotive as before and no longer looking at me with manufactured hate.

"Good morning," she said brightly. She grabbed a towel and wiped the sweat from her face.

"Morning." I matched her tone although I couldn't fake her enthusiasm for mornings. Not before a couple of cups of coffee and a sugar high from my morning pastry. I made coffee, grabbed two donuts and started chomping on one. I'd missed her so much that I enjoyed the look of disdain at my breakfast choice.

"What do we do next? How do we find Conner? I want to get that son of a bitch." The frost and steel in her voice made my eyes widen.

"You're not going to do anything. I plan to find him and"— breathing deeply, I calmed myself enough to give a more acceptable answer than my stock one of "kill him"—"bring him to justice. He needs to be handled by the Supernatural Guild."

"Yeah, because they 'handled' him so well the first time they had him." She was right; he'd broken out the last time. "How many Legacy and Vertu are there?" she asked, sliding in her chair in front of me.

"I don't know. We were going to look for more when we were sidetracked. I recently met Elijah. He's a Vertu and helped me find you." I told her about his skills and how he was staying in the city to help me.

"When is the last time you spoke with him?" she asked, her voice strained.

"A couple of days ago."

"Call him," she instructed, concerned. "Conner's desperate. When he took me, he wasn't even the same person. Before he was at least a charismatic monster; now he's just a monster. Emotions so rabid and vengeful I could feel them. All the hate and thirst to conquer have been directed at you."

This made me remember the same anger that Savannah had fixed on me the day before. "You can do magic," I pointed out.

She shook her head. "Conner seemed quite interested in what I am. He showed me how to hijack magic. But I have to be connected the way we were. I think it only works if the person performing it has a great deal of it."

It was something we needed to explore and I added it to my ever-growing to-do list. I was sure Blu would enjoy helping me look into it. Before I could get excited about Savannah's newfound ability, I had to worry about what it meant to other people. No one, besides Conner, who saw her do it yesterday could use it. I'd have to make sure it remained as unknown as her supernatural title.

Savannah slid into the seat across from me and gave my breakfast another scathing look. "I think he's working with whoever is spreading that virus. I'm not sure if he was there at the beginning, but he's definitely working with them now."

Slumping back in my chair, I expelled a rough breath. That was another set of problems. Who had the ability to orchestrate such a strategic plan, persuading enough people to blindly follow them and wage a silent war against supernaturals?

Before I could state my worst fear, Savannah did. "I'm afraid someone will kill me. I don't doubt they'll start trying to kill off any Vertu and Legacy they find as well. After all, we're the reason their plans are failing."

Grabbing my phone, I called Elijah. He picked up immediately. "Levy, is something wrong?"

"I was just checking on you. Um…" I knew I was going to sound paranoid and overprotective, but I had to do it. "You should be careful."

"I'm always careful." His response was simple with a hint of arrogance that reminded me of Conner. Perhaps something intrinsic in Vertu gave them unyielding confidence. "Would you like to practice more? You were so close to learning to transport with accuracy."

Learning to change my hair color was a nice parlor trick but didn't have any value. I needed to learn to transport with accuracy and without cues or assistance from Elijah. It was a very handy skill to have and another weapon to use against Conner since he managed to pop up anytime. "Can you come here today, after I get off work around five?"

"Yes, of course." He hung up without saying good-bye. It was his odd quirk. You weren't going to have long conversations with him, and if you forgot to tell him something, too bad—he'd hung up before you could add it.

It was hard trying to go back to business as usual when I knew about a group of people determined to kill supernaturals, and Conner, who was set on making me pay for my interference. But I had to work, and the many days I'd taken off was siphoning off my savings.

"Are you going to work today?" I asked Savannah.

Oddly, she'd gone to work while she'd been under the shapeshifters' care and had a great deal of explaining to do regarding their presence in her building and outside it. She worked in a casual setting, but over-the-top shifters hanging around wasn't something taken casually.

"I think you should still stay under the shifters' protection."

"Are you kidding me? They're a little...no, they are a lot extreme."

"Believe me, I know. Do you remember the entourage they had for you when you went to the hospital?" I teased. "There I was expecting a chart-topping diva or an award-winning actor and all I saw was you. I was so disappointed."

"Whatever." She leaned over the table and playfully hit me on my arm. "Maybe I'll stay with Lucas." She didn't sound very confident in the suggestion and her face lacked the enthusiasm it usually had when she spoke of him. Guilt shadowed her face. "I don't think he's going to forgive me. I treated him awful."

There was a familiar knock on the door before I could offer comfort. I'd seen how hurt Lucas had looked when Savannah wouldn't let him near her, but he'd forgive her. He was more hurt by it than angered. I wondered how my roommate had enthralled the Master of the city in a matter of weeks. Speak of the devil: He was at the door when I opened it. He wore a dark blue suit, and one button was undone on his slim-fitting light blue shirt. For Lucas, that was as casual as wearing a tattered t-shirt and jeans.

"Lucas, you could have at least gotten yourself dressed before you came here. Man, have some respect," I said, grinning, which made me the only person doing so. Standing behind him were his usual guards. I referred to them as Suit Number 1 and Suit Number 2 but No Smile 1 and 2 would have been just as appropriate. Just like Lucas's, their faces were emotionless.

When Lucas finally addressed me, his tone was chilly, a reminder that I was dealing with a very old, very deadly vampire.

"Levy, it would have been good of you to keep me updated on Savannah's state."

It would be good of you not to treat me like I work for you. The sharp look he gave me kept me silent. I reminded myself that he was worried about Savannah and that having him there to watch her was a good thing, although part of me was dying to set boundaries. Lucas needed boundaries. Boundaries he'd probably ignore.

"Savannah." He said her name with the smooth rhythm of a song and approached her cautiously.

When he started to nuzzle her neck, I was reminded why I often left when the two of them were together.

"Stop. I need to shower," she informed him, pulling away. Lucas was close behind her as she headed toward her room.

"Hey, lover boy," I called after him before he could disappear down the hall. Then I jerked my finger in the direction of the door. "What do you plan to do with your packages at the door?" With a quick snap, I closed my mouth as it dawned on me that I had just called the Master of the city "boy." Shrugging, I owned it. Lucas turned and fixed me with another sharp look. I squared my shoulders and stood taller. "Master lover boy?" I corrected with a grin.

"Levy, let's remember I'm still quite displeased with you. Don't make it worse."

"Don't forget, I'm displeased with you as well," I snarled right back at him, baring my teeth in the same manner. I wasn't, but I wasn't above deflecting and being fake enraged to get him off my back. "And you know why!" I stormed off, tasked with finding a good reason to give him if he ever cared to ask.

Heading back to my room, I was able to hear him instruct the Suits that they were to wait out in the car. I wondered who they'd pissed off in a past life to earn the job of Lucas's guard or what ridiculous amount of money they were being paid. It had to be the latter.

Blu's face brightened when I walked through the office door. With a great deal of effort, I forced mine to do the same. Midwest Barbie was out of my desk chair, moving with ease in ridiculously high boots that made her tower over me. A scarf was around her head tying back her hair, displaying hoop earrings. I felt bad for being jealous that she seemed to have replaced me. I wasn't sure how, though, because neither she nor Kalen was the type to do the work of crawling through tight attics, dirty barns, and messy basements to get our goods. She was likely to be ecstatic about accompanying Kalen to any auction he wanted to attend. I'd happily give up that position and let her be the one who had to get dressed up to attend them, but despite all my complaining, I enjoyed the other part of the job.

"I knew you'd be fine. I just knew it," Kalen greeted me. It was the same thing he'd said when I'd called him after Gareth and I had returned home from Menta Island. Repeating it was his passive-aggressive "I told you so" to Blu. Her brows rose and she gave him a look; rose coloring inched along his cheeks.

"What was it like?" Blu asked, taking a seat on the desk.

I spent nearly twenty minutes describing the trip to them and answering all their questions. When I finished, Blu gave me the same look of sympathy and shock that Kalen did whenever he saw me fight. His theory was that behind every good fighter was a tragic story. In my case it was true.

"Savannah is okay?" he asked.

I nodded. "For the time being. She can do magic now." I went on to explain what had happened during my spell.

Blu scowled. "She can't really do magic. Once you disconnected from her, the source was gone." She seemed relieved by it, and I was, too. It was comforting that Savannah was more human than supernatural. She could pass for human. A naïve and too wistful part of me wanted to believe the less magic inclination she showed, the more likely it would be for her to survive if a Cleanse should ever happen again. There wasn't anything to support my theory, but letting it overtake me, even for a few minutes, was comforting.

"I need to find Conner," I admitted. I wanted him dead, but realistically we needed him to find the people behind the virus and the attacks. "I just can't believe that this is being done by a random person. It has to be someone who is well connected, charismatic, and linked to supernaturals. They knew about Jonathan's death and used that as a way to get to his sister. Humans don't typically follow the change in supernatural regimes that closely, especially since he was replaced within days. As far as most were concerned, a mage was a mage." I moved from my desk and paced the length of the room. "Conner gave Jonathan's sister three arrows with the virus, and she infected Gareth, Victor, and the fae who was with us."

"Did he give them to her?" Blu inquired. "All you all know is that she had them in her possession. Would it be a stretch to consider that Jonathan's sister might have a similar interest—to incite a civil war between humans and supernaturals? Create a virus that can only be treated with the blood of a Legacy and an *ingnesco*? I'm willing to bet that combination is very similar to the blood of a Vertu."

Blu's speculation had me wondering on the drive to the SG if we could use the *ignesco*/Legacy combo to find Conner. He could block it if I was trying to find him doing a blood search with my blood, but could he do it with the combination of Savannah's and my blood? Armed with the new information, I wanted to try it, but I had to make sure that if I could locate him, I had enough backup to apprehend him. On the drive to the SG, I contemplated the pros and cons of getting backup. Backup meant there would be witnesses. Witnesses to what surely was going to be a crime.

Apprehending Conner permanently meant killing him. I had no intentions of coming in contact with Conner and allowing him to leave alive.

I waved at Beth as I rushed past her, getting a quick glance at her flushed appearance and cautious look. Gareth, Victor, and a group of heavily armed police officers and FSR agents met me in the hallway to Gareth's office. I was quickly surrounded, with at least seven guns trained on me.

"Put them down," Gareth ordered.

"Maintain your position," Victor boomed with authority, daring anyone to disobey it. Out of my peripheral vision I saw two agents ushering Kalen and Blu away; they looked as confused as I was.

"What's going on?" I kept my hands in plain sight. I was quick with magic, but I wasn't faster than a bullet.

Gareth's voice was calmer than he looked, the glow of his shifter ring bright, his gaze predaceous, and it seemed like he was just seconds from exploding into his lion form. "They think you're responsible for the attacks," he snarled, incredulous.

"I'm the one who saved you all. I've been working with you to stop it. People are alive because of me. What do I gain from this!"

"There was another attack this morning. Your blood was found at the scene and inside one of the arrows left behind. A sai, which is your weapon of choice, was found with your fingerprints on it."

"My weapons are in the car," I said, but second-guessed whether they were. Had Conner slipped in and switched them? I wouldn't put anything past him. When I'd been unconscious in his presence, had he taken my blood and fingerprints? Planned to make me wanted or hated so vehemently that I would come to him for succor?

I started to feel caged, afraid, and ready to protect myself. Defensive magic pricked at my hand, slivers of it wrapping around my fingers. "Test it again," I demanded.

"They've tested it four times upon my request," Gareth said exasperatedly. "You're being set up for this. I don't know how. I've had people monitor the testers. It doesn't make sense."

"What do you mean, it doesn't make sense?" snapped one of the FSR agents, a mage. "She killed Harrah, and she's a Legacy with a great deal of power. You've allowed yourself to be compromised, but you won't do it to this department. The rumors are true: She killed Harrah because Harrah found out what she was up to. Harrah handled it poorly by calling in a Mors, but she was taking care of the situation. Levy is dangerous and you're too busy bedding her to see it. She's been playing you the whole time. Helping us? She always seems to be in the right place at the right time. If she and Conner were actually enemies, why hasn't he killed her?"

He was right. This looked bad.

The mage glared at me as he tossed accusations. Responding that Conner wanted me as his broodmare and companion didn't seem like a good answer. The agent had found me guilty, and no matter what I said, I wasn't going to change his mind. I pushed aside feeling betrayed by Victor to try to reason with him. "You're a shifter, listen for my vitals, see if I'm lying."

"Olivia Michaels or Anya Kismet, I don't believe even I'm skilled enough to tell whether or not *you* are lying. You seem to be quite proficient at it," Victor responded darkly. My alleged betrayal of the supernatural world was clearly taking its toll.

"I'll let a fae question me."

The mage who'd accused me earlier scoffed. "We know what you are and that our magic would be ineffective. We have no chance of getting the truth out of you."

My eyes dropped to his crotch, exactly where I wanted to deliver a striking kick. I was tired of proving myself to them, and my temper started to get the best of me. "Then since you know what I am, you know there aren't too many places you'll be able to hold me. I'm walking out of here. The next time you're attacked, don't call me. When you no longer have an antidote, just let the virus run its course and leave me the hell alone. Maybe after several of you assholes die you'll realize I was on your team all along—" I pushed back the rest of my words at the audible cocking of a gun.

Could a bullet penetrate my protective field? I knew that magic couldn't, and the way everyone was looking at me, I knew they were willing to find out. Surrendering was a hard pill to swallow. Victor took a step closer; his eyes had softened and his scowl relaxed. "Just agree to stay in custody for a few days while we figure this out."

"That'll prove nothing. Whoever is setting me up—and we know who it is—will just hold off on any further attacks while I'm in custody, which will support the implication that I'm behind this." Harrah had said that I was careless with my blood, but there had been so many attacks; surely I hadn't left that much around to be used. Focusing on Victor's eyes, I tried to determine if he was under the same manipulative spell as Savannah had been.

"If you take her into custody after all she's done to help us, I'm done. Find the person responsible, or don't. I won't help anymore," Gareth snapped.

"You've been abetting her. Do you think we really want your help?" offered the mage, who seemed to be angling hard for a thorough ass-kicking. The way Gareth looked at him, it seemed like he was closer to getting one than he imagined.

"You're not going to speak again," Gareth asserted, shifting his attention to the mage for just a moment before redirecting it to me. He frowned and moved even closer to me, in front of the guns. "What do you want to do?" he asked me softly.

"I don't know," I whispered. The mages and fae might not have heard but I felt sure the other shifters had. It was one of the few times that I'd felt utterly devoid of a plan. I was about to concede when I heard a high-pitched feminine command: "Don't you put your hand on me!"

Gareth made a face and sighed heavily, recognizing Savannah's voice over the crowd as it spilled down the hallway. Her heels clicked against the ground with purpose.

"Excuse me!" Her voice was closer—much closer. She'd bogarted her way through the agents. My eyes widened as I watched her navigate through them as though they weren't holding firearms.

She was always a little spunkier than most humans and possessed an audaciousness that most were too shocked by to respond. She stalked her way to Victor, who had over seven inches on her. He dwarfed her in height only. A fiery and angry Savannah was like an uncontrollable wildfire; it was difficult to get a handle on it or figure out where to start.

"Savannah," Victor said sternly.

"Don't you *Savannah* me. It's Ms. Nolan, and in less than an hour, you'll be speaking with my father, Jacob Nolan, Esquire. You all will need to have a reason why she's being arrested."

"First, you have nothing to do with this," Victor started in a coarse voice, his thinning patience obvious. If he'd been a more perceptive shapeshifter, he would have quickly realized that was the opposite of what to say to Savannah. It was equivalent to telling her to sit down and shut up. And she looked like he had, face the color of a ripe strawberry. Her emotions lent her as much power as magic did its wielder. She was a rising firestorm, blistering and undeniable.

I feared she was just seconds from escalating the situation to the point of no return. Most of the people in the room were staring at her as if they were thinking the same thing. "No, here's the first. When you had strange creatures running through your city, who the hell stopped them? It wasn't you guys. When the Maxwells were on the loose wreaking havoc, who the hell apprehended them? Or what about the time two cave lions were about to destroy each other in the middle of the street and were stopped? Can you recall who handled the strange, deadly creature traipsing through the city destroying anything and anyone in its path? I don't care what evidence you have—it's wrong. So. Fix. It. We're leaving. You have no reason to arrest her and you're not going to," she commanded heatedly.

"Ms. Nolan," said an unfamiliar voice. A human police officer who'd squeezed himself through the crowd started to read her the Miranda rights.

Damn. Damn. "Please don't," I said to Victor, my mind going a mile a minute as I attempted to make sense of the whole situation. I didn't have a plan.

"Stay in our custody for a few days. Let me figure this out," Victor beseeched. His tone had lost its edge and he seemed conflicted. His inner turmoil didn't squelch my feelings of betrayal.

"Don't arrest Savannah," I said.

Being cuffed and escorted away didn't quell her defiance at all. "They'd better not arrest—"

"Savannah, stop. I'm fine. You can't help me if you're in jail." I turned to Victor. "I'll agree to stay in custody, just don't arrest Savannah."

Victor nodded once in the direction of the police officer who had cuffed her. He removed them. Keeping his voice even and tepid, Victor continued the conversation he'd started with Savannah earlier. "You are very aware that the rules in the human world apply to us. Levy is a public safety concern and will be contained."

"Or killed," the mouthy mage offered. It was the last thing he said before Gareth pushed him so hard he crashed into a wall several feet away.

"I said you were done talking."

A flash of anger lit Victor's face. It was safe to say that Gareth's job security was in question.

"I'll go. Just let Savannah go." I turned to Gareth. "I'll be fine. Find out who's behind this."

"It will just be for a few days," Victor offered. He inched closer to me, his voice a barely audible whisper. "I don't think it's you, but I can't let you stay free. We just need a few days to sort this out."

I nodded.

CHAPTER 16

*I*f Victor thought I was innocent, he was doing a horrible job showing it. Barathrum was where they kept the most dangerous supernaturals, and I was now being held there along with such luminaries as the Maxwells, the chaos mages. It was like being sentenced to eternal solitary confinement. Each section was a separate multiroom, with a great deal of magic used to keep it secure. Secure for most—Conner apparently didn't have a problem breaking himself or others out. After eight hours inside, I was convinced that the Maxwells might not have started off as bad as they seemed, but had been driven to madness. It was too quiet and the pulse of strong magic that coated the air irritated me, especially since I was saddled with large iridium manacles that restricted mine. They weren't fooling around.

Victor was on my list and there weren't too many things he could do to get off of it. If I'd known this was where they planned to hold me, I'd have railed against it. The silence just gave me more time to think about the situation. I walked along a long hallway with rune-decorated peach-colored walls. The color made it seem less institutional, but the limited space was definitely a reminder. Off to the right was a small room for dining, to the left a larger one, a multipurpose area. There was a TV, exercise equipment, and a flimsy bookshelf with few books on it. The wall coloring was a little cheerier, blue. I assumed it was to give the illusion of being outside. It didn't.

I went over all the things that had transpired. Someone had used my blood to make the virus. Contrary to what Harrah had believed, I couldn't have left much of my blood at every scene of battle. But I hadn't been careful—not as much as I should have been. Familiar magic brushed against my back, and I whipped around and assumed the defensive position with only the manacles available as weapons. Conner stood at the other end of the hallway.

Rolling his eyes, he exhaled a breath of exasperation. "Sometimes I believe you are more savage than woman. I'm still drawn to the idea of taming the savage."

"Each time we've met, you've attacked me or tried to make me your consort to be nothing more than an incubator for your self-proclaimed wunderkinds. I think we know who's the real savage."

He chuckled, a stormy, bristling sound that definitely put him up there with every super villain imaginable. "So this is where they keep you after you've done so much to curry favor with them." He waved his hand around. "You're locked in hell."

"I agreed to be here."

"Of course. Like a good little Legacy, you do what you think they will want. Someone with your level of magic should never be told what to do. Ever. I wish I could get you to see that. I am not above forgiveness; seeing that you are here, I imagine you see the error of your ways. There are more of us. I guess in your misguided way, you've emboldened them." He smiled, one hand casually placed in his pocket as he maintained a good distance between us. Was he being courteous or did he know that if he came close enough I would strike him?

After several minutes of silence, he closed the distance but left several feet between us. "Savannah is whole again," he said. "Resourcefulness is what I find most alluring about you." Turning away from me, he looked farther down the hall, then into the two rooms. I could see his frown in profile; he still had it when he turned in my direction. "Savannah is a woman of great beauty and refinement. Too bad she's human."

I started to correct him but decided against it.

He went on, "What if I told you she could come with you if you agreed to join me? She's proven to be worthy. Would you reconsider?"

"No matter what package you wrap that crap in, it's still a big heaping pile of compost. I'm never going to agree to kill a bunch of people because you have a distorted, and I might add, possibly clinically insane, delusion of your greatness."

His typical haughtiness settled casually over the planes of his face. In silence, he studied me. "You do realize you will be rejected by the others. I will see to that. Your blood was found in the virus. The next time it won't be yours, it will be another's. One by one, I will force them out. Others won't be screwing the head of the Supernatural Guild, so they won't have your advantages. They will turn against other supernaturals. They will side with me, seeing the need to separate."

"You overlook the reason that the Cleanse failed before. It was because of the humans. Those conditions haven't changed. Do you think there are fewer people who have some link to the supernaturals? You'll fail again. I do believe a bomb or being riddled with bullets will be something you can't walk away from."

Sizing me up, he said, "You seem to think you have all the answers. Such a problem with youth. I can assure you that I've taken precautions as well. It would be good to have you join me, but if you maintain your staunch allegiance to others, then your death is well deserved."

"You know who's behind the virus, don't you?"

He smiled. "Of course. It's me." He was lying. Only he would think it was a good idea to take full credit for something so ruthless. There were others. He might have helped with the idea, had a major part in it, but there was more than magic at work. Others were involved. Ironically, the one time I needed him to monologue about his diabolical plans, he chose not to. In a flash of movement, he was just inches from me. When he reached up to touch my face, I blocked his hand.

He spoke softly: "You know you survive because I will it to be."

He is more than textbook nuts. He's giving psychotic egomaniacs pause with this behavior.

"Really. Because you seemed to be *willing* your creatures to kill me and trying rather hard to do it yourself as well."

"Not once have I doubted your ability to succeed," he said, giving me a wry smile, "which is why it bothers me that you require so much coercion."

"Are you on drugs? How many ways must I tell you that I'm not interested? I don't want your world of solitude, surrounded only by people who believe themselves to be gods. Anyone who agrees with you and is willing to help you suffers from the same delusions of grandeur. What do you think will happen when they grow tired of you being the leader? When they feel they could do a better job? They will come after you. How many times must you fail?"

"Did I fail?" he asked, a brow hitched up in amusement.

I shrugged. "Well, since you were on the floor with your chest sliced open, I'd call it a decisive failure, but then again, I'm sane."

"You question my sanity, I question your virtue and your intelligence. We are linked and you chose others. You're here because —" He turned in time to catch the burst of magic heading in his direction. The mage had another ready, which he shot the moment Conner caught the first. Conner pushed a wave of magic toward him, so strong the walls rumbled and wavered. Conner wore astonished rage as he turned in my direction. "This betrayal will not go unpunished."

Betrayal? I had no idea what was going on. As defensive magic soared through the air, Conner returned the assault. I picked at the manacles, looking for a weakness in the metal. There wasn't one. An orange bolt hit me in the chest, throwing me back and knocking the wind out of me. Its currents ran through me as I lay flat on the floor. I'd felt Conner's magic, and this was similar. I blinked back tears of pain. Pushing up on my elbows to get a look at the assailant, I saw Elijah's eyes widen and his mouth gape as he realized he'd missed his target. Before he could correct it, Conner returned his assault. Strong, wrathful magic consumed the room, making me feel helpless because I was without mine.

"Levy, give me your hands," Gareth whispered standing next to me. Behind him were Victor and someone I didn't recognize, a tall woman with short, dark hair. A dust of reddish brown freckles covered her nose and cheeks. Her oval face and gentle chestnut eyes made her seem warm despite the small frown on her face. Or perhaps it was her magic. It crept over me, ushering me into a false place of tranquility before I completely realized she was doing it. Gathering that the unknown woman was Harrah's replacement, I inched back away from her.

"Alysa, this is Levy," Victor offered as Gareth removed the cuffs.

"I told you he would show up," Alysa said.

Gareth's features were pinched so tightly, I didn't see them relaxing anytime soon. "Whether you knew or not, you used her as bait. We both deserved to know."

The edge to Victor's voice matched Gareth's: "No one knew but me and Alysa. We needed to keep it that way."

I couldn't tell if the flashing colors before me were from the magical battle taking place a few feet away or my anger. They were both violent and tumultuous. Only when I heard Conner gasp and then a thump did I pull my attention from Victor and the fae. Conner was on the ground, stilled. Magic inundated the air, but also the strong scent of metal. Iridium. Several oddly shaped darts were sticking out of him. It wasn't long before his legs and arms were shackled.

CHAPTER 17

*G*areth was still wearing his anger when Victor and Alysa entered Gareth's office, where I had been taken. Keeping a cautious eye on the fae, I readied my shields in the event that she decided to play games with my mind. I realized she wasn't Harrah and perhaps wasn't nearly as fiendish as her predecessor, but she still had the job in public relations, and was charged with maintaining the innocuous image of supernaturals. If one of her first actions was to use me as bait to trap Conner without informing Gareth and me, I wasn't likely to trust her.

"I apologize for any deception that we had to utilize. Your blood was in fact found after an attack. But based on Conner being at the scene when you were poisoned, I suspected he was involved. We needed to do whatever was necessary to apprehend him." Alysa started off slowly, her voice mild and gentle, delivering her admission of betrayal with a calmness that entreated understanding. Working in her favor were sincere eyes and a pleasant countenance. She was dangerous. Anyone who held her position couldn't be too nice and would have to be a masterful liar. Being a fae, she innately had one ability: to manipulate. She could do it to minds and with her appearance. The face she'd chosen worked. She looked innocent, which would belie her nefarious act.

"If you had told me, I would have helped. There was no need to keep me in the dark."

"Ms. Michaels...or do you prefer Kismet?" she asked, the implication she placed in her words pointing out that I'd lived in two different worlds. I was a Legacy, something no one seemed to be willing to forgive me for. As if I had something to do with it.

"Michaels is fine."

She nodded. "Ms. Michaels, I am still learning the extent of your capabilities, and from my understanding Conner's abilities exceed yours. If in fact that was the case, he would have been aware of everything and wouldn't have stayed."

"We can't read minds."

"Perhaps you can't and maybe he can't, either, but we weren't going to risk it. He's behind this. We needed to apprehend him. If history has taught us anything, you all are capable of extraordinary magic. As a fae, I can sense a lie, and I can touch the mind and find some information. I can imagine you possess some cognitive ability; after all, you all are the forbears of magic. Am I correct?"

I was having a hard time buying her innocent act, but I had more pressing things to address. The number of people willing to ally themselves with a sociopath who wanted to commit genocide boggled my mind. Humans First were bad, and I hadn't missed their constant rhetoric, but compared to whatever we were dealing with now, they were harmless.

"The virus was proven to be linked to me?" I inquired.

Victor, Alysa, and Gareth nodded. "Elijah was found to be as well, which is why he was willing to help us. He wasn't happy with Conner setting him up, too," Gareth added. "That's what's so troubling. I'd implicated the Brotherhood—"

"Trackers," I corrected Gareth.

Nodding in acknowledgment, he continued, "Trackers. But

there are so few now since—the incident." The incident being that Conner and his acolytes had killed all the Trackers they'd been able to find. I wondered if the one who'd made an attempt on Elijah was one of the few remaining. A person so radicalized that despite the death of the organization's body, they were the limb that continued to move.

Was Elijah helping the SG a sign of false optimism, something I'd had just weeks ago? It was fading too quickly as I started to believe that humans and supernaturals weren't going to live in perfect harmony.

Mason knocked on the door and then peeked in. "He's not talking. Even with the braces on I can't get anything," he admitted.

Victor's gaze slipped in Alysa's direction. "Would you like to try?"

She smiled. "Of course."

CHAPTER 18

I made a mental note that wherever Alysa was, I would be nowhere to be found. It took her less than an hour to get the information from Conner. An hour. I was having a hard time deciding which was scarier: Conner willingly giving the information, which surely meant it was a trap, or Alysa being magically strong enough to acquire it from him.

Conner had given a location of where the virus was being made as well as where the artillery was being held. I was confident we would find the next would-be assassins and followers.

My discomfort with Alysa led Gareth and I to take a separate car to the location. The place was exactly what I expected: A large room stocked with ammunition, targets, scopes, and stacks of camouflage clothing. A war room. An empty war room. Weapons in hand, a large group of Supernatural Guild and Federal Supernatural Reinforcement agents went through the building. It was empty. Shifters stood in the middle of the room, brows furrowed, listening for any sound that would give away the locations of the people inside.

"They're still here," Gareth whispered. Sai positioned to strike, I listened for whatever he heard.

"Are you sure?" I asked before a blur of camouflage dropped in front of me. I dropped to my knees, the shot he'd fired barely missing me. Glass shattered from the impact of the bullet. They weren't firing darts with the virus, but actual bullets. A mage behind the shooter hurled magic at him, sending him careening forward. I shifted my weight to get out of his way as he fell face-down on the floor. With a smooth movement, he was handcuffed, had his legs zip-tied together, and was dragged against the floor.

Following the shifters who were tracking the others by scent, we moved outside. Clusters of trees surrounding the building made it difficult to navigate the area, and when a shot zoomed past me, I quickly realized that was by design. Gareth cursed and fell to the ground, blood spreading over his shirt where the bullet had torn through it. I looked in the direction of the shot and saw the gunner aiming at me. Magic wasn't faster than a bullet, but it hit him in time to throw off his aim. The bullet grazed my leg and pain lanced through me. It was a hell of a lot better than the bullet going through me.

A deep, threatening voice ordered the assailant to drop his weapon. Another shot was fired off and whizzed past me, followed by a succession of several more. Another man in camouflage dropped to the ground, eyes blank. I turned from the grue-some sight just as one of the virus-filled arrows traveled toward Gareth. I hit it, striking it out of the air with the side of the sai. Another arrow soared and I hit it. Throbs of pain moved through me with each movement. I decided not to spend any more time knocking arrows out of the air. A ball of magic pushed through my sai and hit the shooter hard enough to knock the wind out of him. He gasped for air that didn't readily come and stumbled back. Before he could react again, three agents had guns trained on him. He gave each gun aimed at him a hard, scrutinizing look before he surrendered. Dropping his weapon, he lowered to his knees and was handcuffed.

Shots being fired, bodies dropping, the rustle of people

running through the grass, and sounds of aggression became a collective din that I had to ignore to assess the situation. Gareth had scooted back and was resting against a tree. Before I could start toward him to help, his eyes darted past me and narrowed. Following his gaze, I saw Gordon Lands run out of the armory and throw a bag into the passenger side of a car. Sai in hand, I ran toward him. He was behind the wheel and about to drive off, but I stabbed a twin into one of his back tires and yanked it out. The car sped away but swerved to the side as air gushed out of the tire. Gordon continued to drive until he was riding on the rim. By the time he'd made it to the end of the road, there was a blockade of agents waiting for him.

Gordon was the diametric opposite of Conner as he was apprehended. He didn't spew an over-the-top monologue about his unhinged and nefarious plans, eyes alight with anger and malice. In contrast, Gordon's eyes were gentle and innocuous. The small, hospitable smile on his lips as he was cuffed didn't strike me as that of a person who would orchestrate such an attack or even ally themselves with the likes of Conner. Staring at the unmarked SF car as they drove him away, I couldn't smother an unsettling feeling about him. Something was off.

That thought stayed with me as I returned to help Gareth. Grimacing, he had his hand over the bullet wound. Once I saw it was more than a simple flesh wound, I reluctantly dismissed thoughts of Gordon.

"Are you going to go to the Isles and let them look at it?" I asked.

"It's fine." He yanked a knife from his shoulder holster. My eyes widened when he stabbed it into his shoulder. I screamed. Not just any scream—a scary-movie, being-chased-by-a-person-with-a-chainsaw type of scream.

"Levy," Gareth groaned, digging even farther into his shoulder, coaxing more screams out of me. "I'm the one with the bullet and knife in my shoulder," he said as he rooted around for the bullet.

"And I'm the one who has to look at it. Stop that. What is wrong with you?" Finally I had the presence of mind to close my eyes, and after several moments I heard groans.

"You can open your eyes now." I didn't immediately, and when I did, there was a bloody mass of metal on the ground next to my knee. Bile tickled the back of my throat. I'd been injured enough that seeing my own wounds didn't bother me too much, but watching a person dig a bullet out took things to a place I'd never go again.

"It's not my first bullet wound. I'm a shifter. I'll heal soon."

"I won't. I will be forever traumatized by that. Thank you."

"You live with a person who's dating a vampire. Surely you've seen him feed from her. How is this worse?"

"First of all, I suck-block *all* the time. If he so much as has a hungry-looking glint in his eyes, I'm there like bam, pow, block, and weave. I'm playing defense like an NFL all-star." My skills had improved significantly over the weeks, which was why Savannah spent most of her time at Lucas's. If I didn't see it, I could pretend it wasn't happening. "As for you—warn someone before you decide to remove a bullet. Okay?"

He rolled his eyes. "Levy, ten minutes ago, I was thinking about removing a bullet from my shoulder that was bothering me. You've been warned," he said, flashing a roguish grin.

"No one thinks you're funny."

"I'm pretty funny," he countered, resting back against the tree. He closed his eyes, and I watched as his skin began to mesh, the beginning of the healing process. "What's with the look?" he asked, moving closer to me, taking in my brow, which was furrowed in concentration.

"It seems off—this whole scenario. You all questioned Gordon and were sure he wasn't behind it. He wasn't an extremist like the rest of them. He was rational and driven mostly by grief over the loss of his friend at Conner's hands. Of all people, why would he work with Conner?"

"Maybe he didn't know that Conner was behind his friend's death."

"That's possible. But the total one-eighty in his personality is unsettling. He looks different. His eyes were blank, missing something, like—"

"Like Savannah's," he interjected.

"We still have some *Culded*. I think we should use the spell on him."

Vacant eyes stared back at me from the other side of a double-sided mirror. Gareth stepped closer to examine Gordon through the glass. "I think you're right, Levy. There is something different about him." Gareth looked at the clock. "If you're going to do it, it should be now before Alysa gets here or the police find out he's here. I assure you, they won't let him stay long, and it's doubtful they'll even prosecute and will instead cite some BS that they don't have enough to go on."

"Will you press to allow him to be tried in the supernatural courts?" I asked.

"Of course, but we haven't been successful once. These last few weeks are going to require a hell of a spin."

"That's why I'm here." Alysa's voice now seemed too sweet and airy—too much effort placed on seeming innocuous. The magic breezing off of her served as a warning. Tensing, I shifted slightly when she took up a position next to me, watching Gordon through the glass.

"I'm disappointed that he was able to evade your staff. The fae aren't as good as I was led to believe. Perhaps it's time to recruit better," she suggested.

"They are good. In fact, the best the city has to offer," Gareth responded. His voice was as professionally cool as hers.

"*I'm* the best the city has to offer," she retorted.

"And modest about it, too," I mumbled.

Her mask of cloying smile, charming freckles, and gentle eyes dropped for just a fraction of time as she shot me a sharp look. "They hired me because they knew I could do the job. I am Harrah's replacement because I can do what she could, perhaps even better. And I have no intention of meeting her fate." The chill in her voice sent shivers through me. *When they post the job, do they require the person to be devil spawn, or is it just a preferred quality?*

"I don't want him leaving here," Alysa said. She slipped into the role of heartless harpy pretty easily. Was there an academy where they trained people like her?

"What do you propose we do with him?" Gareth asked.

"He's dangerous. I propose you treat him like the extreme danger to supernaturals that he is."

Moving closer to the window, I looked at Gordon, who still possessed the strong features, welcoming countenance, and relaxed persona that had catapulted his career. They made most people believe he was a shoo-in to attain any political position he chose for the future, and his humanitarian efforts had made him a legend in the city and a well-known name globally. I couldn't believe that he was behind the virus. He was reasonable, not a radical with stark tenets. He was driven to take over Humans First only after his friend was killed.

Like Savannah, he seemed like a shell of a person.

Looking over my shoulder at Gareth, I said, "We need to do the spell—now."

Alysa's brows hitched up. "Spell?"

With a great deal of reluctance, I shared our thoughts about Gordon and our plans to use the spell to see if I could remove whatever Conner had done to him.

"If you are right?" Alysa asked.

"That exonerates him and you have the person responsible for the virus: Conner. There might have been someone else in the beginning, but I'm willing to bet anything that the moment he aligned himself with Conner, he sealed his fate. You might find a body, but that's it."

Alysa looked at me as if she was questioning Conner's ruthlessness. If she was, she wasn't as good as she thought and was too naïve to deal with someone like Conner.

"Conner doesn't care about anyone except Legacy and Vertu and is perfectly content killing off every other supernatural. It's to his benefit to do so. Kill off the very people who were able to break Legacy wards. Without magic to assist, the humans would have lost against the Legacy. Conner wants power and separation. The fewer supernaturals who exist, the more likely people are to acquiesce. At the threat of a war, humans would be more agreeable to segregation. It would give him an advantage of getting the Legacy and Vertu that exist to side with him. We would live our separate lives and procreate to increase our numbers. What do you think happens with the next Cleanse or even war?" I said.

"Conner's a pain in my ass," she acknowledged.

With a mirthless chuckle, I offered, "You've only been dealing with him for a few days. Wait until you've been dealing with him as long as I have."

Gordon gave me a doubtful look as I explained my theory.

A light smile flourished on his lips and made its way to his eyes. "You think that I am under the lure of magic and everything I've done is because of it." Humor laced his words. Perhaps he did think my theory was utterly ridiculous, but I had a feeling this was the beleaguered protest of a man who had been in control of his life and didn't want to think that his actions weren't born from his own thoughts and desires. He'd rather think himself the type of person who would do something horrendous than be under the will of someone else, even if it was because of magic.

"If it's not magic, then doing the spell won't have any effect," I said simply, grinding the *Culded* in a small metal bowl to make it into a dust as I'd done before with Savannah. Gordon split his attention between me and the people moving the furniture out of the way. As the commotion continued, he looked as if he were ready to change his mind about participating.

Seeing hesitation cast a dark shadow over his eyes, I didn't give him a chance to say no. Whispering the incantation, I blew the flowery dust into his face, and he inhaled. In a matter of minutes, he was on the floor, sedated, his eyes moving busily behind his lids. The hours crept by, and when he awoke, there was a difference in his eyes.

When the smile fell from his face, I realized he probably also remembered everything he'd done under Conner's influence. I couldn't help but wonder if those memories were clear and explicit or hazy bits and pieces. It was something that Gordon quickly answered.

"I shouldn't have met with him," he whispered. Then he went on to describe his many meetings with Conner and how he'd help recruit people. Conner was there with each recruit, using magic to manipulate the situation. He'd used tactics I'd used before—implanting false memories and cognitive manipulation. They were illegal—well, illegal in the real world; the SG seemed to follow a different set of rules. But when dealing with Trackers, it was justified. I figured in Conner's warped mind, cognitive manipulation and implantation of false memories were justified as well.

No one objected when the mayor, ignoring all protocol, called to request that Gordon be released. It was expected. What was surprising was Victor's response twenty minutes after Gordon's departure. I'd wilted into the corner of the office, hoping Alysa, Victor, or Gareth wouldn't take notice of me and ask me to leave.

Victor scrubbed his hand along the stubble on his face, probably the result of long hours at the office dealing with Conner. "He's a problem beyond redemption, and if you think for one moment he can be handled like anyone else, then you are foolish. He needs to be handled like any volatile weapon and destroyed."

It took a great deal of effort to refrain from showing my enthusiasm. As much as I'd like to believe I was being covert, skulking in the corner, part of me knew that my presence was known. Victor's gaze found me. "We need to be more diligent about the Legacy coming forth. We can't allow this to continue. The way things are unfolding will open the path for another person like Conner. Once he's gone, I don't want another of his ilk popping up." Pulling his attention from me, he turned to Alysa. "Please handle it as quickly as possible."

With his last instruction, he started out of the office.

"And you will be handling..." Alysa started, knowing the answer by the determined look on his face.

"Conner. I will be handling Conner," he said, without breaking stride.

CHAPTER 19

"*N*ow that's what I'm talking about." Kalen beamed, giving me a once-over. I'd been pulled, tugged, primped, and coiffed until I was almost unrecognizable. His stamp of approval confirmed that I looked like Barbie, innocuous, sweet, Legacy edition. I was itching to put my hair in a ponytail instead of having the loose curls brushing my shoulders. I took a quick look at myself in the mirror and saw what the makeup artist and stylist had transformed me into. A dark business suit might have seemed too portentous, so they'd opted for a light tan skirt and a pearl-colored shirt instead. I didn't look like a powerful wielder of magic but something trite and palatable. It annoyed me. I'd agreed to the press conference and coming out on television, but being paraded around as the adorable person who "happened" to possess powerful Cleanse-evoking magic grated at my thinning tolerance.

Sensing my discomfort, Savannah sidled in next to me. "People are silly. Just do this, and after it's over you can put that horrible plaid shirt and jeans back on. Why not give Kalen a conniption?" She pulled a slouch hat out of her purse and grinned.

"Conniption, he's likely to catch the vapors and pass out at my assault on fashion." I laughed, loud enough that it got Kalen's attention. I held up the hat and made it seem like I was about to put it on when he donned an expression as if he was about to witness a horrific accident that he couldn't stop. *"Just kidding,"* I mouthed, handing the hat back to Savannah.

"He's so easy." Savannah chuckled. "You seem to be having a better day than Elijah."

My heart went out to him. It wasn't as if he looked out of place in slacks and a dress shirt—they looked good on him. His clothing was nice and professional, but the scowl fixed on his face wasn't. It hadn't relaxed since Gareth had asked him to do the press conference with me. Victor, Gareth, and Alysa believed he and I would be good at it. I'd agreed with them about Elijah; his quiet power made him approachable and alluring. But his power didn't seem so silent now. It was raging and he looked like a person who could start an apocalypse.

I wondered if it was the situation, or if he, like I had, figured this press conference had already been set up days before. It was hard for me to believe Alysa could have this all ready to go under eight hours after Victor had requested that she handle it. She'd orchestrated this faster than Victor would be able to get rid of Conner. There was more involved than just walking into Barathrum and destroying him. The Magic Council wanted to question him. I couldn't understand why. What could they want from him that would justify keeping him alive?

Moving closer to Elijah, I brought my fingers in front of my face and drew them out, a gesture to tell him to smile. After several beats of silence and consideration, he ushered one onto his face with great effort: a peculiar mix of grimace, scowl, and grin. "Your smile makes you look like the Joker, the dark goth one. Not the one where you don't know if he's really the bad guy."

I was immune to the eye roll. He and Savannah had hit it off nicely and were always giving me collective eye rolls whenever I commented about a comic book.

"This dog and pony show is ridiculous," he huffed out, tugging at the sleeves of his shirt.

"Well, you two are the best dog and pony at this show," Savannah said, giving him a playful nudge. He smiled—a genuine one—and I was thankful Lucas wasn't around. He wasn't a fan of Elijah, solely because of his comradery with Savannah. Lucas intimidated most people, but not Elijah.

"I thought they would send out a tweet or something," Elijah grumbled.

"You couldn't have thought that at all." I laughed.

"Maybe not something that informal, but I didn't think it would be this big of a deal."

I agreed with him on that account. It seemed like Alysa could have just gone out and smiled for the cameras; fluttered her eyes a little; hit them with that kind, melancholy voice that elicited calm; given them an update on the state of the supernatural world and the alliance; and ended with, "By the way...you know the people who were responsible for the Cleanse and who we thought were extinct? Well, they aren't, they've just been hanging out among you all. Okay, then. Good day to you." Then she could have left without answering any questions and referred them to a website. This meant the press were going to demand answers, and no amount of questioning that Gareth, Savannah, Kalen, Blu, or Alysa had lobbed at us would have adequately prepared us.

When Savannah glared at the person approaching from behind me, I knew it had to be Victor. I was still upset with him for detaining me in Barathrum, but from the looks of Savannah's flushed skin, steely gray eyes that homed in on him with unfettered anger, and snarl that would make any shapeshifter proud, it was clear that she was planning on taking her grudge with her to the grave.

"Play nice," I whispered to her.

Eventually a smile spread over her face, and it was obvious she was putting a lot of effort into it.

"Agent Victor Matthews," she acknowledged in a sharp, cool tone.

Like any shapeshifter faced with a challenge, he mirrored her greeting with a cool undertone of authority. "Savannah Nolan, as usual, it's good to see you." He dismissed her as soon as he'd greeted her. "Are you nervous?" he asked me.

"No," I lied.

My lie coaxed a half-smile from him and the same brow raise that Gareth gave me, a subtle reminder that shifters could tell when a person wasn't truthful.

"A little," I amended with a frown. Elijah's tweet idea was looking a lot more appealing.

Everything went smoother than I thought for the first ten minutes. The typical questions: "How many are there?" "Do you know how to do the spell that caused the Cleanse in the first place?" "How can we trust you all?"

Then there were the questions directed to Alysa about the supernatural community and what would be done to prevent the Cleanse from occurring again. She assured them that the Legacy had agreed to be braced with an iridium cuff that would diminish their magic significantly. I looked out at the crowd of people for anyone with a shifter ring to see if they bought the lie. It concerned Gareth that he couldn't detect lies from Alysa. Her physiological signs stayed steady—even during times we knew she wasn't telling the truth. Like now. I'd agreed to the brace; Elijah had refused. Conner's words echoed in my head: how I was a "good little Legacy." Was I? Or was I just pragmatic, under-standing the tradeoff involved in us being accepted? A minor display of goodwill wasn't that difficult and it would be even easier since the thin band they were requesting we wear wouldn't do anything to stop our magic.

The questions fizzled until there were just a few hands, most of the curiosity sated in the first fifteen minutes. We were coming to a conclusion when one hand shot up; Alysa hesitated before directing her attention to him. When he stood, I understood her apprehension—a cool drift of animosity consumed the room. Unmistakably human, he wore his disdain for us, all of us, heavily on his face. Sharpening his gaze on me, he started, "Do you want us to believe that we aren't in any danger from you all?"

"You wouldn't be in any danger anyway. You're human," I offered in a neutral voice, hoping it belied the grimace I had to struggle to keep off my face.

He shrugged. "To the naked eye. So were the ones who died. We don't shift, change our appearance with a shrug of our shoulders, or create magic with a wave of our hands, but since the alliance, there has been a significant amount of intermingling." His disgust lingered after his last words. Doubting that he had any supernatural in him but was simply raising the question to incite strife, I listened, forcing all the emotions off my face as he continued. Elijah was having a harder time. It took him a moment to relax his frown.

The reporter continued, "I'm sure people want to ignore the increase in extraordinary events over the past weeks. Odd creatures roaming the streets. Dangerous supernaturals who were 'supposed' to be locked away in the strongest containment facility we have causing havoc after escaping. Magical fights that nearly destroyed the city. At least when the other magic users get out of hand, we can count on the shifters to resolve things since they are immune to most magic. But not to yours. Who will protect us when you go rogue?"

Grimacing, I watched all eyes focus on him. He looked down at his notes. "On more than one occasion you've been seen fighting another supernatural. I've been told he is a Legacy who has attempted the Cleanse." Again, he looked down at his notes, but I was convinced he'd memorized his arguments and was well versed in anything he had to say. "Also, what was your penalty for killing three people in the middle of the street? It seems like a person who did that should be in the Haven, not the poster girl for magic acceptance."

Swallowing the bile that had inched its way up my throat, I remembered the time I'd been attacked by three Trackers and passersby had witnessed my self-defense. From a distance it had looked like I'd killed three people in cold blood, but in fact they had orchestrated an ambush to block me in on a rarely traveled street.

Alysa edged in next to me and eased her way to the microphone. "I appreciate your concerns. First, I will address the most pressing issue. Olivia isn't a cold-blooded killer. She was protecting herself from an attack by an organization called the Brotherhood of the Order. I'm sure you are familiar with the name since you've worked with them before." Fixing him with a hard, knowing gaze, she continued, "They had planned to kill her, and she protected herself. She was found innocent because it was self-defense. Which leads to the next problem. When people are forced into hiding, they don't have the benefit of our protection—it lies on them. People die when things like that occur. The Brotherhood has been linked to several murders and attacks. The Legacy no longer have to hide, therefore there is no need for people like the Brotherhood of the Order to exist."

"What about the strange happenings over the past few weeks?"

As she maintained her pleasant façade, her lips curled into a kind smile. "We had a rogue Legacy, just as we've had rogue humans—the ones responsible for violence at the Solstice parade. There will always be those who continue to do things like that because they thirst for that divide. It gives them power. You want to know why a *rogue* like Conner existed and would have been successful if it weren't for Olivia? Because he, like others, was tired of hiding. Please remember the Cleanse was stopped and the Legacy were defeated because of the collective effort of supernaturals and humans. I don't think we would have been as successful without both. Remember that." She looked down at the name on his press pass, and I was positive I could see the mental note of him being put on her crap list.

When his shoulders slumped, I suspected he knew, too. With the new ruddy color on his face from being called out about his membership in a rogue vigilante group, he looked as if he wanted off the list and out of the room.

"Finally, Conner has been apprehended, and we've taken extra measures and are confident that he won't escape."

I wished I shared that confidence. Watching them taking him away, I'd seen that he didn't seem concerned. Even though he'd been cuffed with enough iridium to render him magically help-less, I'd felt like he had something up his sleeve. A man who'd eluded death as many times as he had wasn't likely to go quietly. It still bothered me that he hadn't made an escape attempt. Sent briefly into a moment of paranoia, I'd questioned everyone, including Elijah, who had fought against him. Guilt clutched my chest as I realized that the only way I'd feel confident that Conner wasn't a threat was when I saw him dead. Really dead. A confirmed kill.

Alysa concluded the press conference, and Gareth, Victor, and the SG escorted us out past the cameras and the enthusiastic jour-nalists who had more questions. In the car, I wondered how Gareth did it. What I'd experienced on a smaller scale, he was apparently intimately familiar with as one of the most sought-after men in the city.

"What's wrong?" he asked.

"I don't like the attention," I admitted.

"It'll wane soon."

"How do you deal with being the city's most eligible bachelor? The man all the women swoon and blog about?" I teased.

"It's a struggle, but I don't blame them. And at least I'm not getting the level of hate you are. After all, you have all of this." He waved his free hand over his body.

"Yeah. I'm the luckiest woman ever!" I said with mocking

enthusiasm. "To have Gareth Reynolds, the most modest and humble man, with me most nights. The impossibly beautiful shifter who makes Adonis pale in comparison and walks around as if he's just mere man when he is a god. A freaking god, I say. How will I be able to pay adequate tribute to your glorious presence?"

A mischievous grin crept over his face and made his eyes twinkle, and he licked his lips. His brows arched. "I'm sure you can find a way."

"Did you just make that dirty?" I asked, rolling my eyes.

"Since you're the one who wanted a way to praise me, I think *you* made it dirty."

I just wanted to wipe the grin off his face. Directing my attention outside, I asked, "Have you seen Conner since he went to Barathrum?"

"Yes, once. He asked to see me."

"And you went? Why?"

He shrugged. "I was curious."

I turned from the window toward him to give him my undivided attention. I waited for him to continue. "What did he want?" I pressed.

Frowning, he dismissed Conner with a wave. "Just a bunch of threats. What's your favorite saying, 'super villain'–style. He went on and on about how he'll get his revenge. It was just ten minutes of ranting from a desperate madman."

It wasn't what he said, but what he hadn't. "Threats against me, right?"

"He's not going to get out."

"He wasn't supposed to get out the last time, either."

CHAPTER 20

Don't think about it, I scolded myself as I followed Kalen toward the small brick home, a new job. It didn't help.

Seeing my unease, he slowed and said, "There's a reason they are keeping him alive. Alysa must know something about him that she's not sharing. That's the reason Conner's still alive."

"Nothing he knows is worth him staying alive. They have the virus; it was in Gordon's car. Conner has nothing else to offer. They need to get rid of him."

Shocked by how cavalier I was with Conner's life, Kalen stopped and gave me a look.

I softened my voice and tried to take the chill out of it. "He's escaped every time they've had him, and I'm the one he comes after."

The fact that Conner no longer requested to speak with Gareth bothered me. He'd found resolve, but in what? I needed to know. Had Conner finally been broken? Were they foolish enough to consider the possibility of keeping him around—using him in the future? The thought made me ill. The political maneuvering baffled me. Conner shouldn't be part of political negotiations. He was strong and one of the most knowledgeable supernaturals ever to exist. Perhaps that was an asset they wanted, but they should know that the cost would be too high for the benefit.

"But he's also been so many steps ahead of everyone. What if he has another group of acolytes just waiting to avenge his death? I know you hate that he's still alive, but if they can, they need to find out everything he has planned. If he escapes this time, you find him and do what is necessary," Kalen said. If I wasn't mistaken, I would have suspected that he wanted Conner to escape—a small part of me did as well. I wanted to get my justice. It didn't make me a good person, but I was several wounds and far too many attacks down to care when it came to Conner.

And the past week Legacy and Vertu were going to SG offices around the country, making their presence known. There weren't nearly as many as I'd thought there would be; Gareth said that there was a total of fifty. The work was being done for Conner. He didn't have to find them; the SG had a way to do it for him.

My mind raced trying to come up with a plan to get into Barathrum. Everything came to mind, from the mundane, like requesting a visit to see him, to doing something bad enough to get me placed in there. They weren't good plans, but rather the musings of my overactive, frantic mind fully aware that if he broke out again, I might not survive it.

Shrugging off the thoughts, I attempted to slide into my typical routine as I stood next to Kalen on the doorstep of the house, waiting for our client to answer the door.

A wiry old man greeted us with a wide grin. Hunched over, he relied heavily on a cane.

"We could have let ourselves in and saved you the trip to the door, Mr. James," Kalen told him, rushing to the man's side to assist him when he looked as if he was going to lose his balance.

"Nonsense. I'm a lot more spritely than I look." Unless he was talking about a can of soda, he wasn't. Even the magic that came off of him was faint. Witch probably, maybe even a low-level mage. "You deserve a proper greeting. You're celebrities around here"—he smiled in my direction—"I've seen you on the Internet, Facebook. Everywhere, really."

Ignoring the twinge I got every time I was recognized, I gave him a weak smile. My newfound celebrity was a little overwhelming. Either I was met with fascination or aversion, and sometimes an odd combination of both. Mr. James was vastly intrigued.

"Legacy," he said, getting closer to me, inspecting me as if to see what made me different. It was an exercise in patience when he leaned forward a little and smelled me. Kalen's brows inched together, curious.

"Your magic is strong," he acknowledged. Again, I felt the weight of his appraisal.

"We have paperwork we need to fill out," Kalen informed him, his tone assertive and loud enough to yank the man's attention back to the task at hand. Mr. James's gaze continued to flick in my direction.

"Yes, yes. Of course. I don't want any of it. Most of it I've accumulated over the years, and the items that have been classified as illegal I made sure I surrendered to the Supernatural Guild." He flashed us a grin, his teeth discolored from excessive coffee drinking—or at least that was what I gathered from taking a whiff of the house. It smelled like a coffeehouse and I could hear a pot brewing in the kitchen.

The man was weird, without any concept of personal space. But at least he was honest. He reviewed the paperwork, going over it in more detail than any client we'd had in the past. Usually if the person was shifty and using us to clear out their place only to request the return of most of the goods, they read over it in detail, asking questions that easily gave them away. "What if I didn't know about the item, can I keep it?" "Do I get a percentage of it if I didn't know about it and its value?" "Is this legally binding?" The last question always earned an eye roll from me. *No, it's not legally binding. We just have you sign it to get a look at your penmanship.*

Mr. James's questions were thorough and well thought out. He inquired how the items would be used, the process, and where they would be sold in the event we found something he wanted again. Were our clients humans or just supernaturals? Kalen always maintained a businesslike approach during the questioning and let the person know that they could purchase goods back, but in reality, he'd never made anyone pay. One wistful puppy dog look from a customer had Kalen handing over the goods without so much as considering the cost. As much as Kalen blathered on about this being his business, it was a hobby that brought in some money. Not nearly enough to support his lifestyle and not even a percentage of his designer clothing. It was a good thing he had a trust fund that took care of those things. It also took care of my griping at him every time he gave away an expensive item. More often than not, I had to point out that I didn't have a trust fund I could resort to. Each time, it bothered me. I was content in supporting his delusional belief that he was the common man. Like a "common" man would wear Tom Ford to rummage through someone's attic. I guessed he wasn't since most of the time he "delegated" that part of the job to me.

Directing us to follow him, Mr. James took us through his house. Colorful walls made the house vibrant along with the sunlight that spilled in from the large, curtainless picture windows. Along with the strong scent of coffee, magic moved through the air, getting stronger the closer we got to our destination. Powerful magical objects were near. Studying Mr. James as he led us to the basement, I couldn't help but wonder if he was deceptively stronger than I'd been led to believe. Young, powerful mages become older, powerful mages.

Basements didn't bother me, but for some reason Mr. James's

did. The magic was too strong; it prickled at my skin, raising the hairs on my arms.

Even Kalen noticed it. "You have a lot of magical objects down here. Are you sure you want to part with them?"

"Magical objects are only as good as their practitioner," he said, waving his hand. "I stopped using magic long ago. It was too much trouble. Damn Legacy made me realize that maybe magic shouldn't be used." Giving me an apologetic smile, he continued, "Not everyone's bad. I know, but sometimes it's really hard figuring out who isn't. You know, from the moment you walked in, I've wondered what you really look like—fae. You are all so darn pretty, but I wonder if that's just the glamour. Do you look like little hellions when you drop it? Each time I deal with one, I just figure my mind's been tampered with or something. Probably not, but it's fun to think about it."

Another weak smile lifted his lips. He threw open the door. Rows of cabinets filled with stones, rods, balls, and various magical objects lined the entire right wall. Two bookcases of books were on the left side.

Hesitating at the entrance once he stepped in, I watched as he went over to one of the cabinets. He opened it and began picking items up, smelling them, and then frowning. *What is his deal with sniffing everything?*

Kalen looked at the neatly stored magical objects. Some of them were illuminated, offering wafers of light in the dark space.

"You've been collecting magical objects," I said, moving closer to him to see if I could identify them. There were several summoning stones, Hearth Stones, which witches used to call forth ancestral magic, and then a blade that looked like a Necro-spear. Before I could grab it, Mr. James picked it up.

"This one was a gift," he said as he examined it.

Without warning, he shoved it into my stomach. Stumbling back, I clawed at it, trying to remove it, but it latched on to my flesh. A wave of magic sent Kalen and me back, pressing us against a wall. Heat simmered in me. The blade felt like it was cauterizing the injury. Calling magic was a fruitless endeavor. I felt empty, devoid of it. Mr. James's lips moved slowly as he performed an invocation. Gold and amber flashed off the few inches of exposed blade that hadn't been embedded in me. Fatigue took over and I collapsed against the wall, feeling the drain of magic, the way heavy doses of iridium felt. With iridium, I could still feel my magic, like pent-up energy that needed to be expended. This was siphoning it out of me. Trembling, I tried to gather whatever magic I had to free me. Nothing.

"Stop fretting; you will make it harder on yourself. I think it should be over soon." Mr. James looked around expectantly as my stomach blazed. A cyclone swept into the room, magic fluttering through the air.

Conner appeared before me.

"You can't bear to look at me, darling."

I cringed at him using words of endearment to refer to me when all I had were curses and hate-filled names for him.

"I can't possibly disgust you that much," he mused, taking in my appearance.

"Even more than you can imagine," I snapped angrily. I made another useless attempt to free myself. He chortled, which heightened my blistering rage. They should have killed him.

"No more magic. That was your promise, right?" Mr. James said to Conner. I winced. Another person had fallen for Conner's promise of a beautiful magicless utopia.

"I've given you my word. I will end magic," Conner promised. The sincerity in his voice demonstrated what convinced people to follow him, to sacrifice their souls and toss away their ethics to do his bidding.

"I can't do anything like this," Conner said to Mr. James as he wiggled his fingers, exposing his shackled wrist. "Do you think you have a key that would fit these?"

"Of course. Of course." Retrieving a ring of keys from a

drawer, the old man went to work trying different ones on the lock on the cuffs. Unable to find a key that worked, he resorted to picking the lock with tools.

Great. He's a misguided man of many talents.

He slipped the manacles off Conner's wrists. The Vertu then gave me his undivided attention. As he whispered an incantation, color shone brightly from the blade. I narrowed my eyes to soften the blinding deluge of colors and bright light. A magical pull jerked the knife out of my stomach. Pain curled my toes and jolted through me as I crashed to the floor. Conner was holding the knife he'd retrieved from my gut.

"Thank you, sweetheart," he cooed, finding a perverse enjoyment in me cringing at his endearments.

Willing my body to recover, I kept my focus on the knife in his hand, planning my movements so I could disarm him.

"You want to drive this straight into my heart, don't you, my little warrior?" His slow movements were purposeful and dramatic. "I'm better than you are."

Anger-riddled, I lunged at him, hitting a magical barrier he'd placed between the two of us. The shield held despite my pounding on it, and it felt as though I was hitting a wall.

I coaxed whatever magic I had to the forefront.

Laughing, Conner watched, amused, as I attempted to break the barrier. "You're not going to have access to powerful magic for some time. You have no idea how much it takes to break out of Barathrum. I had the benefit of others helping when I did it. Mr. James had to use the blade to source all the magic from you to break me out. You didn't know that could be done, did you?" he taunted. "I could have taught you so much, and you squandered that. Right now you're weak, defenseless. An unkind person would take advantage of it." He looked at the knife in his hand, examining my blood that overlaid it.

"Thank you, love, for getting me out. That place was dreadful. But you already know that, don't you?"

Rarely did I allow myself to feel defeated, subjugated, but now I did. Conner was better than me, steps ahead of me each time. I glared at Mr. James; the hopefulness his face once held was extinguished. I wanted to kick him while he was down and tell him he'd placed his trust in an unscrupulous man.

"You have to keep your promise. You *said* you would keep your promise. No more magic." I winced at what the man was asking for—another version of the Cleanse. While Conner wanted to divest the world of magic for his own selfish desires, Mr. James wanted to do it to rid the world of what he considered nefarious.

"I made that promise to you and I will keep it," Conner said. His voice was so earnest that in that moment, I could see what his acolytes did. He was charismatic, charming, and confident to the point it seemed like he could do the impossible and possessed godlike abilities that made him seem invincible and capable of performing miraculous tasks.

"No one will get hurt? You promised," Mr. James entreated as concern wavered in his voice.

Really, a knife in the gut isn't someone getting hurt?

"I will do all that we discussed," Conner confirmed, giving the man a gentle pat on the shoulder. I wanted to despise Mr. James— he deserved it—but he wasn't a person with reprehensible intent. Self-hate was something entirely different. While most could see the beauty and mystique of magic, he saw its cruelty, tenebrosity, and obscurity. Blood soaked my hand as I glared at Conner, searching for a modicum of magic that I could use against him. Magically depleted, I relaxed onto the floor, closing my eyes for a moment, hoping the few minutes of inactivity would restore my magic.

"You said this wouldn't kill her. She seems like she's going to die." Concern coursed over the older gentleman's words.

Conner didn't display the same worry; his voice held a cool sharpness. It drifted through the room with conviction. "I assure you it will take more than a stomach wound to stop her. She possesses more tenacity than you will ever see." Admiration and intrigue were in his last words. My gaze lifted to find him looking at me with an odd combination of wistfulness and anger. And cruelty. I couldn't ignore that. It was the look of a megalomaniac who'd been denied, and he was struggling to commit to an emotion, seemingly overwhelmed by so many.

He dropped his wall and inched closer to me. Narrowing his eyes on me, he said it again. "Yes, it will take more than a knife wound to kill Anya." There wasn't the promise of death in his words. Hatred works just as good as adrenaline and in an explosion of it, I lunged at him, only to grab air as he disappeared from the house. I paid dearly for it as pain ripped through me. I just needed a few minutes and then I'd be able to heal myself. Or at least I hoped I would.

Mr. James pressed his warm hand to my shoulder and said, concerned, "I'm going to call an ambulance." I didn't want him to be kind and misguided; I needed him to be cruel and callous. I could work with that. It wouldn't make me feel bad about wanting to take an old man down. But a kind, gentle man, who was misguided enough for Conner to persuade and use, made me feel sorry for him. Dealing with the irony of pitying someone who had just stabbed me in the stomach was difficult.

"Don't call an ambulance. Call the Supernatural Guild and ask for Gareth. Let him know that I've been injured by a—" I waited for him to fill in the blank so I'd at least know what was used on me and if the loss of magic would be permanent.

"Quardon blade," he offered softly. "It redirects magic."

"Redirects?" I panted, becoming increasingly weaker from the loss of blood. I looked back at Kalen, who had just come to his feet with a moan. Hitting the wall with such force had knocked him unconscious. Rubbing his head, he glared at the older gentleman as he made his way to me.

"Are you okay?" he asked, approaching me slowly. Each step

was pained and forced, making me wonder if he'd injured his legs when we'd crashed to the ground.

"I don't know. I don't have the use of magic," I admitted in a pain-rasped voice.

"Your magic will return," Mr. James assured me. "You should go to the hospital."

"I want to go to the Isles," I said firmly. At the hospital, I'd get stitches, but at the Isles I'd get a gifted mage or witch who could seal the wound with magic, leaving me without any scars.

"I think you should go to the ER," the elderly man pushed.

"I just texted Savannah. She'll get Gareth," Kalen said. Anger reverberated. A tinge of magic flickered from his hand. Fae magic was strongest with cognitive use and glamour manipulation; the defensive magic he possessed was so negligible that it was useless.

Seeing the flicks of magic that danced over Kalen's fingers was more impressive-looking than what harm it could inflict. Mr. James stood taller in defiance or acceptance of guilt. I had no idea which, or if there was a combination of both.

"Kalen, don't," I said softly.

"You shouldn't rely so heavily on magic. It will soon be gone," Mr. James warned.

"No, you've made a deal with the devil. Conner has no intention of *just* getting rid of magic. He'll get rid of the people who possess it as well," I told him as I made a futile attempt to come to my feet. After several tries, I made it but staggered. My hand was coated in blood; it was only a matter of time before I'd lose too much to stay conscious. The booming sound of the door being broken down thundered, followed by loud footsteps. The elderly man remained reserved, but even I had to cringe a little at a pissed-off Gareth, whose attention went to my blood-soaked hand and the wound that wouldn't heal.

My weak objection to being picked up went ignored. "I can walk."

"I'm sure with the amount of blood you've lost you think you can fly, too. I'm just going to take your foolish talk as the incoherent babble of a terribly injured person."

"I've had stab wounds before."

"I'm not sure why you're bragging about that," Gareth shot back, his anger at the situation hardening his joyless, dark chuckle.

CHAPTER 21

*H*eat traveled along my skin from Gareth's hand that was placed lightly over the now-healed wound on my stomach. It was distracting as I attempted to give a detailed account of the story. His other hand was on his phone, scrolling through objects in the Magic Council's database as well as the prohibited ones in the national database.

"I don't see that dagger mentioned," he finally admitted, scowling.

"Maybe it's an unknown," I said.

I made an attempt to sit up, but he added enough pressure to discourage it. "Levy, give yourself time to heal."

"I'm healed." I lifted his fingers to reveal my unmarred stomach.

"Do you have access to magic?"

Reluctantly, I shook my head. For the past twenty minutes, I'd been trying to use it, wondering if that was the reason I hadn't been released. It had been close to four hours since the doctors had seen me. The first two hours I wasn't conscious to notice the minutes passing. I woke up to a healed wound and Gareth hovering over me. Something he was still doing. I wasn't sure if it was a shifter thing or a Gareth thing.

"Gareth, I'm fine. I give you my word."

"She's always fine." Savannah came around the corner, holding a basket and balloons. I was willing to bet the brightly colored balloons were her idea and the basket of goodies was Lucas's. When it came to gift giving, Lucas was an all-star and Savannah was in the minor leagues, peddling her bags of granola, sugarless abominations, and gluten-free whatever. "Oh, it's just a stab, give me the duct tape. What, my arm's dislocated? Give me an ACE bandage," she mocked in a falsetto voice. She placed the basket on the counter and came closer to me. "May I?" she asked Gareth, who removed his hand to let her see the nonexistent injury.

"How bad was it?" she asked him, giving me a look as if she wasn't willing to accept anything I said because I tended to downplay my injuries. It wasn't as if I didn't think they were serious, but whether it was major or minor, Savannah behaved as if I needed to be airlifted to the hospital for life-saving medical attention. And then for days afterward, I'd get her overzealous nursing treatment. She approached it with the same gusto she did yoga and her need to push her honey-sweetened muffins.

"What is Conner up to now?" Savannah rolled her eyes as she scowled. Something she did every time his name was mentioned.

"He's taken Levy's magic," Gareth said.

"We don't know that for sure," Kalen corrected from his place on the sofa where he'd been sitting and fuming over Mr. James's betrayal—not against us, but the magical community. He'd tried to understand it, look at it from the man's perspective, but Kalen, who loved his magic, didn't understand how someone could hate it or make an effort to eliminate it from the world. He wasn't willing to accept my explanation of the man being misguided.

"There's misguided and there's willfully ignorant. He's the latter if he chooses to see the world in black and white when magic has so many shades of gray and can't be placed in a box and labeled bad," he'd seethed an hour ago, when I'd made my last effort to explain the man's actions. Anger had clouded Kalen's ability to be reasonable and he'd seen my explanation as acceptance. It clearly hadn't been. My perspective was different because I came from a people that had been villainized for the actions of a small group. I would never do the Cleanse, but everyone treated me as if I was five seconds from doing one. Conner wasn't helping.

I kept looking at my fingers for that spark, or the lively feeling of magic awakening and pouring through me, ready to be used. There was a flicker, like a lighter being ignited but not quite catching. For several minutes I kept at it until my fingers glowed a weak blue and white. Relief flowed through me, even when the colors fizzled and died as quickly as they had kindled. My magic wasn't gone, and that was a relief.

"It might take a while. He used your magic to break himself out, and based on what was reported, it was explosive," Gareth said.

"I'm ready to go home."

Gareth made a face.

"You can't possibly think I'd be safe here."

"Safer," Gareth whispered. "I don't think Conner will come here."

"No, there's nowhere I can go to get away from him."

Gareth knew this and it seemed to weigh heavily on him. "We need to stop him." Gareth shook his head. "What was Mr. James thinking?" he breathed out, exasperated. I had a feeling he was team misguided, while Kalen stuck to his opinion and Savannah, who had gathered the gist of what had transpired from questioning Gareth, seemed to have sided with Gareth. Once the Supernatural Guild was done cataloguing and checking Mr. James's collection of items against the databases, Kalen and I became their owners, per the contract.

I couldn't wait for Kalen and Blu to get their hands on them.

They were useless at digging through boxes, negotiating the confines of an attic, and cleaning out barns to find things of value among the garbage; however, when it came to research, the fashionistas were a power couple. Anyone could tell their similarities didn't just stop at their fashion sense. They loved magic and had a huge thirst for knowledge of it.

"Conner should never have been sent to Barathrum." I evaded saying what I wanted to but Gareth got the picture.

"When we catch him again, he won't." Menace and anger reverberated in his words.

"Is this what you're going to be like from now on?" Savannah asked as I approached her, emerging from my bedroom after my second nap of the day. My recovery was taking a lot of energy. I'd been released from the hospital two days ago and my magic had just fully returned.

"Give me a break, I've only had full use of it for fourteen hours."

Taking a seat next to her at the kitchen table, I allowed magic to curl around my fingers in a rainbow of colors. She watched me as I played with it, surging it into a ball of power only to extinguish it with a flick of my finger.

"The agents at the SG are nervous. You had your magic pulled from you. No one wants that. You know what that means for anyone who isn't a Legacy."

Frowning, I wasn't so sure that it didn't mean death for us, too. The Legacy and the Vertu had hidden behind a nearly impervious ward while the world had collapsed around them. I suspected the Cleanse would have had an effect on them as well.

Not using my magic was one thing, but the inability to use it was another. It was a part of me, how I protected myself, and without it I was left with only the twins, which I'd kept with me the whole time.

"Are they still out there?" I asked, frowning, jerking my head at the door where Victor had placed two of his agents in cars. Gareth, I assumed in an effort to show that his was bigger, had three of his agents—two high mages—at our door, and a shifter doing perimeter sweeps.

"They were out there when I took them beverages and snacks."

"Stop feeding them and maybe they'll go away. Or better yet, give them your muffins. That will make them hate us so much, they would be glad to let us be assassinated."

She made a face and stuck out her tongue. "We need to find Conner before he does whatever he plans."

"The SG and FSR are looking for him."

Several minutes passed as Savannah chewed on her lips. "If they find him, they'll just arrest him, again." Her voice was low, crisp, and dark. Enough so that my eyes widened on her. It cast a dark shadow over her usually bright features. It was the first time I'd seen raw, unfettered anger and spite in her in regards to Conner. What he'd done to her was a violation and his egregious acts only added to it.

I searched for a vehement response to dissuade her, but I didn't have it in me. I wanted Conner dead as well. Not in a prison where he'd find a way to escape. Dead.

The silence between us spoke volumes; we'd settled on a silent pact. We would see to it that Conner died and stayed that way.

Our silent pact was one thing, but letting Savannah be actively involved was another. When you killed someone, it took something from you; it didn't matter whether they deserved it or not. I wouldn't let Savannah be burdened with it. Conner was my problem and she was caught in the crossfire.

Watching the SG guard as he passed my window for the third time that hour, I wondered at what point my neighbors would start a petition to get us evicted. In the past few months, Savannah and I had brought our share of violence and extra police surveillance. They were still polite, or as polite as one could be while casting looks of suspicion every time they saw one of us. Our dating choices hadn't made things easier. We'd quickly devolved from the quiet ladies in the building to the freak show that no one wanted anything to do with.

After sheathing the twins at my back, I checked the knives I had at my ankles and flicked magic at my fingers, testing it again. The last thing I wanted was a magic mishap going up against Conner. My plan relied heavily on Conner wanting to be found. Thinking about the look he'd given me at Mr. James's home, I knew he couldn't wait to get at me any more than I could him. His ego was his weakness. He wanted a fight, to know that he'd conquered and bested me. I waited for the guard to get far enough past my window that he wouldn't see me. It was the mage doing the sweep. Patiently, I'd waited until they traded shifts, knowing that the shifter would be able to smell and hear me.

"Is the shifter gone?" Savannah whispered in the darkness, before turning on my bedroom light. I jerked my attention from the window to take a look at my roommate. Her "quest bag" draped over her shoulder, she had on calf-length yoga pants and a pale blue shirt with "Namaste" scrawled across the front. A knife was sheathed at her waist. She had a butcher knife in her hand. "No one saw fit to get me proper weaponry, so I had to make do."

"Why are you holding that knife like you're about to dice vegetables?" I gave the woman who wanted to be my partner in vengeance another sweeping look. She looked dangerous but only to herself. Taking the butcher knife from her, I laid it on the bed. "You're not going. I'll be back soon."

Before I could launch into my list of reasons she needed to stay, starting with the butcher knife, my phone buzzed. Lowering my voice to a low drowsy sound, attempting to make it seem as if

I'd been awakened from sleep, I mumbled into the speaker, "Hi, Gareth."

"You weren't asleep. You're standing at your window watching my guys, chastising Savannah for carrying a butcher knife. Let me guess, she has her quest bag to take on your adventure."

I looked around the room. "Do you have a camera in here or something?" I fumed.

"No, one of my agents heard you."

Damn shifters!

"Gareth, I need to do this. At least see if I can find him. We don't have time on our side because we have no idea what he's planning."

"You're going to use yourself as bait," he growled.

Calm down, kitten.

Victor had. I'd rather be the person to do it than someone else.

I didn't want to fight with Gareth. He had every reason to be afraid, but I'd have to deal with more than fear if I didn't stop Conner. Gareth was reasonable and I knew he'd understand. After several long moments of silence, he said, "I can't talk you out of this, can I?"

"No."

"Be careful." He breathed out an exasperated sigh.

CHAPTER 22

Savannah looked around the small cave that was once my personal sanctuary where I could perform magic without discovery. She was an interloper. Best friend or not, it felt just as peculiar to have her in my spot as it had when Gareth had been in it.

"What are you going to do?" she whispered from just a few feet away.

"I'm going to track him."

"You've done that before, and it didn't work without Elijah."

Sucking in a breath, I had to admit the obvious. "It worked because together we were stronger than him." I glanced over my shoulder at her, the large flashlight minimally illuminating the midnight space. Shadows formed over the worried lines of her face. "I won't need to be stronger than him; I'm sure he wants me to find him."

He'll try to find me.

Standing up taller and gripping her weapon with purpose, Savannah was ready to take on a psychopath who wielded powerful magic and swords—with a kitchen knife. If I wasn't so concerned for her safety, it would have been comical. She looked ridiculous holding it, as if she was going to swing it like a bat.

"I really wish you would leave and let me handle this," I pleaded for what I believed was the fifth time.

"I wish you'd stop sounding like a broken record. I'm not leaving you to fight Conner alone. He comes after you, he comes after me. Period. We're in this together."

I shifted from her, making room to perform the locating spell. Space was the least of my worries; once I did the locating spell, I'd open myself up to him finding me as well. He could transport, and my skills at that still required some honing. I could do it now, but I wasn't exactly sure where I'd end up. I had a ways to go.

As I pulled the knife from the sheath, a blinding flash of pale white blasted in the cave, illuminating it enough for us to see Conner's extravagant entrance.

"I thought I'd save you the trouble," he cooed.

I was distracted; a wave of magic hit Savannah in the chest, sending her so far back I couldn't see her in the unlit, cavernous area. The sound of a body hitting the ground and expelling a sharp breath was my only indicator. She groaned. At least she was alive.

"How will it end? Three people come in, one leaves?" he taunted. The low light made his features look more ominous. The embers of light that came off his fingers held my attention more than the sadism on his face. A sense of finality swept through me as his hate-filled gaze narrowed on me. Before there were still slight cinders of interest and allure, reverence and adoration. Now there was only unadulterated hate. Cool air swooshing through the dank area brushed against my cheek, magic buzzed against my nose, and fear rose and fell in me like an unsteady wave. I didn't like being afraid but knew that at times fear was good. It ignited the instinct to protect myself, and that was what I needed.

"*You* destroyed us," he accused in a cold, venomous voice.

"Really? I thought you trying to do the Cleanse again did that." Whipping out the twins, I refused to be on the offensive as we rounded each other. We both knew how it was going to play out. Sai pointed at him, I sent magic through them, sharp and hard. It fizzled against the wall he'd quickly erected in front of himself.

"I'm stronger than you," he pointed out, as if I needed that. After all, he'd never made a secret of that. His lips curled into a rueful snarl, disgusted at my very presence. His feeling of betrayal was apparent.

"I have all day," I said, waiting for him to drop the barrier, refusing to expend unnecessary energy to break a wall I knew he would eventually drop. He couldn't perform magic against me behind it. His eyes promised a painful death.

His wall fell and magic burst from him like a wrecking ball, hitting me in the chest and knocking the wind out of me as my back crashed into the wall on the opposite side of the cave. Dirt broke from it and fell over me. I caught the edge of the sword that had materialized in his hand between the shaft and the side prongs of a sai. A quick strike with the other penetrated his extended arm. He yelped when I pulled it back. Retreating, he seemed to be in pain as he handled his sword.

"You are truly a warrior." The longing in his voice returned. How sick and twisted did he have to be to long for someone who wanted him dead as vehemently as I did? The time it took to make a few steps back was all he needed before the wound closed and the blood disappeared, revealing an unmarred arm. *Pierce the heart,* I reminded myself, but I wasn't convinced that was enough. There was no way that Gareth had missed his heart when he'd mauled him. I'd do more than just pierce it; I'd cut it from his body if necessary.

"Are you afraid, Anya?" he purred sadistically.

"Nope. Just trying to figure out how to kill you in the most efficient way. Can I borrow your sword? I bet you can't live without a head."

A deep rumble of laughter reverberated through the caves. It sounded more maniacal when it resounded.

Rolling his eyes, he scoffed, "The lover."

Expecting to see Gareth, I was surprised when Lucas emerged with such speed the ball of magic lobbed in his direction streaked past him. Up close, he struck at Conner, the sounds of striking metal filling the small area as they aggressively attacked each other. Conner advanced. Half-turning, Lucas avoided the strike. Conner's hand punched into Lucas. He wailed. The energy of the magical current that Conner shot through him made the hairs on my arms rise. It loosened Lucas's hand from around his sword, giving Conner the advantage to send it soaring several feet away. We both heard the scuttering of movement. Savannah, her hands moving into sight enough to grab the lost sword. Conner's sharpened gaze went in her direction.

"If I get a hold of you this time, I will destroy your mind to the point that Anya can never save you," Conner threatened. His last words were forced out with a grunt as I threw a tightly coiled ball of magic. It hit him as hard as his had hit me, knocking chunks of dirt and rocks away upon impact. I charged at him before he could recover enough to use magic or respond with his sword. The sai slid into his stomach, not enough to pin him, but deep enough he had to work at removing it. Blood soaked his shirt and molded it to his body. Panting as he squeezed his eyes shut, he removed the sai with a swift move.

I replaced it with the other twin. He folded over, lifting his head just enough to look me in the eyes. The jolt of turbulent magic that wracked through me was worse than the hateful glare he gave me. It felt like a bull was rampaging through my body, using its horns to clear the way. Tears sprang to my eyes and my knees buckled. I tried to gather the energy to stand, but it felt like it had been siphoned from me. My legs felt like lead as I pulled myself to half stand. Conner dislodged the sai from his stomach and turned it to me, blocked by the barrier I'd shielded myself with. It wavered upon his impact. Weakened by the magical retaliation, I knew he'd eventually be able to get past it. It was difficult to find the balance between holding the barrier and conserving my energy to fight. Conner had one sai, I had the other. A quirk in his lips emerged as he watched me struggle. Just as I'd waited for him to drop his barrier, he waited for my energy to fail. I refused to give him that pleasure. Out of the corner of my eye, I could see Savannah easing forward. So could Conner.

"Savannah, I will destroy you if you interfere. Leave your mind so wrecked you will need someone to care for you. Do you think your vampire will stay to look after you in the infantile state I will put you in? Stay."

He'd just ensured that she'd do no such thing. I didn't need to see her to know she was flushed with anger and her lips were drawn back in a scowl. Reminding her of his violation wouldn't make her fear him. It would only ignite the flames of her ire and desire for revenge. She moved slower. Arrogance and self-satisfaction placed a haughty smile on his face.

Easy, Savannah. Easy. As if she could hear me, she stopped. He grinned, satisfied. Savannah looked afraid. He was enjoying her fear too much. I dropped the barrier and threw magic hard into him. It was weaker than earlier, but in constant succession, it packed a punch. Savannah eased next to me, dragging the sword with her. She placed her hand on my shoulder, and the surge of power that ran through me yanked my breath away. It hummed, like an electric wire, with energy that needed to be expended. I'd felt Savannah's magic enhancement before, but this had me amped more than anything she'd provided previously. Was it because she was running on endorphins and hormones from her fight or flight response? Using the upsurge of magic to my advantage, I pummeled him with offensive magic until he was against the wall. Again, I planted my sai in him. Lucas moved toward him, less graceful than usual.

Savannah's screech, shrill with frustration, anger, and thirst for vengeance, reverberated in the enclosed area. Conner's wavering strength was showing—the magic that came off him was weak, a strong wind instead of a violent storm. Savannah tore through Conner's withering magic and swung. I turned, feeling a wet splatter on my face. I didn't look. I knew what had happened before Conner's body collapsed to the ground. Savannah looked and kept looking. Her lips were parted, her eyes wide and glistening in a state of awe and terror. Wiping her hand across her face smeared the blood rather than cleaning it away.

Gareth's head poked down from the cave's opening, and he gave a sigh of relief.

"We're fine," I said.

"I see that."

I'd spoken for my well-being. I wasn't as sure about Savannah's. She hadn't moved. Lucas's nudging her brought her out of an awestruck state—partly. She dropped the sword and let him help her out of the cave. I was the second to move up. Lucas stayed behind. I backtracked to check on him and felt the heat of the flames as I poked my face in the hole.

Gareth cursed behind me, and several people from the SG rushed down to put out the fire, but I gathered it was too late to do anything substantial. Gareth blew out a breath, he didn't seem too angered by it. I was relieved. Conner couldn't come back from that.

As we made our way to the car, Gareth shook his head; his lips lifted into an incredulous smirk. "Did you really ask to borrow his sword to cut off his own head?" he barked out in a cross between scathing ridicule and a dark laugh. "What is wrong with you?"

"What? All he could say was no," I shot back, just as incredulous. Our mood should have been more solemn. Someone was dead, and my best friend had done it. I'd tried to save Conner and reason with him. Each time he'd failed, he'd had a chance for redemption, which he'd rejected. Now the Legacy and the Vertu had a chance. It would be a new era, and hopefully, like the original Cleanse, Conner's demise would be a cautionary tale. I looked over to Savannah, who was being checked out by a medic. She seemed okay. I hoped she was okay. Lucas gave her the same assessing look as I had. The gentle plaintive smile she gave him was reassuring for the moment. Even against her protests, she'd be taken to the Isles because she was still considered a human. Humans had to be taken care of. Alysa showed up, hopping out of her car before the driver could come to a full stop. Perhaps she was the best; even Harrah hadn't had a driver.

Scanning the area, she took a quick appraisal of everyone there. With the exception of Savannah, all were supernaturals—linked to the Supernatural Guild or the FSR. Moving toward Savannah, she had that look on her face—the fixer look. Gareth moved before I did, blocking her approach toward Savannah. Leaning in, he said something for her ears only. They went back and forth for several minutes, jaws clenched as they pushed whatever they had to say through tightly fixed teeth. Alysa's concession didn't come easily, and for several moments she split her attention between Gareth and Savannah, whose gaze was sharpened on her like an eagle.

Eventually Alysa backed away and went to her car.

"If Savannah goes to the Isles, I want to be there the moment she gets there," I told Gareth once he was closer. Even though I whispered it, Lucas looked in my direction and I knew he'd heard it, too. *Ugh, vampires and shifters make life a lot harder.*

CHAPTER 23

*G*areth's gaze traveled along the room of Devour, something I'd been doing throughout the night, watching the vampires, not out of interest, but because they were coveting my neck the entire time. Savannah accused me of being paranoid, but I found it difficult not to be overly cautious surrounded by people who'd had decades to perfect their charm and allure. I came armed with my cynicism, and the six-inch decorative pins placed in my messy bun. Originally it was a tightly spun knot on the top of my head. It had been met with a frown and an eye roll from Savannah, before she'd rearranged my hair into a loose bun, curls falling from it enough to obscure the pins.

Lucas had greeted us with a teasing smile, his gaze quickly moving to them as they peeked up from the pile of hair. "Oh, Levy. I can guarantee you will be safe. Violence is never used to lure people. Ever." And he was right. The lovely faces, graceful lithe movements, and overt sexuality promised a night of pleasure a person wasn't soon to forget. I preferred Crimson, the club where the younger vampires hung out. They hadn't perfected their allure and adopted their vampire personas from every teen vampire film imaginable. They were usually angsty or broody.

That I could deal with. The deep mesmerizing looks, the throaty entreaties, the way they brushed against a person making something so casual sensual and intoxicating. Watching and noting it all, I made it part of my defense, but Savannah was enthralled by one vampire in particular. Gareth and I couldn't do anything about it.

"Stop looking at them, you can't suck block all night," he teased. I'd spent most of the evening finding Savannah in the midst of the crowd of people in the barely lit room, so close to Lucas I could barely make out where he ended and she began. My attention wasn't just to suck block Lucas; I was concerned about Savannah. She'd killed someone, and he'd deserved it, but nevertheless, she'd taken a life. She seemed okay and I really hoped she was. Perhaps she had cataloged it into that section of things that needed to be done, where she brushed off her ethics and shouldered the responsibility for the greater good. Conner was gone. He'd come back from a mauling by a big-ass cave lion, but he wasn't likely to come back without his head. Just to make sure, because when it came to Conner no one wanted to take chances, Lucas had burned the body.

"Levy, she's fine."

"I know. I expected her to be different. Darker, heavier."

"I'm not sure you're going to get darkness from a woman who wakes up like an adrenaline-riddled puppy." Taking a sip from his glass, he found her in the dark where she caught us looking and started waving enthusiastically. "Yeah, that's an abysmal hole. She's so dark and foreboding—I'm shaking." He laughed and looked at me. "Now you, on the other hand. You're dark enough for both of you."

Stepping back, I gave him a full look, licking my lips the way he loved and dropping my voice until it was deep, sultry. "Am I dark, sexy, and broody?" I asked, teasing.

"No. Not at all. You're dark and geeky—between the plaid shirts and the constant talk about superheroes you left *sexy* and *broody* in the hallway and slammed the door on them." Still grinning, he leaned in to kiss me.

"Yet, I managed to get you," I breathed against his lips.

"I'm easy, remember?" Taking several steps back from me, he gave me a full view. Apparently getting him wasn't as easy as I'd teased him about. He still was of interest to a lot of women and even as we stood at the bar of Devour, surrounded by vampires, humans with an affinity for vampires, and an occasional supernatural, I received looks. Some of admiration but most of them were judgmental. I hadn't lived up to their expectations, and I wondered if a few of the disdainful looks were because of my having come out.

"Do you want to leave?" he asked.

"Yes, let's leave. I feel like I'm on the menu."

Gareth laughed, turned his glass up, and emptied the contents. His fingers interlinked with mine when I felt a cool gust come through the room. Everyone stilled in their positions for a brief moment. It was just a second, as peculiar magic swept throughout the room. Frozen in time for several beats, the clubgoers found themselves separated, their bodies pushed aside, leaving a clear path to me and Gareth. A chill brushed against my nose. Out of my peripheral vision, I watched people beat against an invisible wall. Dorian came into sight, fully human. His face remained the picture of professionalism, unemotional, reserved. Stone-hard eyes homed in on us, as if through an assassin's scope. Magic perked in me, a protective reaction, but I had no idea what I needed to use it against. Dorian staring us down wasn't an attack. Should I strike preemptively?

"Confirmed," Dorian whispered as he stepped back. Time no longer moved slowly. Everything quickened beyond recognition. It was as if I was swept into a hurricane. I couldn't move fast enough, scream loud enough, or call enough magic to stop it. A pale-haired woman was in front of Gareth and me, her presence icy cold—the incarnation of death. The gauzy white gown that flowed behind her expanded like wings. Enchanting icy crystal blue eyes locked on mine and then Gareth's. She was an odd combination of devil and angel, scary and soothing. Gareth and I stood in shock, unable to move until her screech erupted in the room as she took hold of our wrists. A heavy magical jolt shot through me, shocking me into a response. I forced out a powerful burst of magic that thrashed into her; she stood taller, absorbing it, screeching louder. The horrific sound had power, pushing against my magic, infusing more of hers into us. My arms felt like they had been set on fire. Sudden silence fell on the room. As quickly as the woman had appeared, she disappeared.

She left behind an identical mark on both of us. An ash-colored circle with an extension that looked like a clawed finger positioned into a hook.

"What the hell was that?" Savannah hissed, looking at the reminder of the woman's visit on my arm.

Gareth extended his arm and Savannah examined the identical markings. Her finger hovered over mine, reluctant to touch it. I didn't blame her. The skin around it was raw and angry-looking.

She tugged us behind the bar and gave the bartender a look when he dared to be offended by her invasion. I knew his concession had little to do with her angry face and everything to do with who she was to Lucas. Turning on the cold water, she stuck our arms under it. It cooled the inflamed area but didn't remove the mark or soothe the odd sensation that lingered over it. It pulsed a steady beat, a reminder of its existence.

Standing behind Savannah, Lucas pulled her into him when she mustered the courage to touch it.

"Don't," he instructed. Frowning, he looked at the activity in the club. There were a lot of things that could be said about vampires, but no one could ever question their formidableness. The activity had returned to normal, as if a strange, screeching woman dressed in white was just a glitch in a night of hedonism and fun.

CHAPTER 24

Kalen and Blu looked down at the mark on my arm again and then went to look at the matching one on Gareth, who was seated in a chair in the office sitting area. He was starting to let his frustration show. There had been a flurry of activity since we'd been marked the night before. The Supernatural Guild had taken pictures of the marks, a specialist on ritual magic had been called in, and we'd spent several hours with a team of agents, going through books trying to find out what the mark meant. It still pulsed on my arm, and since it was linked to Dorian and a woman who was simultaneously the scariest and most alluring thing I'd ever seen, everyone's curiosity was piqued —until we told them who Dorian was and how we knew him. Gazes became concerned or judgmental, nonverbally chastising us for our excursion.

Kalen and Blu were just concerned as they split their attention between their books and our indelible marks. The third time Blu roughly turned my arm over to look at the mark I suggested she take a picture of it.

"No, I need to see it in real time in case it changes."

"Why would it change?" I asked, confused.

"Why would a magical mark be placed on you and Gareth? Why is it this color? Why is Gareth even marked at all? He's a shifter. There are a lot of whys here." Twisting her lips to the side, she flipped a couple more pages in the book she was referencing before tossing it aside and grabbing another.

"How was magic used on Gareth? Do you think a Legacy did this?"

"We're dealing with magic that predated the Legacy and the magic we have now. *But* the mark is magic, it's not actually using magic against him."

"Mine feels peculiar, like Levy says hers does."

"It still is *just* a mark." After several moments of deliberation, Blu amended, "I think."

Kalen and Blu began pacing in front of us going through books and exchanging looks in such smooth motion it looked choreographed. It was the first time I'd actually seen Kalen look disheveled. His woven silk shirtsleeves were rolled up to the forearm, the bottom half of his shirt was pulled from his pants, and his hair was mussed from running his fingers through it. Watching Blu march back and forth in front of us added amusement to the dire situation. It was the witchiest I'd ever seen her look. Stereotypical bohemian witch carrying a burgundy gold-rune-covered book. Her thick, coarse ringlets were pushed back and secured by a long flowing scarf. A long printed gauzy dress overtook her frame and fluttered in small waves as she moved. She complemented the outfit with rhinestone-studded sandals that glinted in the light.

The mark had a heartbeat, an annoying thump that bumped at a constant rhythm, reminding me of its presence.

Kalen suddenly stopped. Slowly scanning the book in his hand, he jerked his head up. "When the Naga asked you all to stay, did you indicate at all that you would?" he asked, his voice heavy with concern.

"I didn't want to be rude, so I said I would if I didn't have to get back to Savannah," I said.

"Then what?"

I tried to remember everything that had transpired; it seemed like every detail was important. "I told her I needed the *Culded* to help Savannah."

"Did you offer to return once the task was complete?" Once again I combed over the events of that day. With everything that had happened, it seemed like it had occurred years rather than just days ago.

"You did, in a way," Gareth said, frowning. "You were just being polite, but it's easy to see how she could have misconstrued it."

"How could that be misconstrued? I told her I needed to help Savannah."

Gareth's gaze cast down to the floor as if he, too, was going over the scene in detail. Then he repeated the whole conversation with very specific detail. Impressed by his recall, I was glad I was on the good side of it.

"I was being polite," I said.

"I know you were, but that explains her reaction."

"Reaction?" Kalen inquired.

I shuddered at the image of her wailing in pain. "She attacked us as we were leaving. When we escaped, she cried, sorrowfully. It was very odd, and then we were forbidden to return there."

"The mark is a retaliation," Blu offered. Several minutes passed and she continued, "It's beating—like a pulse, right?"

I nodded.

"It's a magical homing system. Now we need to find out what's coming for you."

Gareth seemed too relaxed for someone who had just been told that a godlike creature had marked us. Instead of looking worried, he gave a haughty smile.

"You're not concerned?" I asked incredulously.

He shrugged. "We've had to deal with Conner. I can't imagine they can send something worse."

I would have loved to be more optimistic, but there always seemed to be something worse. I didn't think there could be anything worse than the Legacy, and then ta-da—I find out about the Vertu. Had he forgotten how hard it had been to kill Conner?

Blu and Kalen's faces twisted into scowls as they both looked at a page in the book that Kalen was holding. Kalen moved to the computer and started clicking at the keyboard frantically. "You want to bet?" Kalen frowned, answering Gareth. "This is worse…a Mortem Spiritus."

Then he started to read. "They only take on a form to collect their offering." His gaze flicked up from the screen. "You'll be fighting something similar to a wraith, but deadlier. It doesn't have a discernible form. I think that's harder than Conner."

"Trap them in a jar like a genie," I threw out. Making light of the situation was all I could do to cope. What they described was worse than Conner. No matter how harmless I attempted to make the situation, the problem remained that I had to fix this, which meant I would probably have to make a trip to Menta Island to track down the Naga and give her a less than kind education on the difference between a polite rejection and a promise.

"There are some positive things about this. They are bound to the darkest of night, where they will rule your nightmares before they collect their payment," Blu offered. It wasn't much consolation. *Great, they can only kill us at night.* She read on and then moved to the stack of books and flipped through several others. "So you all are fine, if you sleep in the day."

"What happens if they appear at night?"

"They'll torture you in your dreams and then use the energy from your terrors to take you away."

"Where do they take us?" I asked, no longer able to hide behind a quip or one-liner.

She kept reading and I moved next to her, reading on, finding

Conner less scary with each sentence that went into detail about the victims of their visits. She turned the page. *Yay, pictures.* I wasn't able to see Conner beheaded, and I didn't want to see the results of the Mortem Spiritus torture chamber. Apparently whatever they subjected you to in your dreams manifested physically. Shuddering at the images before me, I wanted desperately to pay the Naga a visit.

"How do you stop them?" I asked, still peeking over Blu's shoulder. I read along with her and five pages later, we knew who could call them and how it was done and had seen visuals of their horrific retrieval—but there wasn't anything about stopping them.

"I should be able to summon one, right?" I asked.

"What will that do, Levy?" Blu inquired.

Nothing, I just wanted to send one back to the Naga. Pettiness at its best.

"We have to sleep in the day until when?" Gareth asked.

"Until we find a way to stop it," Blu said.

"I'm assuming the death of the summoner would do that." Blu's face twisted in disgust. I understood her feeling. Death being the answer to a problem was difficult to accept and I hoped to end it without bloodshed.

Gareth had been examining his mark for the past few minutes, deep in thought. "Even if that were an option, there's no way we'd be allowed back. They would stop us at the shore." His words were a reminder of the disapproving and angry way Dorian had looked at us.

It was midnight and we had several hours before day broke and we could sleep. Kalen left the room, went to the kitchen, and returned with two large cups of coffee and a bowl of dark chocolate. Between the coffee and chocolate, there was enough caffeine to keep us awake.

The problem with being sleepy and forced to stay up was that you were too tired to actually read. The words of all the books I read blurred in front of me and comprehension became a problem until I looked at the book with the pictures and retelling of the torture that the victims underwent.

"Do they not have a form at all until they are fulfilling their calling?" At some point they had to coalesce in order to touch us. "There are two of us; I'm assuming there's more than one Mortem Spiritus."

Blu nodded. "It seems that they travel in threes," she said, frowning. Oddly, it was comforting to know that there was more than just one and that one Mortem Spiritus didn't wield enough power to take out a Legacy and a shapeshifter. Then I had the morbid thought that maybe one was enough, but three came to ensure the job was done in the cruelest way possible. My heart thumped faster at the idea.

When the sun finally peeked through the darkness, I was more than ready to sleep. Not wanting to worry Savannah or get her involved, I decided to stay at Gareth's. Showered and waiting for the caffeine to wear off so I could finally sleep, I heard Gareth's phone ring. He frowned at the number that popped up.

"Yes, Savannah, dear." He paused. "We are fine, we don't need you to watch over us while we sleep."

I couldn't hear what she was saying on the other end, but Gareth made several efforts to interrupt her without success. I'd gathered from what he said on his end that she was at the gate of the subdivision. He bit down on his lips and pressed several buttons on his phone, which must have allowed her entry.

"She is rather tenacious, isn't she?" he opined, rolling out of bed and starting for the bedroom door.

"That's a good word for bossy and overbearing," I said, following behind him.

Savannah, with a very unhappy Lucas in tow, entered with a tote. She'd packed her overnight version of the "quest bag," complete with a bat, stakes—which Lucas must have loaned her because I didn't have any—and a Taser. The Taser was a new purchase and I wondered when she'd added it to her arsenal.

"I brought snacks. This can be like a sleepover."

Lucas looked less interested in a group sleepover than Gareth was. I couldn't take the disappointment, so I didn't even bother looking in the bags for the snacks, which were going to be taste-free versions of something good.

"You do manage to have your share of adventures," Lucas said, shrugging off his jacket and laying it across the back of one of the chairs before taking a seat. Savannah sat where she usually did when Lucas was present, in his lap snuggled close to him.

"We're okay. It's daylight; they move at night."

"Well, that's what the book says, but remember, your books said Legacy were extinct and have no mention of Vertu. Better safe than sorry," Savannah offered.

Gareth scrubbed his hand across the low stubble on his face with a look of sheer confusion. It was the same bewildered look he had when Savannah became upset with Lucas, him, and me and gave us a good "talking-to." It was entertaining watching him try to deal with Savannah. I figured he'd take a page from Lucas's book and concede in silence and choose to see her as amusing rather than annoying. I considered my overbearing, *tenacious* roommate to be both: an amusing annoyance.

Handing them the books we'd borrowed from Kalen, I asked, "Can you go through these to see if we missed anything that can help us send them back or remove the marks?" Then I followed Gareth back to his room.

Slipping his hand around me, he brought his lips to brush against my hair. "Still suck blocking?" he teased.

"Of course not. I'm just giving them something to occupy their time while they're here."

CHAPTER 25

It took over three days to find something that would have a remote chance of working, since I'd destroyed most of the objects that we could have used to trap them, along with many other objects in the Magic Council's possession. Even though one of the objects might have helped save Gareth and me, I didn't regret my decision.

"This is going to work?" I asked skeptically as Blu and Kalen started making a large circle in the middle of Gareth's living room, using salt, tannin, and a potion Blu had made.

Blu made a face of uncertainty. "It should."

Her lack of assurance made it difficult for me to feel confident about the circle that they were forming to trap the Mortem Spiritus. Responding to the magical beacon, the Mortem Spiritus had seeped into Gareth's home at night, in a puff of dark smoke. Their nebulous forms had filled the room, only to find us awake and sitting on the sofa. Unable to do anything more than taunt us, they'd shifted frequently throughout the night, filling the room with the scent of ash and cinnamon as they took on various forms, the most common one a ghostlike human. Having access to extraordinary magic, I found it absurd that my most prudent weapon against them was caffeine, sugar, and a morning nap.

Yesterday the Mortem Spiritus had trickled in through the crevices of the house to find us awake again. Their corporeal forms whipped around us as their unique scent wafted through the air. They displayed their fury at finding us awake by making the odor stronger and more noxious. They'd resorted to making lulling, somnolent sounds to entice us to sleep. When that hadn't worked, they'd swirled and twisted into menacing forms that would have had the desired effect if they weren't just apparitions.

We had about an hour before we could expect them again. Enough time for Blu and Kalen to finish the spell and for us to position ourselves to execute the plan.

Lucas rested against the frame of the door, an unwilling visitor for a fourth night because of Savannah, who wouldn't leave. His look of irritation and disinterest belied any concern about our safety. Savannah stood next to him, acutely interested in Kalen and Blu's preparation.

Gareth had adjusted well to the sleep change. He'd slept for a couple of hours, stayed late at work, leaving Savannah and Lucas to keep me company, and returned in time to stay up with me at night. I could barely function on just four hours of sleep, but Gareth seemed to be doing fine until now.

Seated on the sofa, his head bobbed. He jerked it up, made a face, then looked around the room. My gaze followed his to the gas moving under the door. He covered his nose. Lucas was shocked into action: He rushed down the hall, I assumed to get towels and anything he could find to cover the windows and doors, while Gareth guided me into the other room. Magic didn't work on Gareth, but gas would hit him—and me.

Fuck. Since the Mortem Spiritus couldn't take on solid form, Dorian had to be responsible for the gas attack.

After a few minutes, Kalen called for us to return.

Savannah was sprawled out on the floor, Lucas holding her

close to him. She'd succumbed to the toxic gas. Lucas wasn't immune to magic but toxic gas didn't affect him, a benefit of being undead.

"I guess they enlisted help," Gareth fumed.

Blu was trying to reassemble the circle, which had been disturbed as everyone scattered to clear out and secure the windows and doors, and then waited for the Mortem Spiritus to return with the evening darkness. They crept in as a dark smoke of swirling clouds and poorly shaped figures that stopped moving when they found us, awake and waiting for them.

I whispered the words to evoke the spell, and they were sucked into the circle as if by a vacuum, unable to pass its boundaries. It was their prison until the morning—if they made it that long. As the magical energy formed around the Mortem, they succumbed to it. No, they seemed to have conceded to the magic.

The spell wasn't perfect. It bound them, but they seemed to use the energy from the circle to solidify themselves. The circle was engaged, working as a diaphanous prison.

Blu and Kalen's eyes widened at this. It was supposed to hold them, and drive them out, preventing them from returning. It held them, but that was it.

It became apparent why they gave into the spell. They used the magic from it to perform their own. The smoke formed large creatures, half-human, half-animal mutations. They were bipedal, a little over seven feet tall, and had fingers that curved into blades. Their faces reminded me of a sloth's, but that was where the similarities ended. They moved within the circle with a shifter's swiftness, graceful and predaceous. Sparks flashed as their claws struck the magical barrier. I winced with each blow. Magically connected to the barrier, I wasn't aware that there would be a physical one as well. The animals thrashed and clawed for dear life, trying to release themselves from their prison.

"You can do it," Blu encouraged from behind me. But I wasn't so sure. They continued their full-on attack on the prison. With the three of them fighting to get out, I wasn't sure how long I could endure the assault. Fifteen minutes later, they hadn't tired. Instead, they'd come up with a strategy. Two came in close, their claws striking repeatedly in the same spot, as the other shifted back into his wraithlike form, trying to find a vulnerability. My heart raced. We hadn't known they would be able to take on solid form while contained by the spell—what else didn't we know?

"If they get out, will they be able to hold that form?" I asked Kalen and Blu.

"I don't know. We didn't think they could take this form," Kalen shot back in a panicked voice as the Mortem Spiritus took on their previous incorporeal form. Something had changed. Heat radiated off the barrier that divided us. At first it was just warm enough to be uncomfortable, but as the minutes crept by, there was pain. Focusing on keeping the barrier intact was becoming increasingly difficult, and I figured that was the point.

Sweat glistened on my face as they continued their heat retaliation. When that didn't work, they added the lulling sounds again. Gentle and soothing, the mesmerizing sound was so similar to that of the Mors that Harrah had sent to kill me, I wondered if they were somehow related.

Hypnotic sounds had me swaying along with the movement of the specters, and when my eyes started to close, Blu and Gareth's sharp, loud voices sent a jolt through me.

"This is getting harder," I admitted in a low voice.

Gareth moved next to me, a sword in hand. Lucas, still close to Savannah, who was rousing, stood and assumed a defensive position.

"Then let them go."

"I can't. Not with them like that." As quickly as they shifted to solid form and incorporeal, it couldn't be a good idea to free them. I suspected once we let them go, they'd leave and either the Naga would send something else, or they would find a way to circumvent the spell.

"You're not going to be able to hold it until morning, Levy," Gareth said, worried.

"If you can hold it until morning, you should be okay," Blu said, her voice holding the desperation I was starting to feel.

Holding it until daybreak was going to be difficult; I was worn down and it had only been two hours. They would be weakened once day broke, and the spell would cast them out and block their return, essentially nullifying the Naga's summoning. However, I had a feeling that while I was waiting for them to weaken, they were waiting for the same thing to happen to me.

By the fourth hour, it seemed as if they'd conceded defeat, but I wasn't falling for it and letting my guard down. My head ached: I'd experienced it all, from pounding against the barrier, extreme heat and cold, to every imaginable cognitive spell to induce me to sleep where they would be the strongest.

When one of the Mortem Spiritus took on the form of a minotaur, with a slim body and claws instead of hands, I stiffened. It breathed and a small flame ignited. If he was going to start a fire, it wouldn't hurt anyone but them. I'd feel the heat of it but that was it. Blu and Kalen circled the enclosure, keeping a careful eye on the creature and the smoke-filled circle. I could fight creatures with forms without any problem. My sai could handle that. But this was more challenging. Anticipating their moods was useless.

Slowly, Blu moved back; eyes still fixed on the Mortem Spiritus, she grabbed the salt, tannin, and the brew she'd made and returned to her position near the circle.

"What's wrong?" I asked, lifting my eyes to a very concerned Blu.

"Something feels different."

Gareth, who had taken a seat, stood again, grabbing the sword. I moved back to pick up the sai, but before I could get a firm enough grip, there was a blast of wind from inside the circle, breaking a section large enough for the minotaur to get through. Blu and Kalen moved quickly to keep the circle closed and the other two in. As soon as the circle was closed, I invoked the spell again, dodging the flames the minotaur shot in my direction. Gareth slashed at the creature. His first strike caught the minotaur in the chest, the second in the stomach.

When the third strike brought the creature down, cutting him in two, I wondered if the power the Mortem had exerted to break the circle had left him too weak to take on his other form. Was this their last-ditch effort to get to Gareth and me and complete their task?

Although the minotaur wasn't moving, Blu and Kalen formed a wider circle, enclosing him with the others. Once the spell was invoked, I stepped back and plopped onto the part of the sofa that hadn't been torched by the minotaur.

It was easier to keep the circle's hold when I didn't have anyone fighting to break it. When sunlight hit, Blu said, "Now."

I invoked another spell and unlike the other nights when the Mortem Spiritus had spiraled into dark smoke that shot out of the house, now they coiled together, becoming lighter, pulsing as they futilely fought against the exorcism. Moments later there was a screeching sound, a flash of light, and then an empty circle. They were gone. Worn from trying to break out, the creatures had disappeared.

After their departure, we waited for several minutes. The marks on our arms were still there, but they weren't pulsing.

"Gareth, we need to go back to Menta Island," I breathed out in a low voice as I sank into the cushions of the sofa, in need of a nap and several aspirins.

"We were banned, remember?" he pointed out.

As if I could forget. "We need to talk to her. Maybe reason with her. If we remove the mark, she'll just do something else until we've been punished for our perceived default on a promise."

"What if she can't be reasoned with?"

"Then we'll look at other options." We both knew the other options were violent and bloody. I didn't want violent and bloody. I wanted to end with dialogue, a friendly conversation, an amicable resolution.

"Please," I said. "At least we can say we tried. Then we handle it differently."

Gareth sighed and gave me a look. He thought I was being naïve, and maybe I was, but the Naga felt aggrieved. This was a woman, or serpent woman, or whatever the hell, scorned.

My Batman worked on getting us back to the island, while I sat on the sofa watched by Blu, Savannah, Lucas, and Kalen, all uneasy, hoping I could keep up the barrier for the rest of the night. I was going to because my life depended on it—literally. We were being paranoid, because if they could have disappeared just to reappear and do more, they would have done so hours before.

CHAPTER 26

wo days after we had averted the assassination attempt by the Mortem Spiritus we were on the same trawler boat receiving looks from the captain and crew far worse than I'd imagined. I didn't think "you're a dumbass" was a look someone could give, but they had perfected it.

When we departed the ship for the island, the captain repeated the same instruction he had given us during the first trip. "We stay until sunset and then we leave, with or without you." His tone held a hint of sorrow, disbelief, and confusion, especially since we'd been evasive about the reason for our trip. I'd done it because I just didn't want to incur any more of their looks; my pride was pretty bruised, and I suspected Gareth was embarrassed by the plan. If I hadn't gathered that from his incredulous looks and head-shaking, I'd have certainly picked it up from him constantly asking me if I'd confirmed it would work. I had absolutely no indication it would work. It was a terrible idea—I owned —but we didn't have a lot of options. The Naga could be just as unreasonable as Conner, but I held on to the idea that she'd wept. It hadn't been a pride thing; it had been pain. We'd been the first people she'd extended an invitation to, and we'd rejected it. She was probably tap dancing on the line between sanity and insanity, but I hoped she was drifting a little more strongly to the former and could be reasoned with.

"You were instructed to never return," Dorian hissed, meeting us at the shore with a cadre of nine other horse-shifters with beautiful, shimmering, sand-colored coats and cold, steely, unwelcoming demeanors. Two on each end held bows in their hands and enough arrows in their quivers to cause serious damage, the others swords. Dorian was weaponless.

Gareth's eyes glowed, the ring around them dancing with his irritation, taking in Dorian's signs of aggression. Stepping closer to him, I touched his back lightly with my hand.

"We would like to see the Naga," I informed Dorian.

"You were instructed not to return," he repeated.

I heard you the first time.

Humility wasn't one of my strengths and showing it took great effort. Dorian's sneer of contempt wasn't making it any easier. Watching his cadre of man-horses advance closer, arranging their weapons, made me expend a great deal of effort not to pull out my sai and see how many equines I could take out before they could get off a shot or land a blow. Taking a slow, cleansing breath, inhaling the floral scents and crisp ocean air, I wrangled my emotions.

"We've come to apologize," I admitted softly.

Eyes widened in surprise, Dorian assessed me for a long time and then directed his attention to Gareth. "You came all the way here to apologize?" he asked with obvious skepticism.

You came the same distance to poison us.

I nodded. "We owe her one. We were misunderstood, and it hurt her. I would like to rectify the situation."

His eyes dropped to our arms. "Does your mark have anything to do with the change of heart?"

He was a shifter; lying to him was senseless. "At first, but I found a way to contain your assassins." I smiled congenially. "As you know, they found a way around our strategy—and yet, we are still alive." *No thanks to you, jackass.* "I possess strong magic and extensive resources"—I showed my wrist—"and it will only be a matter of time before we find a way to remove it. And worst-case scenario, if that doesn't work, I could kill her. I figure if the summoner dies, the request is forfeited." His eyes widened at my candor. "I'm not here to kill her. I'm here to apologize because I owe her one. *We* owe her an apology," I said, hoping Gareth didn't make the same sour face he had each time I'd mentioned apologizing.

The horse-shifter's gaze slowly roved over me, then my weapons, Gareth, and the knives he had sheathed in his belt and down at his ankle. I doubted he could see the latter, but he had to suspect that there were more.

"Fine, let me escort you." We didn't take the same direct route; instead he took us on a different one across the small island, with a view of all it had to offer. Small shops, restaurants, and a large brown building with beige pillars with intricate decorative markings of gold and burgundy, Latin above the door. Another building sat nearly behind the others, a white dome shape. Elaborate columns enclosed it, and beautiful, lush green grass so pristine it had to be magically enhanced encircled it. Large trees bearing unfamiliar fruit were interlaced between the houses we'd missed on the first trip. Or maybe they hadn't been there before and someone was putting on a magical show. More people watched us as we made the journey to see the Naga. With the small army of weaponized fake-centaurs behind us, it looked like we were being marched to an execution. Maybe we were.

Once we were at the shore, he nodded to us. "Godspeed." His voice had lost its edge, becoming velvety smooth and cordial, similar to how it had been on our first visit. Even his eyes had shed their menace and were kind, glistening with sincerity. Had his mood changed because he knew it was the end, or because he knew the reason for our journey?

Chimes rang as we made our way to the island. Once again our clothes were dry within seconds of our emerging from the water. The serpent woman whipped about just a few feet away. She still hadn't found any clothes to cover her upper body. Before her movements were gentle, rhythmic, and sinuous; now they were sharp and aggressive as her eyes moved between round human pupils and vertical slits.

"You've returned," she said, snake tongue darting out of her mouth, tasting the air. Her tail shook with the same hostility as her movements.

"Stop," I commanded firmly.

She jerked back, snapping her head as if I'd slapped her. "Stop?" she literally hissed as her split tongue darted out.

"Yes, stop. Now. We've come to apologize, but if you keep acting like this, we're going to leave." Standing at attention, she looked confused and I wasn't sure by what: my command for her to settle down or the reason for our visit.

"Apologize?" she whispered, bouncing her body between us, her eyes totally human along with her tongue, which she changed while speaking, garbling her words.

Sensing the change in her demeanor, Gareth now seemed to be convinced it was a good idea. "Yes," he chimed in. "We owe you one."

"I was being polite when I told you I'd stay if it weren't for my friend. I wasn't truthful, and for that I'm sorry. The island is beautiful but I want to be around my friend, and we can't stay here."

Her eyes became sorrowful, glistening with unshed tears. If she started wailing again, there was no way we were going to make it off the island.

"Can you change to fully human?" Gareth asked.

She nodded and quickly complied. Moments later she stood before us as a simple woman—a simple *naked* woman, unabashed by her nudity. While I averted my eyes from her lady parts, she moved closer to us.

"We can't stay here," Gareth started. "But you can come with us," he added quickly as tears welled in her eyes. She really didn't take rejection well.

"I can't leave," she asserted softly. "This is my home."

"But you want us to leave *our* home to be here with you," I added, keeping my voice level, hoping she'd see the hypocrisy in her request. She looked over the island. I assumed she was taking in the blue-green ocean, the pale golden-colored sand, large fruit-bearing trees, the palm trees that feathered out to shade out the sun, and a few homes that populated the small island that looked vacant from where we stood. Farther back was a dull gray home that reminded me of an oversized bungalow.

"It's beautiful here, but it's not our home," I admitted, watching realization course over her face. Her faint smile disappeared. "We'll come back and visit, twice a year," I promised, hoping the offering was enough to satisfy her. To right her perceived wrong and get her to remove the marks without incident. I kept a careful eye on her and the surroundings, looking for the unexpected. I still didn't trust the island and its inhabitants.

Reaching into my pocket, I pulled out a bracelet; topaz stones circled the band. It looked more expensive than it was. It was free for me; Kalen had given it to me as a gift for her. Her eyes flashed with excitement. Inching closer, she extended her wrist to me and was delighted when I placed the bracelet around it. Holding her arm out, she admired the gift.

"It's mine," I told her. "When I come back, we'll exchange it for something else."

Her smile broadened as she admired the offering. "It's as lovely as you are."

Okay, I've been compared to worse.

The Naga's eyes flitted in Gareth's direction and held his gaze expectantly. "Your offering?" He swallowed, and I knew he had to be replaying our conversation on the way to the plane in his head when I'd urged him to bring something.

Just as he was about to tell her he didn't have anything, I turned and started removing his watch. "This is very special to him. He offers it to you in exchange for your trust that we will return." I placed the platinum watch in her hand, and she admired it as her interest moved between the two gifts.

"You will come back." It wasn't a question but a statement that she repeated with wistful bliss. A broad smile had become a permanent fixture on her face and it seemed impossible that a person with such a childlike whimsy could summon things as nefarious as the Mortem Spiritus.

After she'd clasped Gareth's watch on her other wrist, she looked at it again. Striding even closer to us with the same ease as her snake movements, she looked pleased. She took both of us by the wrists and reminded herself that we would return. I assumed she was doing it for our edification.

"I'd like to say it won't hurt, but I can't." She frowned. Her slitted serpent eyes returned, glowing lime green, and she whispered an incantation that I committed to memory, in the event that I had to use it. Magic washed over me. I wasn't sure what Gareth felt but the pain was obvious as we clenched our teeth. It felt as if she was digging the mark out with a dull knife. For several minutes I stood before her, my body seized in pain, until she released our arms, which were now unmarked.

"I will see you later." And with that she turned, admiring her gifts again as she assumed her serpent form and slithered away.

"That was a twenty-thousand-dollar watch you just gave her!"

I smirked. "Well, you should feel awful...not about me giving her your watch but that you'd pay such a ridiculous amount of money for a watch. Apple has a watch, you know? And it costs way less than that and does more."

Gareth glared at me, but our conversation was cut short. A soft mellifluous voice rang through the air, gentle and sweet. Dorian's scowl had faded into a smile. "She's happy."

Nodding, I looked in her direction. I couldn't see her. "I don't think she's all there, but I'd rather have a happy psycho then someone set on revenge because of some perceived slight."

I smiled. Answering Gareth's raised curious brow, I supplied, "I've dealt with two possible arrogant psychopaths; this encounter didn't end with a beheading and a burned body." Call me a wimp or naïve, but I was more than happy for it not to.

Dorian and the pseudo-centaur posse accompanied us to the shore. In a choreographed, smooth move they all bowed in our direction. Gareth and I looked at each other, shrugged, and returned the display of reverence. I supposed it was the horse-shifter's apology for trying to gas us, or marking us, or banning us from the island. Maybe it was the number of things they'd planned to do and now felt a little guilty about. I didn't care. I took Gareth's hand and we headed for the boat.

It was even more satisfying watching the crew's shocked faces as we boarded.

"We definitely didn't expect to see you again!" the wide-eyed captain admitted.

Thanks for your encouragement.

CHAPTER 27

*V*ictor's professional countenance made it very evident that this was a business meeting. Despite that assertion, Savannah, who was still holding a grudge against him, didn't want me to go. I didn't blame her. His invitation wasn't exactly hospitable. It sounded more like a command when three days after our second return from Menta Island he asked me to meet him at Chauncy, a restaurant a few blocks from the Supernatural Guild's building.

Sipping on an iced tea, he slid the menu in my direction once I was seated. I glanced at it to see if they had added any new entrees before I ordered my usual. Chauncy was a chain; I'd eaten there more times than I could count. Typical American-style food, so I ordered two cheeseburgers, fries, buffalo wings, a side of onion rings, and a salad with extra cheese—had to have my vegetables.

Grinning at Victor's surprised and disturbed look, I said, "You're paying, right?"

"Of course. It's a business expense."

Is it? You mean you don't typically look like you have a stick shoved up your rear?

He did. Professionally stoic, he watched me for several

minutes, glancing around the room periodically before settling his full attention on me. "We haven't had a lot of Legacy come to us. Gareth suspects that most of them probably still don't trust government officials."

"I'm not sure if that's it. There aren't as many as people might have suspected. Imagine how many Trackers have killed us; those who lived undiscovered were probably afraid to procreate because of it."

Victor made a grunt of disgust and took another sip from his glass before occupying his hands with drumming on the table. I suspected he wanted to wait until our food arrived, but he definitely shouldn't have to. I tended to get distracted when fried goodness was in front of me.

"What did you want to talk about?"

Leaning forward, he gave me another appraising look. "I would like you to consider joining the FSR."

Surprised, I snapped my mouth closed. "What?"

"You're talented, smart, and skilled. Except for the overabundance of smart quips and snarkiness, something I'm sure training will fix, you would be a great addition to our team."

"I...What...I..." I never stammered but I was really shocked by his request. My mind went into overdrive, considering training, having to leave Savannah, quitting my job, and being away from— I stopped myself from that thought but it slipped in anyway. Gareth. I didn't want to be away from him. Kalen and Savannah were big parts of my life and I knew that if I ever had to leave, I'd miss them. Gareth was different. Caring about him was different. Realizing how much I did shocked me.

"I don't know what to say," I admitted. "It's a great offer."

"Well, technically it's a suggestion. You'd still have to go through training and pass the test, but I don't think that's a problem. I believe my recommendation will work in your favor." Silent for several minutes, he looked like he was mulling something over. His voice tightened when he continued, "Gareth would like you to join the Supernatural Guild. He's floated that idea past the ethics committee and me."

They had an ethics committee? Justice was supposed to be blind, but the SG turned a blind eye to a lot. Had that committee been on vacation when Harrah'd been working? There was absolutely no way the things Harrah had done in her career had been evaluated by an ethics committee.

Noticing the note of interest in my voice when I said, "Really?" Victor frowned. "I advised him against it, and the ethics committee frowned on the idea. Your personal relationship puts the agency and him in a compromising position. I think the Supernatural Guild has more biases against the Legacy than we do."

I highly doubted that. They all had their biases. I doubted that was going to end overnight. Shapeshifters would dislike me because I was able to use magic against them. Others would because of the history of the Legacy. I wasn't naïve enough to believe otherwise.

Working with Gareth had piqued my interest and made the idea of joining the Federal Supernatural Reinforcement less appealing, something Victor obviously sensed. "You won't be able to work for the SG," he asserted. His shifter ring glinted—he was irritated. Perhaps he couldn't imagine anyone turning down the opportunity to work with the FSR—which I hadn't.

"He fired the mage who kept insulting you when we apprehended you."

Keeping the perplexed, shocked emotion off my face, I kept my voice even when I spoke. "Really?"

"Yes, really. He had every right to do so because of the mage's insubordination, but Gareth's reaction to the display of insubordination was inappropriate. Based on his reputation, out of character as well. He reacted that way because of you. That's not a way to run an agency. Even if hiring you wasn't ethically ill-advised, it's a bad decision no matter how much of an asset you would prove to be."

The mention of the mage made me relive Victor using me as bait. Did I want to work for someone who'd done that? Could I overlook that for this opportunity? "When do I have to make a decision?"

He shrugged. "I'd like to know something by next week."

I nodded. He waved for the server and asked for the check. Grinning, he said, "No worries, dinner is still coming and it's on me. Gives you some time to think about it. Levy, your talents need to be used for more than cleaning out attics and selling little knickknacks."

"Those little knickknack excursions have found many illegal magical objects, some that have been and will be of great help to the SG and the FSR," I pointed out.

He nodded an acknowledgment.

My lips quirked into a smile and I could picture the smirk and eye roll Kalen was giving me as he responded to the news about Victor's offer and Gareth asking Victor's opinion about me joining the SG. "I wonder where I will find a plaid-wearing curmudgeon who managed to be grumpy and snarky at a level that some might consider artistic. You mean I might be able to work with someone who won't visually assault me with their wardrobe on a daily basis?" he teased in theatrical exasperation.

"Maybe you can hire Blu and you two can spend the day posing and strutting down the hallway like it's a catwalk," I shot back.

"There she is," he quipped. Then there was a long, weighted silence. "I will support whatever you decide to do. You really deserve to be happy."

"I was happy there, you know."

"I know, but I want more for you. This is more."

Breathing a sigh of relief, I couldn't believe I'd been worried that he'd be upset. He wasn't—he wanted the best for me. I hung up the phone, feeling lighter as I made my way up Gareth's driveway. He was waiting for me at the door with a knowing grin. He knew about the meeting. I wondered if Victor had asked for his blessing. I highly doubted that.

Gareth pulled me to him and kissed me before I could make my way into the house. "You look troubled, what's wrong?"

I shook my head.

He groaned. "You're going to make me do the vitals spiel and tell you how I can use the changes in them to determine if you're lying, aren't you? Maybe I should make up cards and hand them to you each time you need a reminder," he teased. Edging his way closer to me, he placed his hand on my waist. "What has you troubled?"

"I was offered a job today."

"I'm aware. What are you going to do?"

Shrugging, I found myself staring at him. I didn't want to—it would only add fuel to the flames of his arrogance—but there was no denying he was nice to look at. "It depends."

"On what?"

"If there is any way to join the SG. I don't want to leave. This is my home, and I want to be here with Savannah and Kalen…" I let the rest of my words fade into silence as I said his name under my breath.

"And me? Is that what you said?" He cupped his ear to hear me better, as if he needed to do that. A pin could drop in another room and he would hear it and tell who dropped it based on their scent.

"Yes, and you," I admitted quietly. *You don't make it easy, do you?*

His smile faded as he was drawn into his thoughts. Eventually, he looked past me at the door. Watching him intently, I wondered if he was making the same pros and cons list that I had. My list wasn't very long. Victor was right, I was good at this, but I hated politics. That was a con. Would someone like me last in law enforcement, either at a city or federal level? The biggest benefit would be greater visibility as a Legacy; those who were reluctant to come out might be emboldened by my presence. I'd be in the public eye, but after being plunged into it as the face of Legacy and because of who I was dating, I'd become used to it.

"They don't think I can be unbiased when it comes to you," Gareth started out slowly, then he frowned. "And frankly, they're right. There are people, even in the agency, who won't like you because of what you are; I won't stand for it."

"You think I should apply for the FSR position?"

He shook his head. "No, I said I'm aware that I'm biased. Knowing it will make me more cautious. The ethics committee never said you shouldn't work here; they said it wasn't a good idea. I disagree. You would be an asset to the Supernatural Guild, and if I need to step down, I will. If you accepted a job with us, I would take the necessary precautions *not* to give you special treatment." Flashing me a smile, he added, "Some might say I'm unfairly harsh on you."

"I would expect nothing less. You had your own nephew pulled over by the police. You're capable of anything."

"He stole my car," Gareth reminded.

"The word on the street is that he borrowed it and you over-reacted."

"I would like nothing more than for you to work here." He moved closer and kissed me.

"I'd like that, too."

"Good, tomorrow go online and apply." He moved to the sofa and took a seat. "What are you going to tell Savannah?"

I shrugged. "I have no intention of telling her; you'll be the one who will have to deal with her impromptu visits checking on me…on us. That should be fun."

Rolling his eyes, he scoffed, "So much fun." Flashes of Savannah walking into the Supernatural Guild with her quest bag demanding to help in dangerous situations to make sure that I'd be safe flashed in my head. I wondered how long it would be before she'd try to apply. The thought of Savannah with a badge brought a smile to my lips. A hint of one curved Gareth's, and I was sure he'd probably encountered a similar image.

Relaxing back, he asked, "Who will be applying for the job, Anya or Olivia?"

That was a good question. I'd been Olivia most of my adult life; it was who I was and had become. I'd acquired my bumps and bruises, my war wounds and lessons, as Olivia. Anya Kismet was my beginning, Olivia was my ending.

"I'm Olivia Michaels—Levy—and I'm a Legacy," I said with full authority and without any apprehension or fear.

It was a good feeling.

MESSAGE TO THE READER

Thank you for choosing *Rogue Magic* from the many titles available to you. My goal is to create an engaging world, compelling characters, and an interesting experience for you. I hope I've accomplished that. Reviews are very important to authors and help other readers discover our books. Please take a moment to leave a review. I'd love to know your thoughts about the book.

For notifications about new releases, *exclusive* contests and giveaways, and cover reveals, please sign up for my mailing list at mckenziehunter.com.

Happy Reading!

www.McKenzieHunter.com
MckenzieHunter@MckenzieHunter.com

Lightning Source UK Ltd.
Milton Keynes UK
UKHW041849281218
334719UK00001B/7/P